The Stonecutter's Daughter
Laura Coe

Love and Eternal Gratitude to:

Sugarfoot, Jettie, & Cody

I owe you all debts I cannot repay, but if you ever find you need something...name it and I will lay it at your feet.

Prologue

I had followed my father to work to watch him as he set his latest masterpiece at the head of an open grave. As I ran through the silent tombs, chasing the last of the morning fog from the sleeping ground something caught my eye. Laying in the grass was a fallen dove, a twisted wing jutting from its body with spatters of crimson on its breast. As it fluttered to no avail, I stooped to pluck it from the grass.

I believed then that my father had the power to fix all things and I brought the wounded creature to him with tears standing in my eyes. He looked at me and the bird in my hands with an expression of profound sorrow. Shaking his head he wrung its neck, ending its pain and pulling a wail from me that would have woken the dead.

He took me in his arms then, I can still remember the way he smelled of tobacco and that unnamable scent of ground stone that seemed to cling to every part of him. As my tiny frame vanished in his monstrous embrace he murmured low against my temple, "Everything dies Gilda, everything…."

Chapter 1

"You had a lovely funeral my dear, it was a shame you had to miss it."

The harsh voice ground out as Gilda's eyes fluttered open to meet the muddy depths of a stranger's gaze. As he raised her hand to his stubbly face and brushed his lips over her knuckles, a lupine grin teased the corners of his mouth. The firelight danced over his mossy teeth and Gilda's stomach clenched in an uneasy knot.

Darting her eyes frantically around the room, she surmised three things immediately. She was alone, she was underground and she needed to leave this place. A fire danced on the open floor, a few stray coals glowing on cobblestones weakly as they strangled in the open air. There was a pile of clothing in the corner with shoes of various styles and levels of wear. A gate with cruel spikes stood sentry on one side of the cramped room while across the way a hole lined with broken and falling bricks led to an untold abyss.

Carried on the foul breeze that crept up from the depths of this place Gilda could hear crying. Not the wracking sobs of a panicked survivor, but the keening moan of a soul that is truly lost and has given up all hope.

He savored her fear, watching the realization and confusion bloom like rare fruit. It certainly wasn't his job to scare her, but no one told him not to...his singular taste strayed far from what even the most seasoned aficionado would call exotic. To Maddox, a lass was at her most comely and irresistible when she was terrified.

This one was well on her way, she wasn't a chatterer like some of the others who fired off question after question in a shrill voice with hot tears staining their cheeks. She was taking it on the chin, trying to hold it together. He both admired and loathed her for that. Hauling her from the floor upon which she laid with obvious frustration. He pulled his dirk from his boot and sliced the laces at the back of her gown. Tearing the silk from her body with deafening rips, leaving her bare and shivering as he added hers to the pile of those that had come before.

His eyes fell greedily on the ample swell of her bosom and he helped himself to more than a handful of her flesh as he grasped the bauble dangling from a golden chain around her neck. With a deft yank the clasp gave way, and she cast him a cold glare.

A low whistle slid from his cracked lips, "If looks could kill...." Shaking his head and tucking the necklace in his jacket pocket, Maddox removed a set of heavy keys and moved to the gate. As the lock turned he cast a dismissive glance back at her.

"No one's coming for you, and the only way out is in." With a meaningful look at that oppressive hole in the wall, he left and locked the gate after him. His footfalls fading as the off key tune he whistled followed. Soon the only sounds were that of the fire and the weak hiccupping sobs that crept out of the black.

Gilda did her best to slow her heart, to calm her breathing. She wrapped her arms around her naked bosom, hoping to shield herself from the icy chill. The air from that hole was making her stomach turn, or was it the greasy fire on the floor that was quickly dying?

Soon it will be black as pitch in here...

She thought to herself, and looked around the sparse little room for a lantern, a candle...anything. Gilda dug through the pile of discarded gowns, wincing at the ruins of her own on the top. It was meant to be her wedding gown with lovely white satin with gilded sleeves. Her heart stuttered for a moment, wondering about her family, her fiancé. They must be devastated to think her dead....

Pushing the thought of the women that had worn the other dresses and whatever fate they'd found far from her mind. She wondered to herself if silk actually burned and made her way down the pile to the moth eaten remnants of the very first ones to have been tossed here. Their once fine and lovely threads were now delicate and dry as cobwebs in her trembling fingers.

Gilda's eyes fell on a bottle cast in the corner, the green glass winking at her from its side. Inside was just enough wine to douse the battered dress. Soaking it and winding the fabric around the bottom of the bottle, she thrust it into the weakly swaying flames of the fire with no small amount of hope.

It lit, god only knew how long it would burn, but it lit. Gilda let out a triumphant sigh, she had untold challenges in front of her, and only one behind, but it was a start.

Her own shoes were missing, which was odd. But if she thought about it, undertakers do not put shoes on corpses...that man had mentioned her funeral. If she truly had been thought dead, and laid to rest, it would explain the finery and her lack of footwear. She tried the shoes in the corner but was dismayed to find that they were all sliced up the sides and along the fastenings in the name of expediency, which rendered them useless.

Gilda reasoned that to linger would be folly and on bare and trembling feet, she took a few halting steps to the mouth of the hole. The torch cast precious little light on carved walls with a dirt floor and nothing else. A few more steps in, and the chill from the damp walls started to raise gooseflesh on her exposed skin, *or could it be the horror of the place itself? S*he wondered. Moving further and further away from that sputtering fire she was enveloped in sanguine silence and realized there was no light at the end of this tunnel.

When she happened upon what looked like a puddle in the floor, she approached with caution and then fear as she drew closer. A pit, in the black...a trap. Toeing a stone into it, she listened and heard nothing.

What is this place?

She moved carefully around the hole, never taking her eyes off it as her dirty feet took small steps around its gaping maw. So focused on avoiding the pit that the pile of bones next to it didn't register until her heel burst through a dry and ancient breast plate and her toes became entangled in the curling ribs.

Gilda screamed then, her gaze falling upon the skull with its jaw dangling open in a silent howl. She yanked her foot free and fell against the carved wall only to jerk away at a sharp pain ripping at her naked skin. Holding the torch toward the stone she saw shards of glass buried cruelly in the rock, their jagged and razor sharp edges dripping with her own blood.

Moving at a snail's pace, eyes scanning the floor for the hollows that riddled the place, Gilda quietly moved through the passage. Searching her mind for a trace of a memory, some piece of information locked in her mind of how this came to be, but she found none.

Her thoughts drifted to home, to her father and his slender hands coated in the fine powder of granite from hard day's work. Her mother singing in the kitchen as she cooked, her books, her bed, her life. The torch in her hand was devouring itself in a slow burn and a hissing pop pulled her from her reverie, looking around she was shocked to see no trace of the hole from which she'd entered.

How long have I been in here? How far have I come?

She wondered, looking woefully at her torch, or what was left of it. The once brightly burning fabric had eaten what little alcohol there was and melted in on itself, leaving a few glowing embers along the edges like some rare smoldering flower. As she gazed on, a breeze once again flowed from the unknown end of this tunnel, carrying that damnable weeping with it and as the cool air touched her torch, it expired in a final wheeze of musty smoke.

Darkness, total and complete washed around her, pulling a gasp from her lips. Dropping the bottle with a defeated cry, she heard it roll the way she'd come with a grinding hum as it moved over gravel and dirt, then silence as it fell to its end in one of those foul holes.

Downhill...it rolled downhill, I must be slowly climbing up.

It wasn't much of a realization, but it was something. It explained why the entrance to this damnable place had vanished, and why the other end was nowhere in sight.

On her hands and knees, Gilda made slow and hesitant progress upward, the intermittent breeze in her face reinforcing that there was an end to this journey. Feeling for the traps this tunnel was lousy with, making precious little way through the maze of them. With sweat dripping from her downturned face as she tried in the pitch to navigate the snares that had been laid here so coldly.

With her eyes useless, her ears and skin were firing away, sensitized to every sound and texture. Pushing through a cobweb felt like tearing through a fishermen's net and the scrambling of a rat's feet along the side of the corridor carried all the cacophony of an avalanche.

Her feet were chilled through and her bare toes curled in the sandy grain with every inch she gained. Her knees and hands were torn, bruised and bloody yet still, she crawled.

Through bones, over traps and rocks, piles of glass and nails.

Her palms fell into a soft and yielding pile of rotting flesh. The putrid smell wafting up to her nostrils and pulling a harsh gag from deep within her starved body. Gilda climbed over the remains of yet another nameless victim of this place as best she could.

The current of icy air that teased around Gilda's ears faded and in its place a breathy whisper...or whispers began to build. Weary and woeful in her mind's eye the musical quality of their voices filled her head to overflowing in their frantic tenor. Begging her to help them, to take them away from this place. Warning Gilda to be careful, to stay away and press on all at once.

She swore she could feel their desperate fingers on her flesh, in her hair, tugging at her to gain some focus. Pulling her in every direction until she wanted to scream for them to stop. Their ephemeral presence was beyond her perception, and only a fleeting glimpse of their faces danced across the dank.

In their wake filthy waves splashed on the shores of her starved mind, a flotsam of memories collided into a raft of pain and loss. Reeking waters and broken dreams were floating across Gilda's eyes. Not all of them her own exactly, but in this place they were one in the same.

There in the pit they lined up before her back to the beginning, to the first of the lost and desperate souls that had been thrown in here. Hollow eyes and sallow skin glowed through the darkness eclipsed by the furious aura of a young life cut short. So much wasted and so many moments lost only to be trapped here to rage at the walls in which they rotted.

Unknown even to them in death Gilda trembled to think what unholy force bound them here, away from the sweet release of death, locked from their families and the beyond where we all go when life is finished with us. This was a pit of torment and dying was no escape, as the man had said before he'd left, "The only way out was in." Gilda would take these souls with her, somehow. Resolute in the understanding that whatever turn of fate had brought these women here to die before her bound them together in her mind as sisters, forever.

She only halted when she put yet another tentative and exploring hand in front of her, expecting the soft embrace of the dirt below her palm or the stomach dropping sensation of nothing only to find stone. Patting all around and finally running both her hands along the floor to make sure she wasn't crazy, that it was in fact what it felt like. Stones, laid stones…a man- made floor.

It was little comfort to her, leaving the Hell she knew for one she didn't, but without a choice or alternative Gilda pressed on. The weeping was constant now, it didn't ride in on the wind any longer, it filled her ears clogging her mind with visions of a tortured woman, maimed and in pain, or worse.

It was when Gilda's hand landed not on stone or into yet another of those pits, but on a clammy foot that she screamed. Not wanting to be close to its owner, but unable to move away without putting herself in danger. Gilda clapped a hand over her own mouth, the woman however, never so much as ceased in her crying.

"Who are you?" Gilda rasped, reaching out again for the foot she'd found only to have it yanked away.

"Are you alright? Do you know where we are? Do you need help?" she asked, frantic and scared.

She only wept, softly, weakly and without end.

"Come with me," Gilda pleaded once again finding her foot in the dark, "we can get out together, we will stay together." She implored only to be answered with a hiccupping sob.

It was clear that this woman had been broken by the darkness, had given up in it....Gilda couldn't linger any longer but also refused to leave her to rot. With forceful hands Gilda wrapped her fingers around the skeletal wrists of the woman and draped her frighteningly light frame over her back. The stench of her breath puffed past Gilda's ear into her face and she fought the urge to vomit at the rancid smell that filled her nostrils.

With the strange and limply hanging weight on her back Gilda's progress slowed, her muscles screamed and bones ached. She could feel the knuckles of her addled companion dragging on the stone, imagined the clammy skin tearing on the grit of the blocks that were biting her own knees. A low roaring like the beating of her heart but louder, harsher began to make her head ache until it was all she could hear.

"The mouth of Hell waits...and you crawl toward it." Her strange companion whispered in her ear amidst the tidal wave of her own throbbing mind.

"In our darkest times, we seek to understand, to assign meaning." Her father had told her once, after a widow had broken into hysterics sputtering nonsense about bringing this upon herself. He had listened to her patiently, and allowed her to cry, offering only a handkerchief and a glass of water when she had calmed. As Gilda watched her walk down the street, hollow eyed and runny nosed, he had explained to her how grief and guilt can run people to madness. "You cannot allow sorrow to control you Gilda, life is cruel and it is the soul that not only accepts that cruelty, but expects it that triumphs."

Expect cruelty.

She thought to herself, navigating yet another of those pits, palming around the rim of it and crawling past. Grunting as she shifted the woman on her back before she could slide off once more into the dust, she was a limp as a rag and so cold as her rattling breaths heaved in and out of her. This place was cruel and the people that built it calculating, the tunnel was just the first test, if you made it that far only horrors could await. Gilda accepted that, expected it and continued.

Thirst soon dominated her thoughts, in spite of the chill in the damp air her throat was parched, running her hands along the nitre covered walls between the veins of glass and nails, she found no trail of groundwater creeping along the carved limestone walls from which to sip. With her tongue swelling in her mouth and her dry lips cracking, she did her best to push the thoughts of water and wine from her mind.

Her knees screamed with every movement and her palms were caked with blood. Chunks of hair hung in her face, grimy with sweat and dirt, and yet she crawled. Gilda's thoughts scrambled now, between her father's wisdom and her mother's kind heart. She had a flash of Nathaniel and the day he'd proposed in the garden that sunny April day. Images of Greyfriar's and all the dead whose names she'd written in script, whose names her father had carved in stone.

"We speak for the dead," he had said after he'd thrown a ruined stone out citing a fouled flourish that was to embellish the bottom, "we are their final word on this Earth and that's a weighty task dear girl, its perfect or it doesn't see the light of day."

Gilda was crying, silent tears slipped down her face as she drug herself and the strange woman along that stone floor, through the maze of pits and over bodies of countless women in various states of decay. Some of them slowly rotting, their flesh mush and soupy, others nothing but bones that almost exploded at her touch. Gilda was covered in traces of the forgotten dead of this hole, tiny pieces of them in her lungs, on her skin and hanging in her hair. Half mad with thirst and exhausted, Gilda thought perhaps she had died when she saw it in the distance...a lantern.

Glowing warmly, the flame danced through the beveled glass throwing starbursts of light against the wall. Gilda rubbed her eyes with dirty hands, blinked hard and looked again....it burned serenely, as if waiting for them. The curled and desperate frame of some long dead woman leaned against the wall beneath it. She'd spend her final moments in this world beneath its light, gazing on it in despair.

She moved slowly, feeling for pits and searching the walls for some new trickery, a trap, a snare some spikes...a blade. As she knelt in the pool of light cast by that first lantern, she gazed down the hall and saw more, a twinkling path of golden stars leading the way. Bones and skulls along the floor, obscuring the stones beneath. Countless women had made it this far only to die.

Gently she laid the woman she'd carried on her back next to her on the stones, in the light. Straightening to lay eyes on the face of the stranger she'd drug inch by agonizing inch through this torment the breath left her lungs in a wheezing gasp.

Green rubbery flesh hung off bones in sickly ripples and festering gashes. The putrid stench that came off the half rotted corpse all but rendered Gilda unconscious. The eyes hung open in a milky gaze that told the tale of her demise, this woman was dead, long before Gilda ever found her. It hadn't been her breath, it had been her...the stench of dead flesh rotting atop her own body as she shuffled and carried it with her through this place.

Pressing her filthy palms to her temples as her eyes burned with tears that her parched body couldn't bear to part with, Gilda howled into the black. Frantically grasping at the threadbare strands of her sanity, she sifted through the memories she had. The weeping, and that first frightening touch of her cold skin...she'd yanked her foot away, hadn't she? Or perhaps Gilda's numb and frozen leg had bumped it away from her own hands...? Could the weeping have just been the moaning of the wind as it moved through the pits of this place?

Gilda pulled herself to her feet then, swayed on them weakly and fell to her knees once more raising a shuffling clatter among the bones of her sisters. Her head swam dizzily, she shook it and tried again, holding herself on the wall, uncaring at the bites she earned from the glass that rested there, she made shambling steps toward the light, to the end of this hell.

A harpsichord was plucking out a rich and lovely tune in the distance and she could have sworn she smelled meat being roasted. Dragging herself toward the sounds and smells, stumbling, falling atop those chattering bones and getting up again. Painful inch after painful inch, she made her way along the wall, holding herself up and hauling herself along until Gilda found herself at a large imposing door.

Lanterns glowed from inside red glass on either side of the round monstrosity casting it a bloodred hue, iron hinges ran along the top and bottom however there was no handle, no ring from which to open it. Only a great brass knocker in the center, a ram whose horns flared from his head and jutted madly from his jaw with flared nostrils and hollow eyes that implored her to knock.

On the other side of the heavy wood, she could hear the music and smell the food. People's murmured conversation, low chuckles of men with the musical tittering of women....a party?

Expect cruelty

Gilda told herself, and raised a shaking hand to the knocker where she lifted that wicked visage and let it drop in a heavy and consuming thud, once, twice, three times.

The party on the other side fell silent, the music halted and Gilda held her breath.

She heard a great lock turning lazily in the door and with a low groan of those mighty hinges, it opened.

Chapter 2

"The door itself is made from a single piece of Irish Black Oak which carbon dating places back to the Paleolithic Period. With a diameter of 335 centimeters it the largest known specimen of this extinct genus of wood. Weighing over 900 kilograms the door would have required a tremendous work force to hang, the unusual circular shape makes this a collector's dream. The hinges were not found with this piece, however marks remain that indicate wrought iron spanned both the top and the bottom, an interesting anomaly that remains unexplained are the one sided latch and lock treatment. Finally, in the center a brass ram's head knocker which our curator advises has long since frozen on its hinges, the tooling however is consistent with 1700's metal working...."

Her prim English accent was making an already boring address downright unendurable, Cullen couldn't understand why the people at Sotheby's insisted on grandstanding when an item clearly didn't need the help. He allowed his cobalt eyes to roll around the salon, draped in cerulean brocade accented with an impeccable Persian rug from the Ottoman Empire, he flared a brow wondering if they didn't cherry pick the best pieces for themselves here in London.

His phone buzzed in his pocket again, and Cullen's eyes rolled theatrically, halting the owlish woman at the podium in her endless prattling of dimensional facts. His gaze landed on the screen and he sighed, it was his boss:

"Have they dropped the curtain yet? Send a picture!!!!"

Cullen quickly replied, knowing patience was not one of his virtues.

"Not yet, will send when they do."

Pushing a breath from pursed lips, likely making more noise than the British would approve of, he again focused on Owl-Face, as he'd come to think of her since it sounded like she was about to get to the good stuff.

"As lovely as this piece is on its own, the crowning jewel is its provenance. Excavated from a recently discovered tunnel beneath Montpelier Hill in Ireland, it is believed that this door served inside the building during its occupation by The Hell Fire Club. Reputed to have performed black masses, animal and human sacrifices as well as endless other unspeakable acts of debauchery and defamation before a fire destroyed the building the in 1776. This door is the only known artifact from this locale and time period, rendering it, in our opinion – priceless."

Raising her hand to the stage team in the back, the curtain was drawn back along the sealed glass viewing room where the monstrous door was perched in all its glory. The wood was almost as old as the Earth itself and as the dignified collectors and buyers attempted to remain passive to its presence, the urge to crowd the glass was a palpable pull that Cullen denied again, and again to himself.

This was so much more than a door, it was as if he was looking at a living entity of some type...something old, and powerful...something he felt as if he shouldn't have seen. His thoughts stuttered and all of the world slipped away as his gaze fell upon the infernal ram at its center. A perfectly placed light set the brass aglow and the patina of the metal was sublime in spite of the oppressive countenance of the animal itself. An imposing and aggressive expression creased its face, with flared nostrils and a defiant glare, Cullen wondered if anyone in the history of this door's life had mustered the courage to even lay a hand on the thing, let alone knock.

Cullen sat there for God knows how long, contemplating the series of events that had brought that door into the light of day once again before his phone buzzed insistently.

He didn't even look, just snapped a picture and sent it without further explanation.

The room had cleared quite a bit, a few of the more interested parties lingered, thumbing through the glossy catalog of Sotheby's Fall Auction. While others stood close to the bullet proof glass that separated them from the belle of this ball, unabashedly admiring it for what it truly was, a rare piece of magic in this cynical world.

Cullen however, restrained himself from such behavior. As blown away as he was, he remained professional. In circles such as these, among those privileged few that received hand written invitations from the curators of these fine auction houses, word travels fast and reputation is everything.

He had honed his image, his walk and even his way of speaking to a non-descript, yet pleasing presence. Thin and strong, but not bulky, his sandy hair trimmed but still long enough to highlight his hawkish features, always clean shaven, well dressed and no matter what, so very polite.

His efforts had landed him his dream job this year, a buyer and consort for a secretive collector who wished to keep his own face away from the public. Perhaps it was just the nature of his employer or the very sensitive niche in which he collected. Either way Mr. Baruch paid Cullen quite well to find and secure him any and all pieces of antiquity relating to the occult.

It wasn't an odd fascination, in fact it was a joke that all powerful people harbor an obsession with Satan because if he is real, they'd like to ask his advice about a thing or two.

He was about to leave and make the customary call to Mr. Baruch to discuss the item, the auction and whether or not it was worth what he would probably end up bidding to buy it when she caught his eye. Standing near the podium, regarding the door with an expression he could only call regret, she was singular in her presence.

A tight expression cast an otherwise lovely countenance in a cold hue, she was well heeled, that much was clear. Cullen was an expert on assessing people and she was the genuine article. Perhaps a wealthy heiress, or self-made business woman…still Cullen thought he recognized the Old World in her.

An effortless presence that cannot be bought or learned but handed down from the oldest bloodlines and finest families. She was someone alright, fashionable in a way that defied the current trends, she filled out a pencil skirt to the point of being distracting and a sassy three quarter sleeved blouse in the deepest blue, matched by a pair of pointed heels she echoed the fifties in a room filled with athleasurewear and peg leg pants. Her tawny hair swept up in a French twist, diamonds in her ears and a ruby wedding ring on her hand…she was someone alright, she was his competition.

He ambled over to her, careful not to seem too rushed or focused, another friendly man in Sotheby's and nothing more. But she threw him off guard when she directed her stormy eyes to his, "Can I help you?" she asked tilting her head a little to the side.

Cullen blinked and stammered, "Ummm…no. I uh- do you work here?" he managed, shoving his hands in the pockets of his leather jacket.

She smiled then, and set the room aflame with her husky laugh, "No more than you." Obviously already finished with him, she moved to leave, but Cullen stopped her, his hand out as he introduced himself. "Cullen O'Keefe. Private buyer."

Her eyebrows shot up in hearty amusement and with a stiffened back she thrust her delicate hand into his with no small amount of strength behind it and replied, "Enola Sloan, none of your fucking business." And moved once again, to leave.

Cullen caught the tiniest whiff of rose as she swept by, and her voice, "Is that a brogue I hear, Ms. Sloan?" he asked lightly, examining his nails as if touching her might have damaged them in some way.

She stopped, and turned on her heel slowly, "Almost as faint as that drawl of yours...And it's Mrs., if you don't mind."

"I don't mind at all," he started as he closed the space she'd put between them with a nonchalant stride, "Your husband must be quite the success to be able to even consider buying such an item." He fished, jerking his head at the door in the case.

"Who says I'm here for that old thing?" she quipped.

"Your eyes..." Cullen replied fervently, "I've never seen anyone look at anything the way you look at that door."

Those copper flecked depths of hers flashed, only for a moment though, "Don't mistake interest for want Mr. O'Keefe." She warned, "Have you been to its home?" she deflected.

He shook his head, un-phased by her transparent attempt to distract him, "Your husband?"

She regarded him then, in a way that made him feel like he was being measured in some manner he had no control over. "Oh yes Mr. O'Keefe, he has." Something in her tone, the deepened tenor her voice took on as she replied stopped Cullen in his tracks.

Before he found himself again, Mrs. Sloan was out the door and on the street and Cullen was left to wonder what the hell had just happened.

His phone was already buzzing when he stepped from the stately portico of Sotheby's and into the icy October drizzle as it crept down the busy streets of London. Pulling his leather jacket tightly around him and stepping into the sleet, he found he was unable to focus on the task at hand. His thoughts, which should be on his job, drifted time and time again to her and the way she'd looked at that door. Hailing a cab from the curb, Cullen eased into the seat and pulled his phone from his pocket to dial Mr. Baruch, who picked up before the first ring could be completed.

"Tell me Cullen," his velvet voice implored, "what was it like to gaze upon something older than the pyramids?"

A smile teased the corner of his mouth as he searched for the words to describe it. Part of this job was painting a picture, connecting his clients to these items and creating desire for something they'd never seen. But his eloquence failed him and he remained silent long enough for a deep chuckle to come through the phone.

"Do my ears deceive me Cullen?" he asked, "has this simple door rendered you silent?"

"It is far from simple, Sir." Cullen managed, "but yes, it is beyond description."

"If it looks half as good as the photograph, I'd say it's the find of the century." Mr. Baruch stated, followed by the long pause that could only be him drawing on a cigar. Unaffected by the vilification of smokers, he insisted on enjoying the habit unapologetically and as often as possible.

"To be honest, it's in unbelievable shape, no hinges though." Cullen offered.

"And the knocker, the ram?" he prodded almost anxiously.

"Perfect." He replied, remembering the menacing countenance of the brass creature, "Although not functional." He added.

"No....." Mr. Baruch said in a distracted tone, "I would imagine not."

"There was a woman there, Sir." Cullen stated, picturing the ivory column of her throat framed by the collar of her blouse. Remembering the timbre of her husky laugh, the sea colored hue of her eyes.

"Do tell," there was another long draw on his cigar, "if this job is about anything, it's the fringe benefits." He chuckled.

"No," Cullen said as he paid the cabbie and exited the back seat, "not like that, not some wealthy bird looking for vases and rugs, she's quite different."

There was a long pause on the end of the line and Cullen could imagine Mr. Baruch considering his news in his study, reclining easily in a large wing back chair beside a fire as the smoke from his cigar curled sensuously around his hand.

"I'll trust your judgement Cullen, it's what I pay you for. Handle the woman any way you see fit, but make no mistake, I want that door."

"Of course, and what is the threshold for this auction?" Cullen asked as he walked past the reception desk to the elevators where he pressed the button to call down the car.

"I'm prepared to go as high as 27." Mr. Baruch offered brusquely.

"I understand." Cullen stated, hoping the surprise he felt didn't carry over the line.

"The auction is in two days, enjoy yourself until then. We'll be in touch Cullen."

Chapter 3

An awe struck hush washed over the room as the mighty door swung open before Gilda, her hands trembled, terrified of what would become of her. Her eyes searched the room frantically, not certain what she was looking for, but confused utterly by what she found.

A sea of candles glowed in candelabras, casting halos of light up soaring stone walls. A fire roared in the hearth and the long shadows of those in attendance held eerily still as they looked upon her with a strange reverence. The well-appointed drawing room boasted richly upholstered furniture as well as paintings and tapestries on the walls.

She had hoped that there were answers behind this door, but it wasn't long before Gilda understood she was only to be rewarded with more questions. A gloved hand was extended to her from inside this opulent room and she took it, throwing more weight on it than was ladylike to haul herself clumsily over the rounded threshold.

Stumbling in on her still rubbery legs, a black velvet dressing robe was hastily placed on her shoulders and she gladly closed it over her naked skin. The man who still held her hand gently in his own led her to a settee by the fire, after she was seated Gilda noticed that a crowd had gathered around her.

Expect cruelty.

She echoed to herself, wondering what fresh horrors awaited her in this place. Low murmurs and whispers traveled through the curious on-lookers and quickly bloomed into a chattering that rattled up the walls until Gilda could hardly hear her own thoughts.

A loud gong rendered them all silent once more however, and Gilda braced herself for what might come. Expecting some evil device, or cruel trick…wondering if maybe she was just lying somewhere in that damned cave. Her thirsty mind spinning this mirage as a kind of parting gift before she dried up and died in that hole where her bones eventually turned to dust that some other unfortunate girl might crawl through.

She was pulled from the morbid image of her own demise by the entrance of a man in whose expression could only be described as pleasant. He wore a fine brocade jacket of the palest blue over a high collared shirt and the powdery curls of his wig swung behind his back as he approached through the parting crowd. A merry smile turned his lips as he sat next to her on the settee, holding her gaze in his own and his hands out to her, imploringly.

Not knowing what to do, disarmed completely by this place and the people in it, she laid her filthy, blood caked, shaking hands on his gloved palms and nearly fainted when he pressed fervent kisses to the top of both. On his lapel, a smaller bronze ram regarded her with glittering amber eyes and as she cast her eyes about the room she saw that all in attendance donned the same pin.

"You honor us with your presence," he offered in a hushed tone, "ask anything of us as we are your servants." His eyes fell upon her hands then and an expression of rage filled that jolly visage. Rising stiffly from his seat, he clapped his hands and a valet was at his side in a heartbeat, the man whispering a riotous demand in his ear followed by a slap to his face.

He quickly sat again next to Gilda, "Please accept my humblest apologies for my servants, a doctor has been summoned to see to your wounds. As anticipated as your arrival has been, you are a most unexpected surprise this night."

A ripple of laughter was pulled from the crowd that continued to observe and watch her closely. Clearing her parched throat, Gilda tried to speak but only managed a wheezing cough. A goblet of wine was quickly offered and she took it greedily. Draining the silver vessel she was handed a full one and half way through that, she tried to speak again.

"There's been some mistake," she croaked, "I'm not certain I belong here." She offered, taking more wine as her throat began to feel less like a desert.

He smiled then, and it danced around his eyes and lips as he shook his head, sending those curls coasting back and forth across his shoulders. "No mistake at all, we've been waiting quite some time for you."

The portly doctor arrived and her host rose, "Enough for tonight brothers and sisters, our guest has been through quite an ordeal and needs her rest. Retire for the evening and tomorrow we shall revel in her grace."

Gilda watched as they dispersed, stealing final glances of her before they grudgingly left the lofty room. A basin of water was brought and her tattered feet were laid gently into the hot liquid, she couldn't contain the moan of pleasure that escaped from her lips. Clapping a hand to her mouth, her eyes once again met those of her host, "I'm sorry –"

He was quick to pull her palm from her mouth, "You regret nothing and apologize to no one." He advised sternly.

Gilda was taken aback by his fervent statement, and then too distracted by the ministrations of the doctor who was examining her feet who oddly wore gloves as he did so, soaking them through in the murky water. He only shook his head, made a tisking sound with his mouth and replaced them in the basin to Gilda's delight. A clap of his hands echoed through the stony silence of the now empty room which was only broken by the occasional snap from the fire.

Another two basins arrived, one laid on the seat next to her the other in the lap of this confusing man, she openly sighed in bliss when her hands met the welcoming heat. Unable to fight any longer, Gilda allowed herself to flout propriety and melted into the cushioned back of the settee. Her eyes slid closed and she listened with half an ear as the doctor spoke, "The hands are worse than the feet and I predict she will be in quite a lot of pain tomorrow. Unable to walk or stand for any significant period of time, and she will require someone to help her dress and eat."

Questing hands parted the folds of the robe and her head flew up from the silk upon which it rested, "Easy now," the doctor said, "I just want to look at those knees, they've done quite a bit of work these last few nights."

Gilda's mind seized on that phrase, realizing just how very long she'd toiled in that hole alone with only her thoughts to guide her. There were so many questions that she wanted to ask, but they very fiber of her soul was so weary. She once again laid back, savoring the warmth of this room and the water which was now stinging in the raw flesh of her palms. Gilda couldn't understand this place or these people, but they were kind. She was certain there was some misunderstanding, but it would have to be sorted out tomorrow as she didn't have the strength tonight.

Her wounds were cleaned and dressed, her host was given stern instructions to keep her in bed for most of the day and told that the bandages would be changed when he came back after she'd rested. He was to be called if any trace of inflammation or fever showed and with that, the doctor kissed the top of her bandaged hand and bid her a pleasant evening.

The world had begun to slow down for her, turning her head felt as if it took an age. Her arms and legs weighed a thousand pounds and at the same time her head was in the clouds. The words of her doctor made sense minutes after he had left the room and slowly, like sifting through mud, she understood that there had been something in that wine.

Without a word Gilda was coaxed from the settee and that bone melting fire where in limping strides, greatly assisted by several valets, she was shown to a bedchamber. A fire burned merrily in the marble hearth and the velvet draped bed had been turned down. An onyx framed mirror dominated the corner and over the fireplace, a painting of a hare with amber eyes as it sat stilly in the brush.

The valets left as a pair of young girls entered, to help Gilda dress for bed she assumed. But when they both covered their eager eyes with blindfolds, tying them tightly at the back of each other's heads and pulled on a pair of gloves, she looked to the man with such confusion. Gilda opened her mouth to demand he explain but all that came out what a muffled exhale, even her lips and tongue could barely function under the haze she found herself.

Time began to slip and in small flashes she watched as the girls undressed her without the aid of their eyes. Even with the encumbrance of gloves their clever hands never even so much as faltered as they washed every trace of grime and dirt of her journey from her with perfumed water and soap by the fire.

Weak as a kitten Gilda was quickly dressed in a sleeping gown, her damp hair brushed and the blankets pulled up by her blind handmaidens who quickly retreated, pulling the door closed behind them.

She struggled to keep her eyes open, willed whatever potion she had greedily drunk to fail. Even breathing was a struggle and every fibre of her being longed to rest, to sleep...even for just a second but still she battled in vain. Gilda drifted off to sleep regarding the painting over the fire place and the strange hare that stared at her from his perch.

She was enveloped in a soupy fog then, dense and strangling as her ears strained at a rustling nearby. Staggering from the warm bed on maimed feet, now swollen and tender after being tended to, Gilda made precious little progress in the blinding dim through the maze like corridors and halls. Another crackling turned her attention and after a few more limping steps a scrambling of feet on stone led her into the parlor where she had stumbled naked from that hole.

The great door hung open still, the foul air and firelight from the lanterns inside drifting through the opulence of an expired party. Heavy fog rolled along the carpets to curl around the legs of chairs like a snake in the grass. Her eyes caught the knocker once more in the dim, its eyes flashing at her with menace and before she could reach out to strike the mighty plate once more she heard a rustling across the room and drunkly followed.

Gilda went on like that in the swirling mist, following the trail of an unseen guide as it made its own way through this place. She was unafraid, or perhaps still too exhausted to muster such dramatics after what she'd endured. The silhouette of something small and moving close to the ground darted out the massive front door to the sprawl of forest that surrounded this place. Unable to resist, she followed in a shuffling gate, catching her balance on a candelabra that tumbled to the rug as she staggered by, the flames taking to the finely spun rug in hungry waves.

The scent of fire barely registered over the wild wind rising outside, wincing at a stone beneath the howling sole of her foot, the fog began to thin, and her eyes recognized the snarling bramble of a dense wood.

From a tangle of downed branches and twigs, burst a hare with eyes that burned like fire. His dark ears perched proudly on a chestnut head, he lighted upon a tree stump and regarded her with an interest Gilda found odd. His nose bobbed and twitched at her, his smoldering eyes running the length of her frame. The hare went deadly still then, as if a predator was nearby and his fear had turned him to stone. Without preamble or warning he leapt from the stump, looked back with a questioning expression that seemed to say, "Are you coming?" and bounded toward a clearing with Gilda close behind.

Gilda tore through the woods where she could hear the leaves below her feet as she walked across the cold damp earth. The trees were ablaze in the throes of autumn, shedding their summer leaves in a riot of amber and golden hues. The long velvet robe she wore drug damply on the Earth as she ventured into the frosty chill of the night.

Was this a dream?

Perched high on a lonely hill, she looked back for only a moment to see the lodge from which she'd emerged. Flames had begun a high dance in the windows of the mighty hulk of stone and mortar. The monster on the mountain surrounded by black forest was slowly burning from the inside out and through the lingering haze of her mind Gilda decided it was likely for the best.

A noise called her attention from the structure, her eyes searched but no one was about this place. It was late, and the woods dense…she moved away from the lodge to the trees. A harvest moon hung heavy on the horizon, its honeyed light dripping through the shadowy claws at her feet. Twigs and branches tugged at her hair and nightgown, the inky night sky winking with stars as a loon sang nearby.

In the distance, she caught a glimpse of someone standing in the moonlight with great arms outstretched to the heavens. Her bandaged foot found purchase on a rotten root and as her tender sole broke through the dead crust of it the snap echoed out and into the night sky, shattering the stillness like a stone as she fell into a bramble bush.

The stranger turned to where Gilda was tangled in thorns, effectively trapped. He moved to her swiftly, unnaturally so and in midnight sun she could see nothing of his face, just him coming for her. She tugged and struggled, but it felt like the vines were holding her, tightening her grip, keeping her still...for him.

A desperate sound escaped her lips and he froze a few feet from where she lay tangled.

He held up his hands and turned enough so his face was caressed by the moonlight.

"I won't hurt you." He said softly, "Let me help you."

She regarded him for a moment, he looked kind enough and could certainly have overtaken her should he have wanted. He was tall and quite strong looking, the arms he held up bulged...her silence must have spurred him to continue.

"I'm Adam, the blacksmith from the village....?" He offered, creeping toward her.

"What village?" Gilda asked shrilly, "We're in the middle of no-where!" She gasped yanking her tangled hair free with a cry.

He stopped where he was and a sly smile danced across his lips, "You wound to the quick my lady, it may not be much of one, but there's a village at the bottom of this hill, I should know, I've lived there all my life."

Gilda's eyes wildly scanned below, seeing no lights or rooves, nothing to show that anyone lived anywhere near this place.

"I'm sure you've noticed that the trees are quite dense..?" He added, staying put with his calloused hands in the air and a look of increasing concern on his face.

She stared him square in the face then, and was a tragic sight indeed. Wound up in brambles with leaves in her hair, bare footed and bandaged, "Are you going to hurt me?" she asked in a small voice that trembled.

His face and hands fell, "Why would anyone want to hurt you?" he asked and without waiting for her answer he moved to her and began the arduous task of pulling loose her snares. She'd done quite a job of it and he finally gave up all pretense and pulled his dagger from his boot.

She jerked away from him then, a wild look covering her lovely face in a mask of panic and fear and he dropped the blade to the ground.

"What's happened to you?" he asked in a low voice regarding her carefully.

"I'm not quite sure." Her eyes shimmering with tears, "Where are we?"

His look of surprise was clear, "You mean you don't know?" he asked.

She shook her head and sniffed.

He considered for a moment, and then just blurted, "We're near Dublin, lass."

The expression of panic and fear that crossed her face almost drove him to tears himself, she sagged further down to the Earth and began to cry in earnest. Sobs wracked her body as he made quick work of the rest of the thorns that caged her. Hauling her from the ground and into his large arms, he held the strange woman while she wailed and waited for her to calm.

It took quite a while, and when she finally came up for air she was a mess. He scrubbed her wet face with his calloused hands and pushed her hair back from her face.

"Where have you been?" he asked worrying over the bandages on her hands and bags beneath her eyes.

She pulled in a jerky breath and gestured to the lodge with a healthy stream of smoke flowing from the open front door, "There."

His eyebrows knit together in confusion, "You came from there?" he asked incredulous.

She nodded, concern growing from his reaction.

He looked around, took in the sight of the growing fire and leveled his gaze at her, "We cannot stay there lass, they're bad people, that lot. And I don't want to scare you, but you're not safe...." He pulled his jaw into a stern expression, "Come with me."

"I don't know you!" she hollered, shoving him away with both hands, and feeling more than a little embarrassed that she'd allowed him to hold her so long.

"You don't know them either!" he bellowed back. "And you've no idea where you are!"

"This is ridiculous!" she spat.

He ran after her and caught her arm in a vice grip, "You're in danger."

Gilda yanked her arm from his grasp, "Thank you for your help Adam, it was a pleasure to meet you." And began staggering slowly down the hill.

"I've heard the screaming coming from this place on the wind. I don't know who you are or how you came to be here, but this is a foul place you've found yourself in." He lectured, wagging a cautionary finger in her face.

She lowered her head to her chest, "Gilda."

"What?" he asked raising her chin with the same finger he'd used to scold her.

"I'm Gilda McGregor." She offered meekly.

"Scottish then," he said softly, looking her face over as if it was something new to his eyes, "well, I'll not hold it against you. My offer stands..." he cradled her face in his big hands then, his amber eyes pleading, "will you come away with me, Gilda?"

Chapter 4

Cullen's eyes jerked open at the alien sound of his phone vibrating across the room on the desk he'd left in on last night. It was 11 in the morning and he still felt like he'd only slept scant moments. Groaning as he drug his still dressed body from the bed...or what was left of it, he stiffly walked over to see it was Mr. Baruch calling.

"O'Keefe." He answered, his voice a little more gravelly than he would have liked.

"Sleep well?" The honeyed voice dripped over the line, Cullen could hear a trace of a smirk on his boss's lips as he asked. "Have you gotten our competition's number yet?"

"Unfortunately not," Cullen admitted, scrubbing his face and sitting on the edge of the bed attempting to will himself awake. "This woman is harder to track down than you are..."

"I am disappointed Cullen, I would have thought you'd have that woman taken care of by now."

'Well, there's more than one way to skin a cat." Cullen snapped, a little more sharply than he should have. He winced for a moment, regretting answering at all when he wasn't at his best.

"Indeed there is." He'd replied after an uncomfortably long pause. "You have one day Cullen, to get this lady sorted and away from my door. Do what you have to, understand?"

"You can rely on me, Sir." Cullen replied, and heard the line go dead.

He looked at the phone for a moment and wondered what had possessed Mr. Baruch, he was never so driven to win a single thing in Cullen's experience with him. He couldn't figure out why the stakes were so high on this particular auction, this door of all things...

Why did he want it so badly?

Pushing those questions away his mind returned to Mrs. Sloan, she was a problem and a complicated one. Last night's search had verified nothing about her, he could usually gauge with startling accuracy what kind of money a person would throw away at an auction. What things they were interested in, what they already had and where they came from. She remained one big question mark, a blank space and he couldn't work with that.

His usual tricks weren't yielding any results, it was time to get back to basics. Cullen threw his phone on the charger and started the water in the shower.

He regarded himself critically in the full length mirror, everything had to be just so or this wasn't going to work. It was a formula, a very simple formula and once you knew that the world was your oyster. It wasn't auction day, so he'd toned it down with jeans, but kept it sharp with a short collar button down. His boots could use a polish but it was all part of that Southern boy charm which he'd discovered was universal on this Earth and if he played it right, he'd have Mrs. Sloan nailed down by noon.

It was hard not to call her Owl Face and Cullen made a mental note to never give the people in his industry nicknames like that again, as the horrendous moniker had almost slipped from his lips several times. Deidre, as he'd discovered her name actually was, turned out to be a very knowledgeable resource at Sotheby's, not just about the artifact which would remain on display until tomorrow, but the people that patronized the auction house.

Of course, he'd golly gosh geezed his way into this conversation with some open ended questions about the door and where it had come from.

My how we do run on....

He thought as she detailed with no small amount of enthusiasm,

"...the great effort it took to merely remove the door from what had been its resting place underground for the last 400 years and it was just so remarkable, because it had been buried all that time and with no signs of degrading which is unprecedented for this time period!"

Somehow, she was even more dull when she was excited and that was just a cruel trick of fate in Cullen's eyes. But he kept them raptly focused on her face, a small smile on his lips listening as if he would never hear enough.

"The stain that covers it remains a mystery," she added with a tone of puzzlement, "our laboratories have failed to identify its composition, but can say that whatever it is has tremendously high iron content and a rose oil base."

The light from the windows was landing just so on the thick lenses of her glasses, causing a mirror effect that caught the reflection of the door about which she spoke so fervently up in the sheen.

"And if I have one regret in connection with this piece," she said almost wistfully, "it's that I'll live my life without hearing the sound of that massive door when the knocker strikes the plate..." she drifted off then, her eyes fixed on the case with a small smile on her lips, much like the one Cullen was struggling to hold.

He shook his head sympathetically at this last comment, as if he too would be eternally haunted by the lack of ancient door knockers he'd heard in his life. It would appear that she'd run out of things to say, for the moment at least and lest he spend the day here listening to Deidre he'd best take advantage of her temporary silence.

This was the tricky part and it had taken him a long time get the timing of it right, he waited for her to tear her gaze from the case and back to his own eyes which were fixed on her. When she did, he'd smile and she would too, he'd laugh and so would she and if she was bold enough to still meet his gaze, he'd go in for the kill with a slow bite of his bottom lip and she'd be a goner.

Dedire was no stiff mark, the second she'd looked back to him and caught his eyes for a moment she'd broken out in this nervous laugh that could only described as tragic and a little part of Cullen started to truly feel badly for her. He laughed along and when they wound down he shook his head, as if completely overwhelmed with everything she'd told him.

"I'm just so glad I stopped in here today Deidre," he drawled sweetly, "I truly appreciate all the time you've taken to detail some of the finer points of this piece."

She blushed and swatted an affable hand at him, "It's my pleasure."

"Lucky for me it wasn't too busy, or I'd have missed out. Have a lot of people been by to chin with you about it?" he asked casually.

"Oh my yes," she'd raised her eyebrows well over the rims of those round spectacles at the memory of it, "its caused quite a stir in the collecting community and you could say lots of people have come out from the *woodwork* for it!"

He picked up on her little joke and rewarded her with a good chuckle. "The funny thing is, I ran into someone yesterday and I could have sworn I'd bumped into her before at The Sotheby's in New York, but that was a couple of years ago and I just couldn't place her."

Deidre nodded then her eyes wide, "People I haven't seen in years have popped up for this one, I can't keep track of all of them, what did you say your name was?"

"Cullen, Cullen O'Keefe." He smiled again as she tapped away in the computer.

"Buyer for Mr. Baruch..." she murmured and then stopped abruptly. "Cullen...*you* are Cullen?" she asked with a realization, "I can't believe I almost forgot!" she trotted quickly to the other end of the desk and pulled a small envelope from a drawer. "Someone stopped by this morning, and mentioned that you might come in here looking for them, here's hoping it's your mystery friend from New York...cheers!" she'd said merrily as she handed it to him and sailed over to the glass case where a new set of people were about to be told just everything about the door inside.

Cullen blissfully tuned her out and turned his attention to the small envelope in his hands. His name was written in a fine script on the back, inside a single card read:

Tea?
Hotel
2 pm

Enola

The cab ride back to the hotel had given Cullen enough time to get it over with and get really, unabashedly angry. He didn't like being fucked with and certainly didn't appreciate this woman's personal brand of it which included clandestine notes and too brief to be considered polite invitations to tea.

If he was glad about anything it was that he was five minutes late when he finally stalked into the day room where she was perched at a window side table, happily munching a cucumber sandwich. He felt that same punch in the gut at the sight of her and nearly lost it. Striding up to the table as if he meant to flip it over, he tossed the crumbled note he'd clenched in his fist the entire way over into her lap.

"Just what the fuck do you think you're doing?" He spat out at her.

She offered him a wilting look, "I think I'm eating, would you care to join me?" His eyes were shooting daggers but she leveled it with her own, "Or you can continue to stand here in a room full of strangers while you throw scraps of paper at me and mutter obscenity laced sentence fragments."

Cullen's eyes danced around the room, seeing that he'd already caught the attention of several tables, he quickly sat down and checked his anger, but kept it simmering beneath the surface.

She was pulling the battered piece of paper he's tossed at her apart, seeing it was her note, she smoothed it on the table and once again turned her attention to Cullen. "What is it you want, Mr. O'Keefe?"

He looked away quickly, using his steaming cup of tea as an excuse and a distraction. Cullen preferred to be the one in control, the one asking the questions. He was uncomfortable here, with her and was wondering now if coming had been a good idea at all.

He cleared his throat after his tea was adequately sugared and stirred, "My…uh, my employer…you've piqued his interest." He managed lamely.

"Bullshit." She crowed shaking her head, "I am disappointed Cullen, I though you of all people would appreciate the direct approach." She dropped a few notes on the table and rose to leave, "Enjoy tea, on me."

"Wait..." he'd growled, and she stopped.

She turned, and locked eyes with him once again. It was unsettling how she stared him down, he'd never known a woman to do it and understood just now, what an uncomfortable place he'd put so many women in himself.

She regarded him a moment longer then satisfied he'd been appropriately backed down, she sat and lightly dropped her napkin in her lap, the iron lady was gone and in her place; a smiling tea time companion. "I hope you don't mind, I ordered Silver Needles....my favorite." And with that she dug back in, taking a scone from the trolley and smothering it in Devonshire cream.

Cullen was desperate to have something to talk with her about, "Your necklace," he started motioning to the sparkling orb, "is it old?"

She brought her hand to it and smiled, "Very, it's one of my favorite pieces." She took another sip of her tea and a gigantic bite of scone. "But we're not here to talk about my necklace Cullen, truly, what is it you want?"

He opened his mouth and realized he was going to try and work her, immediately thought better of it and blurted, "Are you bidding on the door or not?"

She rewarded him with a smile then, a beautiful one, "Yes."

He chewed on that for a moment and asked, "I don't supposed you'll tell me how much you have to spend?"

She laughed sweetly, "What fun would that be?"

"I have a lot riding on this auction Mrs. Sloan." He stated, feeling a cold sweat break out. "My employer is adamant that I win him this item."

"I understand Cullen, really I do." She began, reaching a slender hand across the table to his own, "And I know that you're paid to win, but no one wins every time."

He shouldn't let her touch him, he should pull away but it felt nice, her hand on his. It was a simple thing and he didn't have to ask for it or pay for it or trick her into doing it. He turned his palm to hers and curled his fingers around her delicate wrist.

"I know Enola," he said softly, "but I think if I lose, he'll fire me."

Chapter 5

Gilda lost herself in those amber depths for half a heartbeat and then shouting drifted down from the lodge, shattering the moment as torches hastened down the mountain.

"They've come for me." She said fearfully.

"They'll not make the same mistake twice, I'm afraid it's now or never." His body was tensing in anticipation of the fight to come, "We either run now, together or I never see you again."

Gilda looked back, they were in the woods now, the torches bobbing like fireflies through branches and snarls as they slowed. Behind that the lodge was a roaring inferno, the smoke blocking out the moon in the sky. She had a second, a single moment to make this decision, a decision that could mean life or death.

"What were you doing up here?" she asked quickly, searching his eyes for a trace of a lie, avarice, anything.

His neck bowed at the ludicrously timed question, "What was I doing up here?! What were YOU doing up here?" he cried.

"Adam, please." She took both of those big hands in her own hefting their strength, knowing he could kill her with them alone if he wanted, "I need to know."

His eyes rolled and then shot to the ever closer drawing lights behind her, taking a deep breath, his gaze pierced her own and his hands tightened around her slender fingers, "I don't know, I....I was drawn here...to you it would seem."

His answer wasn't any better than her own, but in his eyes she saw that he was just as perplexed and frightened as she was.

"Let's away Adam." She assented, grabbing the tattered and filthy hem of her nightgown and robe in one hand only to have her other seized in his own. Swiftly they ran down and around the slope to the back of the lodge straight toward a marsh rotten with gnarled oak.

As Gilda and Adam approached the tangled wall of branches and vine, the shouting grew ever closer, the encroaching torches throwing their stretched shadows long ahead into the black. As they scurried inside a second night afforded by the twisted canopy of branches and long dead leaves of summer's past, Gilda's bare feet sank into the putrid black mud with a splat.

Leading her with only a dagger at the ready, Adam hauled her through the clutching soup of the marsh one slurping step at a time. Deeper into the stilly silence of this dank place, she could hardly see a hand in front of her face.

She could make out what they were saying now, they were close and the disheartening snap of branches as they tore their way into this swamp with them confirmed how very near they were. A shaft of light from one of their torches lighted on Adam's face, spattered with mud and drawn into a determined snarl.

Their pursuers weren't any swifter in the now hip deep waters of this place than they were, but all of them were inside of it together and a broken branch, or loud noise could give them away at any moment. On and on she trudged behind him, dragging herself through after her tireless companion further and further into the swamp. Her feet were numb with pain and she was shivering from head to toe, and just when she imagined she would drop from exhaustion and drown in the mud, a branch snapped behind them closer than before.

Without pausing, Adam cut a sharp turn behind a massive dead oak surrounded by a dense glade of cat tails. Where he swiftly sunk up to his neck in the mossy water they inhabited. Pulling her with him Gilda allowed the fetid water to climb up and up her face until it was just beneath her nostrils. Shivering in the water, willing her teeth to stop chattering she and Adam waited as the torchlight grew stronger.

"Anything over there?" a strange voice called.

"Not yet!" a voice on the other side of the oak hollered, Gilda's whole body tensed in recognition. She'd know that voice anywhere...

Nathaniel

She froze as the visage she'd gazed upon so adoringly just days before crept out from behind the greying trunk. He held a torch high in front of him and Gilda saw the edge of a drawn blade at his side, those strange gloves on his slender hands. Her heart stuttered as she saw, truly saw what she wanted to deny...her own fiancé, hunting her in the night like some animal.

Before her mind could carry the cruel thread of thought any further, Adam's hand was squeezing her own beneath the water and pulling steadily down. She understood and took a final silent breath of the foul air that lifted off this marsh before slipping beneath its cloudy surface without a sound.

The flare of light from the torch was all around them under the murky water, Gilda had opened her eyes out of fear and necessity and they burned as if she'd rubbed Sulphur in them. Adam's were open as well, through the filmy moss that slid across the top of the water they could see Nathaniel searching, hear his sloshing steps in the underwater drum beats of percussive thuds that struck both of them.

Her lungs began the impatient march toward drowning, and that familiar primal need to surface and gasp freely at the air that was only inches away began to claw at her. Yet still she denied herself, the light was still too strong and she'd rather die drinking deep of this foul place than to see what Nathaniel had in store for her. Her eyes and lungs burned, Gilda clenched on Adam's hand and he in turn clenched back, holding her hand down, begging her to wait, to endure, to hold strong for...just... one...more...moment...

Spots of black began to seep in from the corners of the Earth, a strange weightlessness took over Gilda's limbs and faculties, something akin to being in water yet different somehow. The screaming urge to breathe that had been clawing in her chest was fading and a peaceful detachment washed over her. The black was dropping over everything like veil now, and she was unafraid, no longer cold or scared...as placid as a mill pond and moving toward something in the distance ....

She was almost there when she was jerked from that peaceful place and dropped without ceremony into a freezing, water-logged hell filled with screaming and clashing metal. Nathaniel's torch had been dropped in the water sometime between her near drowning and hateful awakening, leaving the three of them in hideous darkness.

Two men sloshed around each other in the water, the blade of Adam's dagger dwarfed by Nathaniel's sword.

"She'll drown if I don't get to her now." Adam grated harshly.

"You'll not touch her, foul curr!" Nathaniel screamed, "No man is worthy to touch her!"

"She's dying!" Adam wailed, "Please!!!"

Gilda was being hauled from the water by an unseen third, his harsh hands digging into her shoulders cruelly. She retched again and again, the filthy water that had filled her lungs and stomach pouring out of her in a flume of steam. A sputtering cough was all she could manage around the violent heaving of her innards.

"Calm yourself Brother Nathaniel," a familiar voice snarled, "she's wet and sick, but she'll live."

"Take her back to the lodge, Brother Maddox!" Nathaniel ordered, "I'll dispatch this one and join you there!"

Gilda's sloshing mind struggled to recall just where she'd heard that voice before, limp as a sack and slick as a noodle, she was barely any burden at all as he flung her body up and against that wretched oak tree. He shoved her dripping hair out of her face and met her befuddled stare with a cruel grin, "Of all the ladies I've put in that hole…you're the first to come out alive." He sneered, "Must be something special….to crawl from Hell's Throat."

Fear and rage took over her mind then, Gilda clawed at his eyes and face screaming. He hurled her back into the water where she sunk like a stone in her wet bedclothes. Scrambling to get her feet beneath her, she was on his back in a minute, her arms around his neck. Turning smartly he slammed her side into the tree with a resounding crack.

She wheezed as the wind left her lungs, losing her hold she slung low on his back to the loose soil that dead tree was anchored to. Kicking her sharply in her side once, and then again…she weakly rolled away back into the water just to get away from him. He followed in a lumbering fury, kicking water in great fans as he moved. Blood was dripping in his eyes along the scores she'd drug along his face and with both his gloved hands out, he clasped her throat and began to lift her by her neck from the churning water.

Gilda clawed at his arms and face but he was unmoving, that familiar burning rekindled in her lungs, the black spots and swimming head washing over her. Weaker and weaker, she heard Adam and Nathaniel's fight still...and from some secret place inside of her a small reserve of strength shimmered.

Reaching for it through the black, she managed one final kick to his groin which felled him in a moaning heap. Gilda threw all of her weight on his back, and shoved his head beneath the battle frothed water. He struggled to come up, pushing with his legs, which sank deep into the clutching soup of the bottom and with all of her might, she held him under as he thrashed until he went still and through the seizing death that took him...and she was certain that he was no more.

Having no time to contemplate what she has just done, Gilda turned her attention to the two men fighting in the water. One she'd just met, the other she'd known her entire life...or thought she'd known. Nathaniel thrashed wildly at Adam to no avail, they were both winded and wet.

"Nathaniel!" she cried, "Stop this now!" moving between them.

"I've sworn an oath Gilda," Nathaniel managed between gasps, "an oath of blood and bone, I've reaped what they've sewn and must pay what I owe."

"You owe them a woman? Your bride?" she asked shrilly, shielding Adam with her soaked body.

Nathaniel let out another heavy breath and lowered his sword, "You were never my bride Gilda, you were meant for something greater than the life we'd planned...you proved that in Hell's Throat...you stood, stripped before the Ram and he was moved....no Gilda, not my bride...you were never my bride."

"You're not making sense," she pleaded, "none of this makes sense."

"It will," he growled, "Now step aside and I will end this man who deigns to lay a hand on what belongs to"

The dagger landed cleanly in his forehead, halting him on his feet, his mouth open and blade up. Hanging in death for a moment as a final long breath escaped him and he slid into the water, his unmoving eyes searching the night sky.

Gilda watched as the man she'd planned to marry was engulfed in the greedy black waters of this foul swamp, and stared at the raft of bubbles that rose from depths into which he vanished. The final glint of the ram pinned to his sopping jacket giving her a final glare before it too was drowned with its owner.

"You can never really know anyone, can you?" she rasped, her throat hurt and she was freezing and now that the immediate danger had passed once again, the gravity of her situation struck with the fury of a raging storm and threatened to overtake her.

Adam took her trembling hand in his own, "There will be more of them, Gilda. We need to go now."

"Not yet," she said dragging him over to the man she'd drowned. He was firmly planted in the mud below, and slunk over face first in the water the wet and dirty back of his shirt curled out of the water in an awkward hump.

Without really looking at him as she did it, Gilda shoved both her hands in his pockets hoping against hope that it was still there, that he still had it on him.

"What are you doing?" Adam asked, befuddled and anxious to leave.

"He stole my necklace." Gilda said plainly, "But it's not here, so let's away."

Bedraggled and soaked with mud and blood spattering his face, Adam looked the worse for wear. As Gilda sloshed over to him she observed his face critically as they began again to leave.

"Are you hurt?" she asked looking for cuts on his arms and chest, somewhere in the fray his shirt had been sliced, but he looked unscathed.

"Your fiancé is quite the swordsman, Gilda, but I think I held my own this night."

"Former fiancé." She corrected, "I believe this marks the end of our engagement."

Chapter 6

"Good morning, Sir." Cullen answered the phone call he'd been waiting for.

"Good morning Cullen," he'd replied smoothly, "how are you today?"

"Ask me in three hours." Cullen shot back.

Mr. Baruch was his laughing easy going self this morning, 'Remember, twenty seven million dollars...For a door with a broken knocker." He'd joked. "What the hell am I doing?" he'd asked grinning, Cullen could picture it.

"I cannot rightly say, Sir...but we're doing it today."

"Then I'll talk to you in three hours, good luck Cullen."

"Good luck, Mr. Baruch." He'd replied, taking one last look in the mirror.

Sharp enough

He'd thought and walked out the door.

That confidence he'd felt on the phone had held until he reached Sotheby's, it was a bustling swarm of people signing in and setting down for the exhaustion of the Fall Catalog. Cullen went to the front desk and was greeted by Owl Face...Dedire, and she happily signed him in and handed him his paddle.

He'd all but sprinted to the bathroom to retch up what little breakfast he'd managed to get down, he was jittery this morning and that wasn't a good sign. Rinsing his mouth out from the tap in the sink, he stared at himself in the mirror.

You can do this

As he reached the salon he was treated to a second punch in the gut, this one he had expected. Seated in the third row, looking resplendent and well rested in her usual, unusual fashion which was an ivory dress with off the shoulder sleeves and a full skirt that screamed Donna Reid. Without a single strand of hair out of place in a Gibson Girl and her opalescent skin glowing in the light, she was a pearl in a sea of oysters. She noticed him standing in the doorway, met his gaze and offered a friendly smile and nod.

He returned it and hated himself for blushing, he'd cursed at her and thrown things at her and when she'd touched his hand he melted like butter. A confounding woman, Mrs. Sloan, who seemed to be able to reduce him to both boyish antics and unbridled rage.

The auctioneer dropped the gavel three times as is the custom at Sotheby's and all, including Cullen hastened to their seats. He was in a box to the side, where the buyers could use the dedicated hard lines to speak with their employers without disturbing others.

As he settled into the padded chair, Cullen realized he felt better. Perhaps the eggs had been bad or some other small issue, he wasn't jittery any longer, and with a satisfied sigh he crossed one long leg over the other and leaned back to enjoy the show, as his only interest in this auction, was the closing item of the day.

He quite enjoyed the auctioneer's style, having attended auctions the world over Cullen had triumphed in the steaming mosh pits of the open auctions in the bazaars of Turkey and Egypt. Kept his cool in the tight lipped trips to the mixed bag occasions across the continent and howled and hollered to victory in the musical mad house of an auction in the South. That's where he'd cut his teeth on the sport as the cadence of a portly man in suspenders rang off the walls of the place and people bid like mad waving fist fulls of cash in the air.

None of that wildness here, no sir, every word was clear and distinct, and the clean cut man in his late forties had eyes like an eagle for the white of the paddle, if you flashed it, you bought it with this guy. You could hear a pin drop as he politely worked the next to last auction, a homely vase reputed to be owned by Charlemagne or some shit like that. It was down to an old lady in opera earrings in the front and an Italian who stood near the rear, sunglasses still on.

"Alright, I have 52 from the lady, 52 from the lady."

The Italian flicked his wrist.

"Thank you sir, 53 from the gentleman in the rear, 53."

Opera Earrings thought for a moment, considering and waved back with a weak pull on a droopy arm.

"Thank you, that's 54, we have 54 from the lady and it goes back to you sir, may I please have 55?
Will you go 55?
55 sir?
Alright, that's 54 for the lady, its almost gone sir, 54 for the second time.
And I'm sorry sir, it's gone and she took it, congratulations to you my lady, its yours for 54 thousand pounds, and if I may see that paddle number, they'll have it waiting for you shortly."

He carefully wrote her paddle number and the amount on the tablet and the clerks scrambled wildly to disseminate the information throughout the network of the auction house. Verified funds would be drawn and held pending a discreetly obtained signature, shipping preferences would already be in the system and all with the hope of maintaining a seamless experience for those fortunate few who came here to buy.

"Ladies and Gentlemen, thank you and well done."

A half- hearted round of applause echoed through the salon at this platitude.

"We've all but done it, and before we get to the last item in our catalog we'll have a brief recess of ten minutes, thank you." He dropped the hammer and a low murmur rose from the crowd. Opera Earrings was already signing for her vase and The Italian was gone.

Came late and left early, tourist.

Cullen shook a head at that and rose to get a drink of water, there were chilled bottles at a table with napkins and mints. He helped himself to a mint as well and was walking back to his seat when he crossed paths with Enola, that whiff of roses was becoming more and more a scent he associated with her and not flowers.

"I thought for sure you'd be a buyer on Charlie Chaplin's mustache comb." She managed seriously.

"It was tempting, but I resisted." He jabbed back, "And look at you, the very bastion of self- restraint when Madonna's autographed bra hit the block."

She held her hands up as if even she didn't know how she could have resisted and they shared a good laugh.

The hammer fell three times and broke the spell.

"They're playing our song handsome," she held out a hand, "Good luck."

Cullen took it, held on a moment too long before saying, "Good luck Enola."

"Ladies and gentlemen, welcome back and thank you again for your patronage and patience. Without further ado, I am pleased to present for your consideration our final item for auction, the Hell Fire Door."

With a grand gesture the navy curtain was once again pulled back to reveal the ancient door where it perched in a pool of golden light. Seeming to hover under its own power, the ram at its center snarling back at those who dared meet his gaze.

Cullen took one last long look at that ram, and spared a moment to steal a glimpse of Enola looking as serene as ever. Then, resolute as ever he clapped his eyes back on the only person that was going to matter for the next few minutes of his life.

"In my humble opinion it is the find of this age, a piece of antiquity with such mystery and provenance is unlikely to be seen again in our lifetime. It would be my pleasure to open this auction at 5 million pounds."

Paddles flew up in the gallery and Cullen looked on passively, you never open the bid. You watch to see who the real players are after the rubber neckers run out of gall.

"I have 5, 6...thank you – there's 7. Here comes 8 followed by 9."

There was a lull, what Cullen liked to think of as The Hump. Most of the patrons of this place would consider anything under ten million pounds spending money, but past that threshold and you were getting serious. This was where he was going to see who his competition was.

A man near the left with a beard took the plunge.

"That's 10, thank you sir. Who will give 11?"

Enola gracefully entered with a flash of her paddle.

"11 from the lady and welcome to the auction, who will be 12?"

Cullen tipped his hand

"And from the box that's 12, who will be 13?"

The Beard hesitated half a heartbeat before assenting.

"Thank you sir for 13, can I trouble the lady for 14?"

She didn't even think about it.

"There's my 14, what does the box have to say about that?"

Cullen followed suit.

"15 it is...from the rear..? Sir?"

Enola cut in.

"And the lady wants it for 16, does the box beg to differ?"

Cullen held his ground, lifting his chin to the auctioneer in a jerk.

"Perhaps 16 and a half?"

Cullen flashed paddle, but Enola was right behind him.

"The lady says 17 sir."

Cullen flashed again.

"17 and a half, it is."

Feeling his heart start to pound, they were getting close to that magic number. With the exchange rate he could go as high as 20 million pounds without busting the limit…casually he raised a hand to the handset placed next to him and raised it to his ear.

Before Mr. Baruch could answer Enola was ahead again.

"That's 18 million pounds from the lady, I see the man in the box has taken a call, what say you sir, 18 and half?"

"Don't say anything," Mr. Baruch said calmly, "I heard him, keep going."

Holding the phone to his ear in a hand gone clammy, Cullen raised.

"18 and half from the phone, what say you my lady, how does 19 suit you?"

Enola looked at the auctioneer, cast a determined gaze at Cullen and without taking her eyes off his, raised a defiant hand. Her brazen act of breaking the invisible wall that separates all bidders from one another pulled a cloud of gasps and murmurs from the lookers on. It was the Sotheby's equivalent of spitting in his face, and Cullen felt himself flush.

"And she is lovely when she's angry ladies and gentleman, she's got the box in her sights with 19. 19 million pounds from the lady in the gallery, how does the box sit?"

"Damn it!" Mr. Baruch growled into Cullen's ear, "…20."

Cullen raised.

"She doesn't frighten him though, that's 20, does the lady raise?"

Enola did.

"21 million pounds for the lady, and for the box?"

Cullen felt a bead of sweat roll from beneath the earpiece he was crushing to his head, "Mr. Baruch?"

"I heard him..." he spat, "I fucking heard him!"

"And from the box?" The auctioneer coaxed, "We have 21 million pounds from this exquisite lady, sir?"

"Mr. Baruch?" Cullen prodded.

"Hit her again." He snarled.

Cullen's hand flew and a gasp came from the crowd, they were all on the edge of their seats and even the auctioneer had been caught up in the fury, his eyes glittering with excitement, tie slightly askew.

"Ladies and gentlemen, 21 and a half from the box! What will the lady do?"

Enola alone remained unaffected in the fervor, a beacon of calm in the storm of her own making.

She raised that delicate wrist once more and Cullen felt it in his gut. She may as well have been raising an axe.

"She is fearless ladies and gentlemen! 22 million pounds from the lady, 22 sir, what say you?"

All eyes fell on Cullen, and he strained to hear through the line, Mr. Baruch saying anything...something...but he remained silent.

"22 million sir, do you have 22 and half? Sir? I'm going to let her have it, it's almost gone...."

"Mr. Baruch?" Cullen said harshly into the receiver.

No response.

"She could go all night, but she won't have to! Ladies and gentlemen, sold to the lady for an astounding 22 million pounds! Congratulations."

The salon erupted into a thunderous round of applause as people leapt to their feet.

"You're fired." Mr. Baruch said plainly and cut the line.

Chapter 7

Dawn was prying away at the night's final grip on the horizon, heralded by a honking V of geese as they sought warmer climes than these. Gilda watched with bleary eyes as they coasted across a clear sky that had just shaken loose the stars, and wished she could throw a rope around them and be carried on downy wings away from all of this ugliness.

These last hours? Days...? Had left her weary and heartbroken. Far from home, battered, bruised and betrayed, her heart trembled at the thought of what might have befallen her family at the hands of her former fiancé.

Nathaniel Smyth had been a good match, at least Gilda had thought so. A soldier in the Queen's Guard and someone she'd known so long that she could never quite recall how she'd met him. They'd played in the street on summer nights and it was a natural occurrence that their families collided as his parents lived two houses from her own. The effortless freedom of childhood had given way to the awkward strain of blossoming adulthood and things began to change between them.

Nathaniel had grown rapidly into quite a handsome man, eyes the color of glacial ice set off by onyx hair and features so sharp that Gilda almost feared to touch him at times. What started as a wild boy fighting with wooden swords and bringing home frogs had grown into such an earnest and devoted young man. Always wanting to be a soldier, he had studied all manner of combat from a young age and was in possession of a unique strength, being both tall and lithe he was as agile as a cat and had ascended quickly among the ranks.

Gilda had been so very surprised when he'd asked her father's permission to escort her to the Guard's Ball and she and her mother had even made a special trip to the tailor for a gown befitting the occasion. He was a wonderful dancer and she spent the night on his arm feeling proud and admired...he'd asked for her hand the next day and every day after that until the day she awoke in that fetid hole had been entirely devoted to becoming his wife and the mother of his children.

All of that was gone now, and Nathaniel was in the swamp beneath the tea stained water where time would slowly eat away at those unearthly features until he was nothing but bones. That idea filled her with a sort of burning righteousness that stung her heart.

Adam had never slowed, never released her hand and never stopped looking back at her, concern becoming more and more apparent on his blood spattered, mud caked face.

"Will you please stop that?" Gilda moaned as he turned mid stride to steal another glimpse of her shambling form as she limped behind him dutifully. "I'm not going anywhere."

"I'm certain of that." He replied shaking his head, "I'm not letting you out of my sight until we're far from that damnable hill."

"Where are we going?" she asked sounding more than a little like an overly tired child.

"Some place safe." He replied with an impatient tone pulling at his words.

"You've been there before?" she prodded with a distracted air as she craned her head to look around her surroundings coming into vivid relief in the dawn's unstoppable advance on the day.

"That's how I know it's safe." He bit out, pulling her arm a little harder than he should have as he crested over a large rock.

Gilda mulishly let her frame go limp, hanging her weight and twisting his arm back under it. She saw him set his jaw and with a determined yank her head snapped back as she all but flew up behind him. The open wounds on her feet screamed in agony as they scuffed along the craggy earth and with a small mewling cry, she crumpled to the ground and laid there unmoving and limp, her hand still clenched in his.

"Get up." He snarled, and pulled on her arm only to have her flop sadly back on the cold ground.

She shot him an icy look, said nothing and closed her eyes.

"I said GET UP." He over enunciated every syllable, squeezing her hand on every one, willing her to rise from the ground and her childish tantrum to follow him to safety.

"Why?" she brayed.

"Because I said so!" He yelled down at her.

Unable to move away from him as he held her hand fiercely in his grip, Gilda settled for turning her head away from where he towered over her.

Dropping her hand and storming a few feet away, he raked a hand through his still damp hair angrily. He was sucking in deep breaths and forcing them out in great, loud puffs that rose through the chilled air in tiny clouds from his face.

When he was convinced he was calm, he crouched by her side, she was a sorry sight. The tattered velvet robe had crusted mud drying on it in streaks. The gown beneath stained a mottled brown from the horrid water of that swamp. She had bruises around her neck in spots and clots of a deep angry red, bags hung under her eyes and a green tinge had settled on her skin, giving her a waxy appearance that scared him.

"I apologize for being impatient Gilda." He said, holding her small clammy hand in his own massive palm.

Her eyes slid sideways to his gaze and flared a single brow at him but said nothing.

That tore it, anger flared up from deep inside and he dropped her hand, rose to his feet and bellowed to the sky, "I have shod mules that are more cooperative and agreeable that you!"

"So take a mule to your safe place." She sneered.

"Would that I could Miss McGregor," he snapped in her face, bent haughtily at his waist so his eyes looked into her own, "It would be infinitely better company not to mention the greatly improved smell."

And with that he stormed away, shaking his head and dusting his hands in mighty claps as he went, seeking to erase her from his mind with the motions of his body.

He didn't even make it two dozen paces. Halting in his stride he heard her choked sobs and turned to see that she had clapped her filthy hands over her face as she lay where she'd fallen in the marauding morning light. Feeling truly sorry now, he made his way back to her and flopped on the rock beside her.

Clasping her hands with his he pulled them away from her face gently, "Stop that," he crooned and looked upon her once again, "you're awful to look at when you cry."

She stopped with tears still sliding down the sides of her blotchy face, paused a moment and broke out in sniffling laughter, he joined her and they had a good chuckle about it. Adam realized he was still holding her hands and looked critically at her palms, they were bleeding anew, the red shining wetly on her clammy skin. He checked her feet and put a hand across her forehead, in spite of the chill in the air, she was scalding.

"I know you're tired and sad and that nothing seems to be worth getting up," he pleaded with her, "but I need you to find whatever you've got left in that body and do just that."

Something in the expression on his face, that look of worry in his eyes and the too gentle way he held her hands pulled Gilda out of her self-pity and into the moment. This man didn't know her, certainly didn't have to stay or help, but he was doing just that.

Unfortunately, laying down for those few moments had given her body a taste of rest and moving was pain poured over agony. She groaned and broke into a cold sweat just trying to sit up. He clapped one of those mighty hands between her shoulder blades and helped, then holding her up, offered the other and raised her from the ground on teetering feet.

She winced as her weight once again rested on those tender soles, swayed deeply, her eyes rolling up in her head slightly before he caught her and righted her.

"When was the last time you ate anything?" he questioned, looking into her pupils which had opened at the center until there was only black.

She wrinkled her nose and looked sideways in an effort to recall, and finally shrugged shaking her head.

He sighed deeply, threw her arm over his shoulder, wrapped his about her waist and oriented them once again toward the horizon.

It was slow and lumbering and he could have sworn she was sleeping on her feet, her feverish head lolled against his shoulder as they tottered up into the hills where the woods were deep and lush. She was breathing in wheezing fits and laboring coughs, her feet shambling over the now mossy grass as she clung with all she could muster to Adam.

He had to admire her, she was mulish and stubborn but she was a strong one under it all. He didn't know many men that would endure this trek in their best health, let alone after being starved and beaten with a fever clawing at their heels. She never whimpered, never whined, only mumbled and murmured to people that weren't there.

At one point she started crying, apologizing to her father for falling for the wrong man. For not seeing sooner what he was and he felt genuine regret for the girl, this Earth was peopled with men who understood nothing and believed they knew everything. Their actions had wrought this chaos and for what? If a thing is meant to be, it will be...no one has to go to any great trouble to make the fate of one person as it was written. He could go on for days about the misconceptions of men, but it would always fall on deaf ears.

The sigh that escaped his lips when they crested that final hill into a secluded valley with a narrow channel of a lake at its doorstep took with it all the worry and rage the night had created. He directed the now hysterical Gilda toward the cottage at the stony shore and hoped he had the wherewithal to get her through the dangerous days ahead.

The workings of the human body were also a bit of mystery to him, having spent ages at the forge hammering metal and steel, bending to his will the unyielding with heat and brawn...he was worried he may fail her should the body that had gotten her this far begin to falter.

Hewn from pine with a mossy roof and stone fireplace, the cottage was small but sturdy. The walls would keep the chill off if he was good about the fire on the hearth. Fish and hare could easily be caught and they would be safe here until she was mended.

After that, who knows where they could go…where would she be safe?

He stretched her out on a pallet of wool blankets and her eyes rolled one final time before the fever took what little remained of her faculties, and in the welcoming black, Gilda found respite in the rare and untold oblivion of unconsciousness.

Chapter 8

"Cullen.....Cullen! CULLEN!"

He heard the crack against his skin before he felt it and then he felt everything. His head was two sizes too big and throbbing, his stomach churned and bubbled and now there was a burning sting across his face where someone had slapped him.

Opening a tentative eye he squinted into the filtered light of another rainy day in London only to be greeted with the impatient glare of none other than Mrs. Enola Sloan.

"What are you doing in my room?" he groused sourly, belching a little as he did.

"Is that where you think you are?" she asked incredulously, "Look around you Cullen."

Rubbing his eyes he blinked several times in the damnable light and saw cars crawling by behind her, the morning sky as it rained lightly and sidewalk. He was on the fucking street.

"Jesus Christ." He muttered.

"Don't drag him into this mess," she admonished bending to haul him from the doorway he had obviously spent the night in, "you're the one that decided it was a good idea to get pissed."

"Don't yell at me." Cullen moaned rising with her help easily, as he met eyes with hers, another of those watery belches erupted from him and she turned her head in amazed disgust.

"Mr. O'Keefe...you stink." Observing him critically for a moment, still holding his arms she asked "Can you get back to your room?"

"I don't have a room." He mumbled hanging his head, "You won the auction, and I got fired and when I got back here I was told my accommodations were no longer available...so I decided to get drunk instead."

"Why didn't you just pay for another room?" she asked.

Cullen opened his mouth to reply, and was instantly struck with the realization that he had none. Closing his mouth for a moment, opening it again and finally saying, "I don't know, but I didn't."

Enola leaned toward him slyly with a confidential grin on her face, "I think you might still be drunk, Cullen...what do you think?"

He glanced around them shiftily, put a finger to his lips and made a shushing sound before whispering, "Don't tell anyone!!!"

"Oh I won't," she swore with her hands to the damp sky, she pulled him to a nearby water spout that was spraying down a gutter. Wetting her hands she turned her attention to Cullen, washing down his face and slicking back his hair roughly, he stood obediently as she straightened him out.

"Thank you." He said, "Now what?"

She took his hand in her own damp palm, "Now you come with me," she said starting down the road, "you're in no condition to look after yourself today."

They walked a few steps in amenable silence, hand in hand and Cullen recognized the direction they were headed.

"Are we going to Sotheby's?" he asked in a fuzzy tone.

"That we are Cullen," she confirmed, "I know you take no joy in looking at the object that's brought you to this state.

But I must verify its condition before its crated to be shipped and I'm sure you'll understand that if I want to make this afternoon's freight it must be done now."

"I do." He nodded, looked down at her hand in his own and started swinging it in comically large arcs as they walked, "Can we get some breakfast after?" he asked boyishly.

"I'll think about it." She smirked, "but only if you throw up first, don't want to waste good money."

"Says the woman who spent 22 million pounds on a door with a broken knocker." He teased, recalling Mr. Baruch saying the same thing to him.

She laughed then, good and hard with him and though the swinging stopped because frankly, Cullen didn't have the strength for it, she kept his hand in her own slender grasp as they rounded the corner.

The shrill wail of an alarm was the first thing that struck them, causing Cullen to wince and Enola to pull him into a trot toward the stately building. As they approached one of the narrow windows that framed the door shattered into the street a scream following it. Cullen pressed himself against the wall as screaming and the unmistakable sound of gunfire came from inside.

"Call the police and stay here." She said without hesitation and moved for the door. Cullen seized her arm in its filmy blouse, and asked, "What the hell do you think you're doing? You can't go in there!"

She shook him off and repeated, "Stay here, call the police." And began moving once again for the door, which was hanging open at a strange angle. She realized Cullen was behind her, holding onto the fabric on the side of her skirt. She gave him another stern look, "Ok fine, new plan. Stay behind me, don't get hurt."

He nodded at that and felt no small amount of shame in cowering behind a finely dressed woman in a blouse and skirt who barely hesitated at the prospect of being shot. But that was something he was willing to live with if it meant he survived.

As they approached the doorway it was clear from the marks on the hinges that some explosive had been detonated to breach the steel entryway. The cages that acted as a second defense in the atrium were crumpled to each side, as they made it into the smoky salon there was the clear outline of a person laying on the ground. Enola hastened with Cullen in tow and saw Deidre laying on that impeccable Turkish rug.

"Is she....dead?" he asked quietly.
"No." Enola replied looking her over quickly, "But she is hurt, will you stay here with her and wait for the police?"

"Where are you going?" he asked incredulously.

"Where do you think?" she quipped and without waiting, rose and carefully slipped past the clerks desk into the rear of the building where the priceless antiques were stored and more importantly, her door.

Cullen turned his attention to the woman on the floor, her glasses were crumpled on one side and the lenses cracked in spidery lines of white. A line of blood was running from her ear and she was so still, but breathing.

"Sorry Owl Face." He muttered and rose to follow the path Enola had taken from the public area to the vault. Billows of grey smoke rolled along the floor and hung in the air in a haze, emergency lights blazed and their flashes cascaded off the walls and doors. Someone cut off the siren that had been howling throughout the building and the lights immediately ceased. He could hear shouting down the hall and quickly moved toward it.

Through a large set of industrial steel doors, that also appeared to have been blown off their pins he could see the burning light of day coming in through the loading dock. The outline of a truck apparent in the space that the opening afforded. He slunk closer, careful to stay out of sight and behind the massive steel slab dangling loosely from the wall.

Four men, one with a shotgun and two handling the door on the open end of a forklift and the final in the cab of the truck as he sat with the motor running. Wondering where the hell Enola was, he peered a little closer inside the massive room that was rotten with racks loaded down under what must have amounted to hundreds of millions of dollars. He couldn't see her anywhere, and was afraid to move any closer.

The door behind which he was hiding became too much for the lonely hinge on which it hung and with a screeching clang it dropped to the concrete floor, stood for a moment and with a disarmingly slow arc, crashed to the floor rattling the shelves that lined the inner vault with a deafening thud. Four sets of eyes fell on him and he stood there dumbly, all too aware that Enola had been right, he was still drunk...

She sprung out from wherever she was hiding at the man with the gun using Cullen's accidental distraction to her advantage. He was much larger than she, however she took the gun from his hands with all the apparent effort she might have used to remove the cap from a pen. Battering his face with the butt she threw the gun across the room and turned her attention to the forklift operators who were angling the door hastily up and into the box of the truck.

It clattered inside heavily, pulling the truck low on its shocks, the operator ran and hopped into the cab while his companion pulled down the door at the rear. Enola was charging up the ramp swiftly as he was jumping in the front with his companions. As it sped away from the loading dock and Enola ran after it for a few moments before she realized it was too late.

Enola made a beeline for the man she'd knocked out as he lay on the floor, Cullen stood over her as she crouched as his side.

"What are you doing?" he asked as she rifled through his coat and pants for his wallet.

"I'm finding out who took my door." She replied flatly as she hit pay dirt, opening the tri-fold leather wallet she looked closely at the identification card, replaced his wallet and rose.

"No cell phone?" Cullen asked, hopeful, "Because the police can track the calls from a cell phone."

"The police?" she laughed a little, "Will be nothing more than an irritant and a hindrance Cullen. I'm on my own."

"No you're not." Cullen walked to her and slid his hand inside her own.

"That is out of the question," she spun to face him, "I suspect we are dealing with something beyond the realm of pedestrian life Cullen, and I cannot be certain that you would be safe."

"And you're sure that you are?" he railed.

"My safety is not the priority, reclaiming the door is. You were drug into this mess entirely by accident and should go back to the hotel, pack your things and go home." She sighed as the wail of sirens approached, and moved to meet the police in the front of the destroyed building.

Cullen stood in her way, "I'm not leaving you."

"Go home Cullen, find a new job, marry a pretty girl, have kids and never think of me or that door again." Stepping around him again she moved for the door.

He caught her wrist in his hand and held firmly, "No."

"Cullen..." she pleaded, "I'm not sure I can protect you."

He looked deep into her eyes then and saw that she was truly afraid, not for herself but for him. "We'll protect each other Enola, just...don't send me away, please."

She was contemplating his plea when a mighty crash rang through the vault, one of the shelves was likely damaged when the doors were blown and finally gave way under the strain of the thousands of pounds it held. The twenty foot tall piece of steel came crashing down on them both in a hail of vases and paintings and bowls and bells. Cullen braced for the impact and seized Enola's hand, expecting to be crushed and more than a little grateful that he was still inebriated enough to quell his outright panic.

The crushing blow of the heavy shelf never came, opening a cautious eye he saw the shattered remains of the priceless relics on the floor around them and Enola at his side holding the massive structure from crushing them under its weight with a single extended arm. She squeezed his hand then, looking deep into his eyes, "It's all right."

None of this made sense, they should be dead or dying pinned under this monstrosity. Instead, she was holding his hand and holding the mass of iron up like the edge of a tent they were about to enter. Without so much as a strained breath or bead of sweat this beautifully dressed lady was doing the job a hoard of workers, forklifts and chains would have.

"Cullen," she said in an even tone, "I need you to listen to me right now."

He nodded dumbly, feeling a fuzzy detached sensation, then total calm.

"I'm going to let go of your hand and I want you to stay close to me and follow me toward the door."

Cullen nodded and she smiled at him, giving his hand a final squeeze before she released it and raising it to the shelf she was bracing from crushing them both. Hand over hand she and Cullen made their way out from under it, over the rubble of broken pieces of priceless art. Cullen holding onto the folds of her skirt much as he had when they'd walked into this place. When they were finally to the edge of the thing, she made certain he was out of the way and behind her before the let go, and with a deafening crash, it hit the floor in a thunderous clatter that shook the building around them.

Reality was starting to sink in, Cullen's brain was starting to fire at a million miles a minute trying to make sense of what he'd just seen. "What the hell just happened?"

"Cullen," Enola put a hand on his shoulder then, trying to calm him, "if we're going to stay together, there's something I need to explain to you."

"You're damn right you need to explain!" he hollered, backing away from her in wild unsteady steps. His breathing was coming in pants now and the room was beginning to spin around them both.

"I promise I will," she said coming to his side to steady him with her body, "I'll explain but we need to get through the process with the police and I cannot have you on the edge of hysterics while we do that, alright?"

He took a few deep breaths then, and felt his heart slowing. He looked at her as she watched him with a concerned expression on her face, "You mean it, I can..we...together?"

She sighed then with a smile on her face, "Yes, it would appear that's the way it's supposed to be."

The police were swarming in the vault with them now, and she and Cullen stood next to each other waiting for them to clear to room. He looked once more into her eyes opened his mouth to quip some witty comment about sidekicks and vomited down the side of her skirt.

Enola lowered her head and shook it, "Alright, breakfast on me then."

Chapter 9

Adam was hauling another armful of logs into the cottage, it was the third night of Gilda's fever, which showed no signs of breaking and he was truly starting to fear that she would expire from the strain. Walking into the cottage she was still on the pallet of blankets upon which she'd thrashed and moaned these past days, her hair soaked and matted from the chilled sweat that poured from her at intervals.

Another break in the storm that was boiling inside of her, she alternately wept and raged and had managed to escape the confines of the cottage as he dozed in the nearby chair. Crawling on her hands and knees, chanting in a cracking voice that made his stomach clench, "Expect cruelty....expect cruelty."

He'd started sleeping next to her then, holding onto the sour bed gown that clung to her, feeling the heat rise from her sallow skin in waves. He swore he could smell the inflammation that plagued her body at times, a fctid and mossy scent that rankled off her at the most violent pitches.

Doing the best he'd could, Adam had cleaned and bound her hands and feet. Wiped her steaming head and held her as she flailed through the terrors that chased her. This fearsome woman who was trapped in a Hell of her own design, one he could not free her from, regardless of his brawn...and his heart was breaking for her.

A storm was brewing outside, dark clouds coiled over the valley like a snake about to strike and deep thunder rolled from the sky down onto the solitary building causing the planks of the floor to tremble. Gilda stirred under the electricity in the air, her reprieve stolen by the tempest gathering its strength outside, a low moan escaped her then as she rolled weakly to her back, her expression one of pain mixed with fear.

He quickly tossed a few logs onto the fire and laid next to her on the mess of blankets, gathering her in his arms he sought to soothe her with his body. Crooning nonsense in her ear and rocking gently, fearing that tonight she would be stolen from him, just as she'd been found. Tonight she would die.

It made no sense, as he clung to this perfect stranger that he'd found under the harvest moon, running from strange men having emerged from a dark place.

Why her?

He pondered, looking down at her sunken, gray visage. These past days had taken their toll, she was nearly dead and a haunting rattle shook deep in her chest as the great gasps erupted from her in between terrifying moments where she didn't breathe at all. He'd never felt so powerless or weak in his life, all this strength inside of him – so much raw power and yet, outflanked by an inflammation.

His fury rose and Gilda stirred under his rancor, her eyes focusing on his for a scant moment in razor clarity before she was once again drug under by the oblivion in which she wandered.

Inspiration struck him in that second, and while it may just be the end of her, at least she'd die fighting and something in this woman, deep inside of her under the beauty and fragility, wanted the fight...needed it to survive.

He rose and opened the door, welcoming in the wind where it stirred around knocking over the scant pieces of furniture and crockery. The icy visitor lighting upon the trembling body swirling around Gilda as if this was its reason for the storm, as if it wanted her.

She moaned and curled into a ball against its chilled caress, and Adam went to her, nudging her out of her stupor.

"Get up." He said.

She moaned and writhed, a flash of lightning struck and the thunder chased it down the valley, a growling that spread its wings over this sanctuary menacingly.

"Get. Up." He pushed her a little further and he saw her fingers clasp out at nothing, her eyes fluttering wildly.

Now or never.

He thought, feeling the wind rise as the sky tensed for another bolt of fire.

Shoving her fiercely, rolling her to her back again he bellowed into her pasty face, "GET UP!!!"

Her eyes flew open and she matched gazes with him, "Gilda MOVE!" he screamed at her, the wind howling behind him through the shuttering cottage as the clouds roiled above.

Her body shuddered and he saw her muscles clench and release in exhaustion. Her mind would have to overcome her body, she'd have to fight from within.

Adam lowered his voice to a guttural tone, leveling a predatory gaze at the feverish woman for which he'd cared these scant days gone by. "Gilda McGregor..." he harshly spat at her, "I'm coming for you."

Her eyes opened wide enough for them to roll from her head, her pupils flowering to nothing but black as the fear he was stirring inside of her began to take hold. He lunged for her then, arms opened and tense and from somewhere deep inside of herself, Gilda found the strength to struggle to her feet and run.

Out the door she bolted into the thrashing woods as the storm tumbled and shook their mighty limbs. The placid water of the lake thrummed with the raw fury the sky was pouring over this place, over them. Adam gave chase, yelling after her until his throat was raw, watching her stagger and fall over and over again as she sought to escape.

Fight

He thought

Please...fight

Further and further from shelter she lumbered on exhausted legs, away from him and into the unknown. Her fever weak body took the path of least resistance which led her straight to the rocky lake, its emerald depths revealing the stony bottom fathoms below.

She stopped at the shore, yanking her foot back as if the water scalded her flesh. Reeling around at Adam as he slowly approached, stalking her like some wild animal would its prey, cornering her between water and himself.

He locked eyes with her again, the wildly frightened eyes darting between him, the lake and the sky. Her hands shaking madly as she focused through the fever, over the pain and just on him. The electricity rode the wind around them as the clouds gathered and roiled in the blackened sky. Her body finding its final reserve, that tiny shimmering scrap of strength and with a final bloodcurdling scream she ran at him a horrible expression of rage and madness on her face.

They collided and the sky cracked open and dumped rain upon their struggling forms, locked together in battle. He grappled with her, taken aback by the power with which she'd set upon him, quickly righting himself and turning just in time to take a sharp blow to his jaw.

She was in a fury, the storm beating down around them as if the sky were falling. The rain pelting them both, he looked at her holding his jaw and began the fight her in earnest because in Gilda's mind, this was life or death.

She came at him again, and landed another sound sock into his middle winding him and without thinking he shoved her hard. Sending her reeling backward only to have her maneuver her feet back under and rail at him again.

Lighting dove from the sky and set upon the trees that circled the lake. A fire blazing, coaxing itself from their parched bark, climbing the limbs until a wreath of flames danced around them throwing waves of heat down over their struggle.

He reached out with a wide grasp and caught her in a bear hug, hoping she would just wear out and sink back into the sleep that had trapped her. She wriggled and fought, landing kick after kick to his shins and thighs, but to no avail. Their gazes locked in the relentless rain, the two of them soaked and panting and he thought she might be giving in, letting go when an unnerving stillness fell over her.

Their eyes once again locked and Adam stared in the abyss that was her terror seized gaze. He felt her body tensing, clutching at something, gathering the way the lighting was once more around them. The thunder cascading over the valley in an endless wave of soul shaking power as the rain turned to hail and beat over their heads and shoulders, speckling the ground with white. As the fire raged behind them, sucking all the air to feed upon a horrible wind pulling the searing tongues to the sky, Gilda drew a final breath and all at once, unleashed hell.

An inhuman power possessed those fever ravaged limbs and with an ear piercing howl she flexed with all of her might. Breaking the lock Adam had around her, throwing his arms wide, tossing them apart from each other with a power that left him breathless. As he tumbled he saw her falling straight for the water, howling to the wind that danced with the roaring inferno behind her and as she struck the water with a deafening splash that reached the rock bed of the lake, the lighting thrust at the churning water as it engulfed her, the following thunder shaking the valley with the power of the heavens.

And as he looked upon her, drifting slowly under the charged water, the storm that had so suddenly and violently seized upon them, slipped away like the light inside of her, and he knew she was gone.

Chapter 10

A hot shower saved my life today

Cullen mused as he played at getting clean in the massive marble shower Enola's suite boasted. They had managed to get out of the authority's sights much sooner than anticipated, most likely thanks to him regurgitating down her skirt upon their arrival. But it made sense, their story added up and after assuring Enola that they would locate her stolen property, followed by an incessant apology from Sotheby's trembling at the thought of an insurance claim that would bring Lloyd's of London to its knees, they left.

She had taken it all in stride though, the vomit, the interviews, the business cards and the long walk back to the hotel. She refused to subject yet another innocent person to the result of his lack of common sense or self-control.

It was natural that she get the first shower, but had been kind enough to request that his belongings which were being held from his revoked room in the hotel safe be brought up for him. After finally slinking out of the confines of the steaming cubicle, he felt born again and then caught the scent of bacon creeping from the other room and realized there was life after death.

His bag had been discreetly placed in the walk in closet off the bathroom while he washed, he dug through for some clean jeans and shirt and walked into the bedroom to see Enola sitting at the vanity. Her hair was loose and tumbling down her back as she gently ran a sterling silver brush through the waving strands.

She hadn't seen him come into the room and he leaned against the door watching her for a moment. Enola looked like any other woman putting herself together for the day, staring critically at her face. At flaws only she perceived and as she pulled those silken strands up and into a ponytail she finally spied him watching her and smiled.

"It's very rude to stare." She admonished, smoothing her hair from her face and securing the massive swath of it behind her head.

"I wasn't staring," Cullen strolled into the room eyeing the room service cart on the way, "I was admiring you, Mrs. Sloan."

"You're very kind." she allowed as she spritzed herself with a bottle of something Cullen couldn't identify until the consuming scent of roses invaded his senses. She gestured to the cart with a sweeping arm as she rose to zip up the riding boots she had pulled over a pair of tan riding pants.

"You certainly held up your end of the bargain." She offered, pulling the silver top off of a plate of bacon with hash browns, biscuits and gravy.

His eyes almost rolled up into his head and without preamble or hesitation, Cullen sat down at the small window side table and dug in.

"I am sorry about that," he managed around a mouthful of buttery biscuit, "but it couldn't be helped."

"I understand completely Cullen," she winked at him stealing a slice of the crisp bacon out from under his greedy hands, "I myself have felt the wrath of tying one on."

They sat in silence for a moment, him eating and her regarding the London skyline as the icy rain washed over it. Cullen cleared his throat, "You said you would explain."

"I'll tell you what I can." She offered without apology.

"What happened today Enola, what did I see you do?" he asked staring at her silhouette in wonder.

She pondered a moment, tossing the last scrap of bacon in her mouth and wiping her hands on the napkin Cullen had neglected to use, "I saved your life....The same way you would have mine, nothing different in the mechanics of it."

Cullen squinted in a skeptical manner and she held her arms up, turned around. Enola looked like any other person, although out of character for her in a black turtle neck today.

"I'm built from the same things you are..." she offered.

"How strong are you, Enola?" he asked recalling the Earth shaking sensation of the shelf hitting the ground.

Leveling a hard gaze at him, "As strong as I have to be."

"And you've never had this...fail you?" he grabbed at the air looking for the right word.

She shook her head.

"Where are you from?" he had moved onto the hash browns, and other topics, seeing she wasn't going to give him an inch if she didn't have to.

"Scotland, you were right about the accent."

He lowered his head, "And if....if you hadn't found me in the street, taken me with you...if I'd stayed in the salon like you asked...would I be here now, with you?"

Another of those penetrating gazes and a hesitation before she shook her head slowly, "But not because I don't like you...because..."

"You aren't sure you can protect me." He quipped, gulping down more of the muddy coffee.

She crouched next to him then at the table, seeing that she'd wounded him somehow with that admission. "But you are here Cullen," she took his hands in her own, "this isn't what I planned and to be very frank, I have no idea what we might come upon."

He was getting frustrated with her now, he had hoped for transparency, an answer but he realized the question was too large for him to even attempt to ask. If he wanted to find out what he had stumbled into, he would have to see it through and find out on his own.

"You don't have to come any further than this." She said, "I would understand."

"I'm not leaving until I'm satisfied." He stated a little more fervently than he would have liked. An expression he couldn't quite name danced across Enola's features and she left him to finish his meal. Before dragging him through the streets of London with a relentless energy he fought to match.

"Tell me again why we couldn't take a cab?" Cullen moaned as they meandered further and further into a decaying neighborhood of row houses built along a twisting alley. Breakfast had provided an infusion of energy that was now failing him as they walked casually through this crooked mews.

Looking as pert and well rested as ever, Enola sighed and patiently said, "If my time on this Earth has taught me anything, it's that there's a secret dance we're all a part of every minute of every day." She reached back for his hand to halt him, her eyes never leaving a splintered red door across the way, "Speed up or slow down and you'll miss your cue."

Cullen's eyes followed hers and fell upon the shabby entryway, huddled under a set of mossy steps in this twisted neighborhood it was lucky they had found it at all. "Is that the address from the guy's ID?"

Enola nodded, "It looks like the police have already been here." There was a tightness to her expression as she regarded the place, contemplating something she wouldn't say.

"Do we go in?" Cullen pondered, allowing his eyes to take in the positively mid-evil quality of the structure. The stone and mortar stacks curled and flowed around each other into stairs and doors, entryways and corridors. This place was a maze and if they weren't careful it was likely they could become lost inside of it.

"Yes." Was all she allowed, and with the casual stroll of any well- dressed couple out for a walk, they crossed the narrow street arm in arm.

"Where is everyone?" he asked squinting at the sky which had once again opened up and begun to rain. Off balance at the empty silence of this place, there was no sign of life, no people about, all the curtains were drawn and doors locked and bolted.

"I believe the residents of this area are nocturnal Cullen." With a sharp swing of her shoulder to the jamb, the door popped open.

"I could have done that, you know?" he rubbed the back of his neck in agitation at her insistence of always being first, in front, his shield. The Southerner inside of him protested every time she seized the lead, however he realized she wouldn't have it any other way.

"The next door we have to break down is all yours then, I promise." She was distracted as they entered the dim recess of the shabby flat. Dingy curtains filtered dust laden shafts of light through the space.

It was cluttered with a sour smell that hung in the air, walking in slowly on the creaking floor she took in their surroundings with a wince of distaste on her face. "People weren't meant to live this way." She shook her head and began poking through a pile of overdue bills and tattered adverts on an end table. "Look around Cullen, whatever it is the police will have missed it…it will be subtle."

Cullen wandered over to the moth eaten sofa and spied a box shoved carelessly beneath it, reaching he asked, "Why would a person steal that door Enola?" he pulled it out and jerked back in shock. It was filled with crumbled porno mags and cockroaches, the wolfish grins of the nude women as they splayed under the spindly legs of the filthy bugs made a gut turning picture.

"I've been wondering that myself," over by the kitchen now, she was carefully picking through a sink full of moldy dishes, "it's not like they can sell it, even in the black market that would be a trick, getting that thing off this island would be downright impossible. The police are looking for it, the heist made the news and I'm pretty sure that Lloyd's has the Pinkerton's on the trail…so where can they take it that it won't be found, or seen?"

"So if they can't sell it, or even move it…why take it at all? He peered into the bathroom and immediately shut the door with intense regret.

She was standing in the middle of the room, not moving, not really looking at anything in particular, Enola was deep in thought.

"It has value in certain circles by the very nature of its speculated evolution."

Cullen quirked a confused brow at this statement.

"It didn't start its life out as a door, Cullen. What little information I have found and trust me, it's not much, indicates that the door started its life as an altar."

"An altar?" He echoed.

Nodding, "An ancient, Gaulish altar."

"And just what did the Gauls do at this altar, Enola?" Cullen reached for her so they could leave.

Her eyes went wide, "Very bad things…when the occasion called for it."

"Enola, I think this place is just a disgusting dead end." Tossing a jacket that reeked of cigarettes and sweat back over the chair, he reached for the door just as the knob began to rattle.

Together they ran back into the bedroom and crammed into the narrow closet that huddled behind the door, Cullen could hear two distinct voices enter the place.

"Hurry up you dumb sod!" a crackling voice called, "We shouldn't be here in the first place!"

"Shut yer gob," the other spat, "I like this jacket!"

"Sure you don't need anything else, Sir?" the first one teased, "might I pick up your tuxedo from the cleaners?"

"Get off it," his companion groused, "they'll be waiting."

"Right." The first one agreed and they stomped back out.

Enola locked eyes with Cullen for a second as he threw open the closet door, "We have to follow them!"

She seized his hand without waiting for a reply and together they slunk through the flat, out the door and onto the street where the two men were just rounding the corner.

"I think they're heading for the tube station." Cullen noted, holding onto Enola's hand and doing his best to make their frenzied chase look like anything else.

"And you wanted to take a cab here." She teased as they rounded the corner to see their quarry had stopped to light up. Pretending to be lost, she pointed at the street sign and gave Cullen a hilarious look of impatience.

He laughed at her expression and instinctively took her into his arms, she used his body as shield and spied on them over his shoulder.

"Are they moving yet?" he murmured into her ear, helping himself to a lung busting whiff of roses.

"Just about…" she replied, they were shoving each other around on the sidewalk in a mock fight, "these two are apes…why would they want the door?"

"They don't, they want the money the guy who wants the door offered to pay them for stealing it." Cullen pressed her body to his, testing to see if she felt different than any other woman he'd ever held. Her flesh was soft and yielding, she was warm and inviting in his embrace but he could swear there was an energy thrumming through her. Something palpable and unearthly he could feel, only just and because they were so very close.

She broke his train of thought with a pinch on his arm, "Stop squeezing me! They're on the move!" she pulled his hand into her own and saw that they were indeed headed for the tube.

"They must be going uptown." She speculated as they descended the stairs.

"Big money." Cullen offered as he swiped his card and let her through, satisfying the gentleman in him for a brief moment in time before he followed. They hustled onto the train, cuddling up around one of the standing poles near the opposite end.

Wrapping his arms around her and holding onto the pole for support, they made an adorable picture of some amorous couple on the train. Cullen turned a little so his gaze could remain on the scabby looking men but easily be jerked back to Enola if they happened to notice him staring. As the train swept away, jostling all on board, her eyes met his for a moment and she smiled.

"How do they look?" she asked excitedly squeezing his shoulders.

Cullen's eyes slid over them as the car shimmied and rolled on the track, these were hard men. One of them quite thin with a scar over one eye giving him a permanent scowl, the other was big and brawny with a broken nose. Cullen looked again, harder, not believing for a second but unable to deny it. Turning quickly to hide his and Enola's face he whispered in her ear.

"That's the guy you knocked out at Sotheby's...the one with the gun!"

She stole a glance with a coy toss of her head and when she looked back her eyes had gone wide.

"How did he get out of custody?" she asked, "The last time I saw him they were loading him in the back of the police car!"

"He either escaped," Cullen murmured, "or these guys have friends in high places."

Enola and Cullen rode the rest of the way in stunned silence, contemplating the ramifications of the man who they'd both seen arrested scant hours before being on this train with them now. He kept his arms around her, his gaze easy, it was a strange experience to watch a woman who had been the epitome of confidence since he first met her, confused and even a little afraid.

"It's going to be alright, Enola." He said softly in her ear.

She smiled then, it was an effable and shy version of her usual brazen grin. There was a long moment between them, their eyes locked and Cullen felt whatever it was that hummed through her begin to seep into him.

At first it was only a dizzy sensation, easily dismissed on the disorienting ride through the tunnels below London but as that ebbed away a crackling started just below his hearing, a searing heat pulsed from where they touched and through his body. When every nerve and cell was screaming to the rafters and he was sure he was going to faint she broke eye contact and looked at the floor as she whispered in a voice gone hoarse, "I'm glad you're here Cullen."

He shook his head, trying to clear the lingering noise from his ears, started gulping the recycled air that flowed through the carriage as it rocketed through the pitch and swayed a little on his feet.

Enola was already wrapped around him, and merely tightened her hold as a hint of an apology played across her face.

So she was aware of it.

"Where did you come from?" he asked more to himself than her.

"The most humble of beginnings, everything after that however..." she trailed off with a wry grin and laugh.

The sensation of a boat running across a high sand bar at low tide shoved Cullen into her flush again and the heat returned without pause, but he wasn't as disoriented by it this time. It was like being so awake and aware that literally nothing escaped his attention, the world around him slowed down laying itself bare to his designs...and beneath all that chaos and noise, crystalline calm.

"Come on," she started for the doors after them, "I don't want to lose them out there."

Cullen held fast to her hand and followed up the stairs into the dreary London afternoon. Their pace quickened as they navigated through the business district, tall sky scrapers and stately cornerstones flew by in dozens. A turn here, a crossing there and all among the suited dead that inhabited this place living and dying by the clock.

"I think they've been here before." He observed as they walked into a lobby of and entered the lift without consulting the directory next to it.

"There's got to be a dozen people in there with them," she groused, "we'll never figure out which floor they got off on."

"And even if we did, Enola," Cullen took her shoulders to face her fully, a tingling shooting up his hands, "we can't let them see you."

She looked around then, "Now what?"

Cullen spied a coffee shop across the way, "Now we wait."

She sat with her back to the entrance under the umbrella tearing into a scone and Cullen shook his head at her ravenous appetite.

A troubled expression passed over her face, "I don't know about this, what if they come out another way? What if we miss them?"

"We'll see them Enola." Holding his hands up to calm her.

"I hope so." She chomped heartily into what was left of the pastry and looked shiftily from side to side. "I don't understand why you're the lookout either."

"I don't want them to recognize you." He clipped, keeping his gaze on the endless stream of people pouring from the building, he looked at his watch, "Quitting time, everybody home."

"Do you see them?" she was eager to have them back in her sight.

Cullen shook his head, it would be easy to pick them out from all the professionals too but as the stream of workers cried off for the day, the men from the train never emerged.

"They went out another way, I know it!" she was jumping up from the chair when Cullen seized her arm and pulled her down.

"Sit…I think this transaction is one best completed after hours." He directed his gaze upwards and Enola saw a single light in the penthouse of the now dark building.

As evening fell around them the chill in the air started to bite at Cullen's back and arms, folding in on himself in an effort to stay warm Enola remained fixated on the door, unaffected by the drop in temperature. An impatient looking waiter offered an unimpressed sneer at their empty cups and she was quick to offer him a wad of money asking him for refills and to keep the change which transformed him into the most helpful person Cullen had ever encountered.

Sitting there in silence, staring at an empty lobby Cullen's thoughts drifted to what Enola had told him about the door, the speculation of its beginning, its origin.

"Tell me about the Gauls." He sputtered abruptly, shattering the quiet they shared.

She sighed, rubbing a hand absently along her thigh in thought as she gathered the words. "Well, they were a highly respected tribe of mystics, according to Caesar, their warriors were reputed to be unafraid of death. There was even an account of them running themselves upon a blade to get to the man that held it and walking over his corpse with his sword still in their belly."

He let out a slow whistle.

"The world was a more savage place then," she offered in consolation, "their real power lay in their knowledge though. It was believed that the Gauls had tapped into the essence of the universe, understood and could even manipulate its workings. They commanded the power of prophecy and were quite adept astronomers...a baffling feat for that age."

"What happened to them?" he asked sipping from his cup.

"Who could say?" Enola shrugged, "they didn't keep any kind of writings or manuscripts and the accounts of them are so sparse and inconsistent it's hard to speculate. Some say they became what was known as the Druids and were cast to the winds along with everyone else when Rome conquered. Others say they abandoned this dimension, disgusted with the ways of men."

"They weren't men themselves?" he pondered.

"Maybe they started out that way," her expression took on the same quality it had that first day in Sotheby's. The mantle of extreme and soul fracturing regret, "but it only takes a moment for everything to change."

Chapter 11

Gilda was lost now, wandering in the place beyond.

Somewhere most souls pass over, and move through with hardly a glance on their journey to what lies away from life. Locked in perpetual twilight and drained of any trace of the living, she moved through the nonsensical void toward the sporadic bursts of noise and sensation that washed over her.

It was familiar yet, foreign all at the same time, comforting and unsettling all at once.

I'm not supposed to be here.

Exhaustion plagued her, begged her to lie down, to give up and to move on to where we all travel when our struggles have ended. Something inside her knew that her family was waiting on the other end of this place, and all she would have to do is recline on the spongy surface upon which she traveled. Just allow herself to slip though this diaphanous membrane and she would be with them.

The burdens of her short life weighed on her, and her mind sunk into the past reaching for the familiar. The soft methodic chinks of her father's chisel as he worked in the shop with his strong hands and clever fingers...the sight of her mother in the kitchen, her perfectly yellow hair a downy halo in the dying light of day. A fat dog snoozing in the corner near the stove and grandpa snoring in his chair by the fire.

Home

The smell of tobacco, bread and the underlying scent of stone that's been ground to such a fine and exquisite powder that it becomes lighter than air. A perfume on the breeze instead of a rock to be hefted. Standing in the door, her shadow framed in golden light her mother saw her first a blazing smile as familiar as her own beckoned her inside, bid her welcome. Her father emerged from the shop, hair a powdery white from a day's work, moving to her grandfather's chair and waking him, bidding him to see who had finally found her way home. All of their mouths moved frantically in greetings and declarations of love, but she couldn't hear them or make them out, they were too far from where she was and yet only an arm's length away.

Soul searing grief tore at her then, because she wanted more than anything to join them, to rest. It would have been so easy to cross the threshold and leave the waking world and all its toils behind and yet she pressed onward, with nothing ahead no point of reference she willed it to be the right way. Her work was not finished, the world was not done and though it would be a scar she bore in agony for the rest of her life, Gilda turned away from the family she'd always known and the love they've wrapped her in since the day of her birth and journeyed alone into the unyielding bleak.

Time had come loose in this place, with no day or night to mark the hours it was an eternity of moments that tore at her mind, threatening to drive her to madness. In spite of the strangeness of this realm, no fear or pain invaded. Only the heaviness of a soul that hasn't rested in years weighing her down, tempting her to embrace the eternal repose of oblivion.

A garden bloomed around her, vines and blossoms exploding from nothing blazing a palette of blues and violets over a carpet of the deepest green. Nathaniel on his knee before her, a pledge to love her always on his lips and her hand clasped in his own. Shining down in amber light, the sun blessed their union that day and the bells at Greyfriar's rang out in song at their engagement.

The ringing changed somehow, something tinny and sharp and the lively grass below them seeped with churlish water that reeked of mold and decay. Darkness swept around them and a bone chilling cold consumed her. Swords were ringing and as she looked to see their source, to avoid the danger, she looked at her hand clasped in his once more and saw his dead eyes with blood running through them from the dagger in his head. Yanking her hand from his dead claw, Gilda ran away, toward anything...

Shimmering in the distance, a speck of light beckoned her onward and Gilda followed as the sound of stone grinding over and over itself pervaded in growling waves broken by the hollow knock of wood against bone. Drawing close her ears rung with the haunting tones of an ancient chant as a wind rose over the song.

The stirring air led her in a lighter than sky dance toward a massive tree standing in a circle of stones. A fire leaping wildly around its base, casting the shadows of those that conjured it long and painfully thin along the ground in all directions. Unafraid she approached on silent feet toward the robed strangers as they worked their craft in the dead of night beneath the unflinching stars that had begun to come into focus.

Esus bèo bunchur brìocht
Còmhla cruthù cumhacht
Dèithe dil gà scàl

Over and over these words echoed, through the night and into sky invading Gilda's consciousness until all she could hear was the incantation. Obey its command, succumb to the power coursing through this place and into every part of her. All of her body became alive, a coursing rush flowing from the Earth and into her. She surrendered to it, embraced it and submitted to its mighty will.

Circling the tree and the fire, their ghostly voices rose carrying the sacred words. Open hands raised to the sky, imploring the Gods to do as they asked, to answer their call. She could hear the desperation in their plea, the fear in their request…these men were begging for a miracle. Conjuring the Gods to help them. Gilda suddenly felt shame color her soul, she should not be here, should not be watching this. What if her presence here displeased their God? Befouled the rite they were attempting to appease them with?

She moved to leave and found herself rooted to the ground, hard and cold, real. Not the spongey in-between that had carried her here, but the Earth as she remembered. Struggling again to vacate this place and see no more of this ritual she was almost pulled back to the spot she stood upon. Held in gentle bonds that would not harm but refused to release.

The clear night sky clouded over with gusts of wind, the moon cloaked in ebony thunderheads. As the branches of the mighty tree danced and swung in the storm a hard rain as cold as ice pelted the strange sorcerers as they set about their invocation.

Rain turned to hail and thunder threatened into streaks of lighting, the fire now a damp pit of glowing coals and ice. The electricity ran along the wind coursing from the heavens to the Earth over and over again until the ground was smoldering around them.

Still they chanted, unmoving in the hail of thunderbolts that struck a relentless tattoo in the circle they had conjured. Arms outstretched and mouths begging for their will to be done.

An earsplitting crack erupted as a streak the color of the sun blinded Gilda and rendered the world silent. Her eyes burned with the light and she was only slightly aware of the peeling screech of wood tearing from its own grain.

The towering oak that she had been bound to tumbled off its tremendous stump, the soaking branches hitting the ground in a flurry of leaves and twigs. The stump a great circle of countless rings remained. This bastion of time a silent witness to the ages of the Earth was now exposed.

An unseen force urged Gilda towards its fresh surface, she swore she could even smell that mysterious ether of life leaking from cells as she found herself drawn to it.

They brought forth a bull as pale as the winter moon, a wreath of white roses around its swaying neck, a crown of mistletoe atop his head, his hoof falls as loud and thunderous as Gilda's own heart. Laying across the mighty stump, unable to even touch its edges with her outstretched hands, the head of the bull was brought over her frame. The guttural breaths from his great lungs gusted in her face, stirring her hair in the dying gasps of the storm.

Gathering around him, chanting louder and louder as one drew a golden blade from beneath his robe the bull's throat was slit in a glinting slash and the crimson flow that rode over the petals poured over Gilda and the tree upon which she laid as he died.

And still they chanted, over and over, running reverent hands across the flesh of the animal they had slain, the offering they had given. Soothing its suffering as best they could while appeasing the presence that had entered this circle with them, the one that would indulge or deny as it saw fit.

Terrified by the sight, yet unable to move away Gilda locked eyes with the mighty beast as he expired. Watching as the burning in his gaze died away and his strength left him she felt a stirring within herself. A deep, raw power began to stampede through her soul. The hammering of her heart rose within her ears until the pulsing was its own song, invoking her to draw upon this sacrifice, to drink from the river as these men bade her.

She felt the bark of the oak against her back, the heat from the flames flirting on her cheeks and still the thunder inside of her quaked and rattled her very soul threatening to shake her apart. Gilda endured the onslaught over and over, as the bull withered she bloomed.

A vessel that was filled with oil was lifted as white rose petals floated serenely atop its shimmering surface. Taken to the edge of the fire where she was laying in a trembling fury, the chanting stopped abruptly and as its contents poured over the flames in an unearthly hiss that awakened the fire anew.

Gilda was overcome with the sensation of being pulled through something dense and impenetrable. Like a needle drawn through sack cloth, Gilda was being forced from one side of the darkness to another.

In an instant she was seen, locked eyes with this aging man, saw the tiniest glimmer of hope in those haunted depths and then she was gone, into the blackness again...only now a thunderous pounding echoed within her and with a starving gasp, Gilda McGregor once again drew breath in this world.

She sat up into the cold air gasping and was struck in the face with a clod of dirt for her trouble. Coughing on the damp soil that had been thrown in her face, she barely had time to bring her hands to her eyes before she felt someone tugging at her shoulders. Strong hands lifting her from a hole and crushing her to their chest.

"I thought I'd lost you lass!" Adam's voice trembled, thick with tears and tinged with wonder. He was wiping her face harshly with those rough hands and as Gilda opened a tentative eye to the world again "I can't believe it." He was shaking his head and running his palms all over her face and body as if he needed some reassurance that she was alive, in one piece, alright.

Gilda looked down at her hands, clenched an experimental fist and collapsed onto the ground in a consuming pain that buckled her knees. She heard the chanting off in the distance in her head, felt that thrumming in her veins only now it was if she would burst from the vigor of it. She felt that her body simply could not contain the might that had so easily coursed through her soul.

"There we go." He seized her arms and drug her back up to her feet again, "Alive but not well I'd say." Without further ado, Adam hauled her up into his arms and out of the woods where Gilda realized he had dug her a lonely grave among the trees.

I have two of those now

She mused as he lumbered her away from that eternal resting place and back to the cottage on the lake. The trees all around were singed and black and the smell of smoke hung around the eerily still water. Inside a fire burned lazily and as her gaze fell upon it the memory of the bull's eye as he expired near the flame made her flinch.

Adam didn't notice and set her on the pallet of blankets once again. "Washed those after you..." he trailed off and wrung his hands guiltily.

Her mind seized, "How long?" she asked quietly.

Tears suddenly welled up in those amber eyes and he fell to his knees before her, "Four days, lass. Four since the storm, since I chased you out into it!" he buried his head in her lap, clinging to the nightgown she's escaped the lodge in, cleaned as well. "I thought it would make you well, I thought if I could get you to fight, to rear up maybe...." He was crying in earnest now, deep racking sobs against her thighs that shook his body and heaved in his back.

Placing a gentle hand on his head and stroking his hair as he cried, Gilda contemplated his words, his fervor and his regret. "You were right." She said softly.

He sat up so quickly it shocked her, red rimmed eyes met her own with a madness in them that set her on edge, seizing her hands in his own, "I've never in all my years seen anything like that, and I never want to again! As long as I recall, I've cared for myself, about myself but I...Gilda, I could not bear it..."

He was upset, she reasoned, he'd been through so much for her benefit and had asked so little. Gilda shushed him, pulling his head to her chest and stroking his temple, "Rest your head man, the worst is behind us."

She sat with him like that as the sparse sunlight faded, lulling him with the beat of her heart. A small moan escaped his lips and she felt him pass into slumber, balling a fist in her gown, determined even in sleep to hang onto her and keep her close.

Gilda stretched out on the pallet beside him, hearing the strong steady tempo of his breathing as he dreamt. An owl called out to the night, warning all the smaller things of his awakening before he began his hunt. Her mind drifted back to The Bleak and then the tree, those words and the bull, his blood and the roses....Esus.

Looking at him to ensure he was asleep, Gilda once again clenched a fist and felt the consuming pain that had her seeing stars inside the cottage's dark interior. She quickly released and tried again, confounded at the sensation. She sat up to throw another log on the dying fire and gasped when the sizable log snapped in grasp like a twig. Her eyes flew once again to Adam, making sure he wasn't startled from the noise.

Taking another log so gently it pained her, setting it on her lap and considering for a moment the possibilities. She made a fist again and felt the singing pain in her hand, but instead of releasing she endured, concentrated and heard the tiniest crackling emanating from deep within her hand.

I'm breaking my own bones

Her body was exactly the same, that hadn't changed it remained here while she was in The Bleak…and whatever it was she'd left that place with was far stronger than her physical form.

Opening the fist and feeling the sweet relief once again, she held open her arms and looked to ensure there was no change. Then she took the log and slowly squeezed, dents peeling into the wood under her fingers, the bark breaking open and fluttering to her lap. No pain this way, no pain if she directed it onto something else, if she diverted it through.

She was simply the vessel, the conduit though which this power flowed, it could not be yoked or harnessed, merely unleashed.

Gilda McGregor laid there in the night, next to a man she barely knew as his tears for her dried on his sleeping cheeks and contemplated the power raging through her, swearing to herself that no one alive must ever know.

Chapter 12

Cullen had fallen asleep, arms crossed over his chest and legs stretched far out in front of him. The café had long since closed and Enola had spied a bench further down the corner on which they could wait. Long minutes slipped into hours and as the bustling streets emptied of all signs of life, he had drifted off knowing her gaze would never leave that door. The side of his body that was pressed against hers on the small commuter seat was warm in the October night, throwing the chill from the rest of his body as she remained unaffected by the elements.

Vivid dreams came for him in the open air, visions of home and family he'd long forgotten, and sought to erase from his mind. A dirt road curled around the shoulder of a forest and led to a clapboard house with a barn. Two knock kneed nags grazed in the tall grass of the pasture and Cullen was a small boy once again, running barefoot with his sisters through the muddy woods brought to life by an afternoon rainstorm.

As they neared the house the foul stench of rendered flesh invaded, it hung around the house and barn in an immobile cloud that followed them to town and to school in their hair and clothes. No matter how much he washed, no matter how far he ran, Cullen could never seem to get that smell off of his skin.

His father was a tanner and a leather worker, and while he was good at his trade, the world had little use for saddles and boots any longer. He had grown up poor and pitied, teased and reviled...Cullen ran away from home when he'd turned 16 and had never looked back. He'd used the money he'd stolen from his mother's purse to buy a bus ticket to New York and some new clothes, leaving everything that reminded him of that shack in a trash can at the depot.

He'd spent every day of his life since excising every trace of that hell, of that sad little boy from himself. As if he could be transplanted and grow anew, with sophisticated influences and intellect drawn up through his white trash roots. At his core, Cullen hated where he'd come from and tonight, home beckoned.

The green door of the house was open, his mother standing inside of it calling to him and his sisters. She'd been a mother seven times over and her hips, which almost touched both sides of the door showed it. A soft and lovely woman with a quiet voice and eyes the color of the sea, Cullen had loved and hated her at the same time. Adored her gentle patience and sweet countenance, loathed her complicit silence as her husband beat the living shit out of his kids every night for the crime of existing.

An equal opportunity bastard, he'd swung on Cullen and the girls in equal measure, his frighteningly strong body a weapon he threw at them with the smallest provocation. Ennis O'Keefe wasn't a drunk, he didn't do drugs, it would almost be understandable, the way he was if that were the case. But the sad fact was he simply hated his life and what he'd made of it. His wife, his children and that damnable house were all painful reminders of what a failure he was, and rather than change it, he decided to destroy it.

No stranger to pain or poverty, Cullen had lied to teachers about bruises on him and his sisters fearing reprisal from Father should anyone suspect. Sack lunches of leftovers, hand me down clothes from the church donation effort, the long walks to and from school every day. The O'Keefe's were the town charity case and the good people of the community had no illusions about what was going on at that farm, to those kids. But chose to do nothing and soothe their serrated souls with canned goods and old clothes all given in the name of being a good Christian and neighbor.

Little Cullen ran for the door with his sisters on his heels, the smell of casserole and biscuits wafting over the stench to which he'd grown so accustomed. As he neared the steps to the house the red bone hound that slept under the porch, Harvey, started baying at their approach excitedly wagging his tail. A shrieking howl silenced him though, as Ennis walked by and gave the dog a sharp kick. Cullen looked back and saw the old man leveling his gaze on him, he was next and tonight was his night to take the brunt of it.

As those huge hands reached out for him and the snarling face grew closer and closer, Cullen mentally prepared himself for what was to come, the pain would be awful, but temporary…the shame however….

"Cullen wake up." Enola had a hold of his arm and was shaking him lightly, "Wake up!"

His eyes felt as heavy as lead and when he met the stormy gaze of Enola he swore for a minute he saw something he hadn't seen on anyone's face since he was a child, pity. She couldn't know, hadn't seen.

"Look." She jerked her head in the direction of the building they'd been staring at all afternoon.

Two sleek town cars had pulled up to the front door and immediately Cullen's eyes flew to the now darkened windows of the penthouse above. He was wide awake now, and with Enola he watched the door with anticipation that rattled his nerves.

Out of the dim lobby, five men exited…two of them with black sacks over their heads, hands bound behind their backs with zip ties. Escorted by two large men with a smaller one in tow, the smaller man entered the back of the car in front, and the others piled into the second, the doors slammed and they were whisked away into the night like they'd never been there in the first place.

Moving quickly he pulled out his cell phone, pulled up a browser and looked up the transportation authority website. Using the search feature he punched in the carrier number the town cars had displayed discreetly in the rear window and found that the company they ran for was Elite.

Enola's eyes flew about looking for a cab, she wandered into the empty street looking as if she were contemplating running them down on foot, but changed her mind.

Throwing her hands up in the air at Cullen, "Now what?"

She was frustrated, they'd lost them…for now. But Cullen had an idea, looking up Elite he called the number and listened as the line rang.

"Cullen?" she was fuming, "What are you doing?"

He held up a single finger to silence her, listening for an answer, which came after seven rings.

"Elite Car Service." The tired woman's voice said on the line.

"Hello," Cullen flashed a big smile as he spoke knowing it carried over the line, "how are you tonight?" he asked with a little more drawl than he usually spoke with.

"Just fine sir, thank you. What can I do for you?" she asked, sounding bored.

"Well," he started, walking around on the sidewalk as Enola watched him in utter confusion, "It's a little embarrassing, but I was supposed to meet some associates here at The Bachman Building for a ride to a corporate event and…well, I lost track of time and I missed them."

"You said the Bachman Building?" she repeated flatly, the sound of lightning fast typing in the background.

"Yes ma'am." He smiled again, waiting.

"Sir, the cars have already left for their destination, I'm afraid it's too late for them to come back."

"Oh no!" he waved a dismissive hand in the air as if she could see it, "I don't want to trouble the rest of them, I'll get enough chaff from them as it is."

She chuckled a little at that.

"Is there any way you could give me the address and I'll see if I can't sneak in without them noticing?"

She paused, more typing.... "Yes sir, the cars are scheduled for one drop off at Church Lane and West Wycombe."

"Lovely darling, should our paths ever cross, I owe you a drink." He even winked as she giggled on the end of the line.

"Cheers!" she laughed and hung up.

Cullen tucked his phone back into his jacket pocket smugly, "And now, I know where they're going. Church Lane and West Wycombe!"

His eyes squinted as he looked up the intersection on his phone, "That's over an hour away..."

Enola was looking up and down the deserted street she threw her arms up in surrender. "You're robbing this train Cullen," she sauntered over to him and ran her hands briskly over his shivering arms, "how do we get there?"

He regarded her then, in the pool of light from the street lamps that lined this stuffy row of buildings, these titans of commerce. Somehow she seemed larger than the structures that towered above them. His mind ventured back to the vault at Sotheby's, and wondered if the brick and mortar above them should fall from the sky, if these buildings began to tumble, could she shield him from death once more?

"Cullen?" she repeated impatiently, while he'd allowed himself to be swept away by the mysterious Enola Sloan, time was wasting and she wouldn't be denied.

His brows knit together, "They're in a car so that's going to take at least an hour…"

"It's too late for a train." She added.

"Also takes too long," he mentioned bringing a thoughtful fist to his chin. "They could be on their way somewhere else by the time we arrive."

Her eyes were skittering around the place, and lighted on a neon sign, "Come on." Seizing his hand and almost dragging him with her. Cullen saw her destination, an underground car park with a cement ramp sloping sharply down to the levels upon which the workers of this place parked.

The booth where the attendant sat all day was vacant, a fluorescent light flickering on the lonely chair inside the cubicle. They stepped over the spikes that blocked the exit and hugged the wall down and around to the first level, where in a reserved spot boasting a sign that read, "Dr. Huddleston" sat a stately hunter green Jaguar.

Enola nodded, "That will work."

"You've got to be kidding!" Cullen fairly screamed. "We're going to steal it?"

"Rent." Enola corrected, reaching into her boot she removed several notes of cash which she folded and tucked behind the corner of the sign.

Cullen's mouth fell open, this was all entirely too absurd. "And that makes you feel better about this?"

She nodded, "We'll tell him where it is when we're finished, now if you're through admonishing me for solving the problem when you've provided no alternative solution…let's go."

"We could take a cab," he pleaded even as he followed her to the car, "We could call Elite and get them to come get us."

She shook her head as she fiddled with the door latch, "I refuse to drag one more person into this mess, and we don't know what's waiting for us in West Wycombe, do we?" the mechanics of the handle groaned under her grip and she stopped, looking over the car again,

"What we do know, is that two men who were expecting to be paid for something they stole were hauled out of an office with sacks on their heads in the middle of the night. So if that's how these people treat their subcontractors what do you think they would do to a driver, a cabbie?"

She was right, it was irritating and upsetting but right.

"It's not too late to stay behind Cullen, I could drop you at the hotel and you could go home and forget this ever happened." She offered with an expectant look on her features.

"Anxious to be rid of me?" he laughed getting swept up in her eyes again.

"Afraid I will fail you." She stated plain.

His hands went to her face then, framing it in his palms feeling that thrumming that coursed through her seep into him. "Enola, I'm not leaving you."

Her eyes softened at his statement, so fervently delivered, so solemnly sworn, placing her hands over his own she smiled and held them there for a moment before pulled them from her face. She redirected her attention to the car, to a place she could open it without damaging it in a way that was too obvious.

"You don't like to be touched, do you?" Cullen asked as he observed her ministrations. She regarded the hulk of metal and steel as it if were an egg or crystal flute.

"I have grown accustomed to a life without such things." She amended as she fiddled with the trunk which she dented in a few places with her fingers before moving on.

"Don't you miss it?" he asked, picturing the women he'd whittled away countless nights with. Their hands over his own, flesh pressed together breathing each other's breath. Even though they were strangers, and never seen again he'd taken comfort in them. Loved them in his own way for that brief window of time, if only for chasing away the hollow feeling of solitude.

"Of course I do." She was frowning now, frustrated with the car not him, "but I'm not like other people Cullen." As if to prove her point, she tapped the tiny angled window between the passenger window and the rear windshield as a child might pop a bubble and it shattered with musical quality as the shards of safety glass tumbled to the ground. Snaking a hand through the small opening she hit the unlock button and the car doors popped open, with a smile she took the driver's seat, ripped the plastic collar off the steering column and had the car running before Cullen could join her inside.

Throwing the vehicle in reverse and heading toward the exit, she left the car running as she lifted the striped gate that extended from a keypad console where after hours patrons could enter a code to get out. With no more than a touch of her foot, the spikes threatening to tear the tires to oblivion where broken on their mechanism and back below the ground where she needed them.

Re-entering the car and throwing it into gear, they emerged from the parking garage onto a desolate street, she navigated through the business district without falter or fail and Cullen, having nothing better to do, watched her. A confounding combination of femininity and brawn, independence and yet, so delicate in her way, her build. It was confusing.

He ran a hand absently over hers as it rested on the console between them, over the ruby wedding ring that seemed to burn with a fire from within, even in the dark confines of the sedan.

"Where is he?" Cullen asked, framing the large stone in his own fingers, marveling at its quality. Rubies were as expensive if not more so than diamonds and this particular one was quite large and set in a cabochon of yellow gold that was heavy looking and old.

She sighed at the question, as if she'd expected it sooner or later from him, "Dead I expect."

"You mean you don't know?" he asked, watching her face for any sign that she was lying.

She shook her head, "No, I don't."

"But you still wear that?" he pressed.

"Yes."

"Why?" he asked, releasing her hand in frustration, "It's till death do you part, right?"

"I'm afraid it's not that simple Cullen," she pulled the car onto the expressway smoothly and settled back into the seat, "as I've stated before, I'm not like other women."

The Enola Sloan Brick Wall, Cullen was getting familiar with her now, with her way of speaking and throwing up obstacles when he got too close to something, to a secret. She had thousands, of that he was certain but there were some, the ones near her heart that she guarded jealously. And while she might indulge him in a cursory fashion when he asked, it was clear she had no intention of giving him more than that. And she would sooner ride in silence than let him any closer than she was comfortable with.

A breeze whistled through the broken window in the back, sending the strands of her hair dancing across her back. It was making the interior of the car a little cold, but once again she was unaffected, with laser focus she was intent on one thing, getting to that door. Cullen turned on the heater and adjusted the temperature to compensate for the heat that they would be throwing outside all the way.

"You don't get cold?" he marveled.

Changing lanes to get around a rusty farm truck she shook her head.

"Tired...do you need to sleep?" he continued.

"Of course I do," she groused, "but I don't need as much or as often as you do."

Time for the six million dollar question

"Can you be killed, Enola?" he almost regretted asking it when he saw the expression it painted across her face. Somewhere between extreme pain and extreme loss, a memory she'd like to forget but could not.

"Oh yes Cullen, I certainly can."

Chapter 13

I'd be lying if I said you didn't look good in trews." Adam swatted affectionately at her rump as he walked around Gilda. There was a town a day's walk away and she was waiting to pass inspection.

"Think it will work?" she tugged at the rough shirt and marveled at the days that she rued her satin and silk gowns. What she wouldn't give to be pretty for pretty's sake and not getting ready to tromp through the Irish woods in boots that were two sizes too large.

He drew close to her then, his face very close to hers, "A man would have to be blind to mistake you for another man, but it's better than a nightgown."

Their eyes locked for a moment, and Adam slid those large paws down her arms pulling her to him by her elbows for the briefest of moments as he looked once more at that placid water. "You may be able to walk away from this place, but you'll never leave it behind."

Her eyes drifted to the rocky shore.

If he only knew

Without further goodbye's or farewells, Adam and Gilda left the cottage and headed where the village he'd stumbled upon stood against the sea on sheer cliffs of rock. A town peopled with fishermen and boats, Adam was confident his skills would be a commodity. Together in silence they trudged, her hand in his own through the soft moss that covered the forest floor which gave way to craggy hills that finally broke to the unyielding granite upon which the town was built.

As Gilda regarded it in the distance she wondered what would possess a person to live in such a hard place. To build on stone and rock only to be pummeled by the sea.

Adam picked up his pace and she followed, he broke into a trot and she kept time. He finally let loose, dropped her hand and began to run and Gilda was on his heels for a second before she passed him without thinking, letting the bull inside of her run. Feeling that surge of power flow through her and complete a circuit of perfect, unadulterated brawn. Her mind turned off and he took over.

Only Adam's wheezing laugh from behind pulled her from the mindless calm, she stopped and turned to see him far behind bent over his knees, face red and gasping at the heavy salt air. "I think I took care of you too well, and myself not well enough!"

Gilda trotted back to him, feeling herself again, feeling more her than she had while she'd been running. "I believe you are right." she offered an arm and without hesitating, Adam took it, and as he'd done for her countless time since they'd met, she hauled his arm over her shoulder and together they made the last of the trek together.

"You're not even winded!" he complained, still sucking air in jolting gasps.

She didn't reply, just kept moving and kept her eyes on the bustling town. It was larger than she'd expected, out here in the middle of nowhere but as they drew nearer she saw the jagged rooflines of homes and the mighty spire of a church. Spread across the pumping sea, a great dock like a spider web floated atop the surf with ships of all sizes set for the night in the water.

Gilda stopped for a moment and took it all in with wonder. Adam was happy to have the time to recover from his run and they stared together out at the boundless sea. After a while, Adam brought his hand to her face, turning her gaze from the rolling water to his equally fathomless eyes.

"These are good people in this town," he explained with an intensity she'd never seen before, "hard-working, upstanding people." Tucking a strand of her hair that had come loose on the way he let his fingers coast atop her ear almost too gently, raising a hot blush on her skin at the contact. "If we want to make a life here…" his words trailed off as he struggled to put his thoughts to words.

"Adam, what…are you doing?" Gilda searched those amber depths for the root of what he was getting at and saw none.

He opened his mouth to speak, closed it again. Sighed and cast a frustrated gaze to the sky before bringing a palm to his face with a smack. "I'm making a mess of things…that's what I'm doing."

They had come too far and from far worse than whatever he was trying to say, Gilda took both of his hands in her own and with a voice as soft as clouds said, "Talk to me."

He smiled then, and it could have eclipsed the sun in that moment. Shaking his head at her and the way she had of cutting to the quick of things and fighting, even when she was on the edge of death…Gilda McGregor was a marvel.

Suddenly he was on his knee in front of her, his hands holding her own high as if she were royalty. His gaze softened, "Gilda McGregor, I'm not a good man. You need to know that. I drink and gamble, brawl and swear, I'm the original sinner if there ever was and I make no apologies for that. But if you'll have me, I'd be the best man I could for you, I'd work my fingers till they bled and sweat over the forge until I was dry if it meant I came home to your sweet face every night."

Flashes of Nathaniel ran through Gilda's mind, kneeling at her feet, the pretty words and ringing bells. Then of him with bloody tears sinking into the murk of that swamp, where he was rotting this very moment.

"It was a terrible thing that brought you to me, and you've been through so much…let me make you forget Gilda, let me make it right for you, make a life for you." He pleaded fervently, rising from the ground to cradle her face in those hard palms once again.

She was breathless in the face of this passionate proposal, so plainly delivered here on the cliffs of this craggy sea town.

He pressed his forehead to hers then, eyes staring into her soul, "I'll give you everything, if you'll have me…will you have me Gilda?"

She closed her eyes and listened deep down inside of herself, everything she'd thought was good and right in this world, was not. Those she had trusted had betrayed her, her family was gone and waiting in death for her to return but before that happened, Gilda wanted a life.

"Yes, Adam….I'll have you." She smiled at the blazing grin he gifted her with, spinning her around in his arms and squeezing her tight he pulled her away from him quickly and just looked at her.

"Right here and now." He reached into the pack he'd been hauling, pulled a dagger and tore a strip of cloth from that infernal nightgown.

"We're getting married here?" Gilda asked, looking around.

"I've no use for churches, Lass." He offered without much feeling, "if we wed, we wed the old way, alright?"

Gilda nodded, and tried to right herself but ended up laughing at the effort. Adam gave her a mystified look and she held out her arms in abandon, "I was going to try and straighten up for you, to make myself pretty…I'm afraid the cause wass lost before it began."

His features took on a serious expression and he pulled her close to him, "You are the most beautiful woman that's ever walked this Earth. Whatever it is that's inside of you is radiant and it wouldn't matter if you were soaking wet in a fishnet Gilda...it shows with every move you make."

She was stunned at his fervent words, silenced at the hungry way he regarded her, she opened her mouth to speak but found nothing came out.

Holding her close, he reverently kissed the top of her left hand, sliced the wrist with the razor sharp dagger and as the ribbon of crimson flowed from the cut, he did the same to his right and placing them together in a firm clasp he locked eyes with her and vowed, "The blood in my veins, the air in my lungs and my final moments on this Earth belong to you."

The waves crashed behind them and a strong wind kicked up, tossing Gilda's hair about her madly in its dance. She cleared her throat which had suddenly gone dry, squeezed the hand she held and repeated, "The blood in my veins, the air in my lungs and my final moments on this Earth belong to you."

Thunder rolled through the sky as a bolt of lightning scraped the roiling water below sending the ships bobbing on the surf like corks. The sky cracked opened and poured rain over them as Adam pulled her to his chest, ran his unbound hand down the side of her face and pressed his lips to her own in a kiss so gentle and sweet it brought tears to her eyes.

After all the ugliness and pain, kindness, love and the promise of life and home.

When he finally ended the sweet melding of their lips, he smiled as the rain poured down his face and bound their hands, still bleeding and clasped with the piece of cloth he'd torn from her gown, "Its good luck to keep it on as long as we can!" he shouted over the rising storm and pulled her toward the town beneath the now dumping curtain of rain.

They stumbled through the soaked cobblestone streets and into the door of an inn. It was busy enough on account of the squall that had kicked up and as Gilda and Adam made their way to the bar people stopped to stare at the picture they made, soaked to the bone and bound at wrists.

"May I help you sir?" a portly man with a beard asked as he placed a frothy mug of ale before another thirsty patron.

Adam reached into his pack and slammed a bag of coins on the bar. "A room for me and my bride and drinks for anyone that wants to toast Mrs. Adam Flynn!"

The purveyor of the establishment and his jolly wife erupted into a round of applause and calls for good cheer before the hefty bag could even be counted.

"Bless the 'appy couple!" the moon faced woman roused as she hoisted a mug of ale to the inhabitants of the inn.

"To the happy couple!" the occupants replied with cheers and smiles.

A burly man with arms the size of ham hocks, the owner retired to the cellar for a fresh barrel of ale, insisting that his private stock be brought out for the occasion. Meanwhile his wife scuttled about the kitchen in the rear, dragging Gilda and Adam with her in an unshakable grasp. She harried about the stove, stoking the fire and mumbling some wives tale about a good feast for good fortune.

When she was satisfied with the state of the food and had given the scullery maids their marching orders, she regarded Gilda with a critical eye. "Married in a pair a trews with filthy boots on yer feet and the rain on yer face…where's yer mother love?"

Without intending to she had wounded Gilda deeply with that simple question. Having been so far and through so much, her serrated nerves finally crumbled under the weight of that single sentence. She sniffed, felt her eyes water and clapped her unbound hand to her face to hide her tears as they began to spill down her cheeks. Adam gathered her up in his arms and shushed her as she hiccupped sadly.

Just then her husband came thundering up the stairs, a barrel on his shoulder and his face red with effort. Seeing Gilda's state he tossed a sour glare at his wife, "Fanny, ye cruel nag! Our best customers all year and ye have 'er in tears before I can tap the keg!"

Without missing a beat she put her hands on her imposing hips and bellowed, "Shamus ye dumb ox! Get yer arse back behind that bar and start servin the guests...we 'ave a reception to host!"

"With a weepy bride, o aye!" he groused while still obeying her orders. She threw a wooden spoon at his imposing behind as he shouldered his way through the door to the bar and Fanny turned her attention back to Gilda. "I didn't mean a thing by it love, honest. Now, no cryin on yer wedding day." She was wiping Gilda's face with her apron and saw the dirty strip of cloth that bound their wrists.

"I suppose there's no talkin ye outta that so I might make her more presentable?' she asked eyeing Adam with a wizened impatience.

Pulling Gilda's face out of his shoulder with his free hand, Adam leveled his gaze with the tear rimmed eyes of his bride and broke out in a contagious smile once again, "I'm sorry Fanny, but I wouldn't take this fasting off for the Devil himself tonight."

"Figured as much." She harrumphed, "no matter though." She stormed a nearby closet clattering and clawing through it knocking down brooms and pots as she went, "Ye'll be gettin a good enough look at 'er tonight, no secrets between husbands and wives." She pulled her ruddy face out from the mysterious pantry that held an immeasurable bounty of odds and ends to toss a saucy wink at Adam.

"All they're gettin is a good look at that tremendous arse of yers Fanny!" Shamus bellowed as he sauntered back in. "People want to see the lovely bride, what's keepin em back here with ye?"

"She's not lovely yet!" Fanny sniped from inside the closet as she continued to paw, raising a ruckus louder than the party that seemed to have erupted from nowhere. "Ahhhh!" She beamed as she came out with her intended prize, proudly holding up a white lace tablecloth, she swirled it around as she approached Gilda. "A little bit o' thing like you will likely drown in a skirt o' mine, but I think we can make do with this."

Without a single word, Fanny knelt before Gilda and yanked the muddy boots from her feet as if she were un-shoeing a horse. Next came the pants, which fairly ripped under the woman's mighty clasp and in a woosh of damp fabric Gilda stood in a ragged shirt that scantly covered the tops of her thighs and nothing else.

Shamus arched a single brow at Adam, turned and tactfully stood in the doorway of the inn, effectively blocking any view with his enormous girth. Adam bit back a laugh and offered a boyish grin to his now blushing bride.

Fanny was un-phased, with the clever use of a broad belt along with a few strategic pleats and folds, the table cloth swirled around Gilda's bare feet, the dainty lace skimming the floor like a breeze. The shirt was tucked in and the sleeves rolled, after hauling Gilda's tumbling damp tresses into a ponytail and pinching her cheeks she looked rather smart for a last minute bride.

"Its good luck for a bride to be bare footed." Fanny remarked nodding proudly at her handiwork, with no small amount of effort, she hefted herself from the floor and with a frantic sweep of her flapping arms scuttled the bride and groom back out to their guests. Hand in hand and fairly beaming from ear to ear they were received with a tidal wave of cheers and applause, the inn having doubled its occupancy in the mere moments they'd spent under Fanny's care.

Shamus lifted their joined hands, "To Mr. and Mrs. Flynn!"

A roar echoed through the stone hall and from the corner a fiddler began to tune up, the fraying hairs of his bow swaying in the dancing firelight. Fanny busted in moments later with candles and flowers for the tables followed closely by the maids she'd earlier barked at. Shamus handed Gilda and Adam a mug of his finest ale and smiled broadly, revealing a cracked eyetooth beneath his dark curling beard. "First pour of the keg, and congratulations to ye both."

Amidst the chaos and noise, Adam squeezed his wife's hand and looked deeply into eyes, fairly blazing with excitement, "To you, Mrs. Flynn."

She daintily touched her mug to the edge of his, "And to you as well, Mr. Flynn."

They drank deeply, maintaining the now steaming gaze and then the spell was broken as Shamus. Overcome with happiness, either for them or the crowd at his inn, bundled them both up into his bear like arms and hugged them fiercely.

That seemed to be all the encouragement the pressing crowd needed and in a swarm of well wishes, gifts and kisses Gilda and Adam were fairly drowned in the good will of the people of Dunedin. A withered old man carrying a gnarled cane reached her first, and with a courtly bow and a gentle kiss of his papery lips, he offered Gilda a blue satin beggar's pouch.

She took it, mystified but smiling and he was quick to fasten the thing to the belt Fanny had thoughtfully supplied, with a grin and a flourish, he dropped two gold coins in the bag after suggestively rubbing them together as the crowd cheered.

That was the way of it for the next hour or so, kisses and coins, coins and kisses. A small boy with dimpled cheeks approached to shyly tugged on her table cloth skirt. When Gilda knelt down he placed a wreath of white Shepherd's Pearls on her head, stole and kiss and ran back to his mother who smiled, shrugged and helped herself to another pull of Shamus's ale.

The fiddler was in high form and by the time The Flynn's had received all of their guests and the bag was drooping heavily from Gilda's hip. She and Adam were a little more than drunk and before they knew what was happening they'd been drug to the cleared center of the room to dance a reel with the nimble folk still sober…or just drunk enough to attempt such a thing.

Barefooted and tethered to her towering husband, Gilda and Adam managed three of the dances before Adam swayed deeply and almost threatened to drop. Fanny swooped in, dumped them unceremoniously in front of two plates heaping with food and stood between them and their guests to make sure they would eat. All the while barking at Shamus to fetch another keg from the cellar as this celebration looked to see the dawn.

In that stolen moment, their sweating hands still tied to one another Gilda learned some things about her groom that had escaped her all this time they had shared. For one, he was left handed, and for another he hated carrots. Slyly pushing them to her plate when Fanny was turned away and stealing another steamy kiss to the delight of the sloshing guests, Gilda could only smile.

When they'd finished the general consensus was that the guests were tired of the bride and groom and that the bride and groom must certainly be tired of them. With a final haunting air sung by a young girl with hair the color of tar and eyes like smoke, Adam and Gilda were hastened up the stairs to their room, which Fanny had taken the time to fill with flowers and candles and even two bottles of wine.

Adam lifted her awkwardly with the tether still in- tact and carried her gallantly over the threshold. Kicking the door shut so hard the hinges all but broke and with no small amount of satisfaction murmured, "Alone at last Mrs. Flynn."

Chapter 14

Cullen drifted into a dreamless sleep as Enola navigated their ill-gotten sedan to the outskirts of West Wycombe. After her cryptic reply regarding her mortality, he'd settled for silence, internally stewing about what it was she hid from him. Resenting her detached nature and regard that was contradicted by her extreme fear for his well-being, by her insistence that he be safe, always. At the same time he was thirsting for intimacy, craving that electric hum he heard in the back of his head when they touched, the fiery gazes that blazed from within and her secrets ...to know her in any way she would allow.

When the car began to slow he stirred, his fitful state hinged on the soft sway of the car as it rolled along the expressway, the whistling of the wind through the broken window and the hum of the heater. A delicate spell that was broken as Enola jerked the car into park and leaned over the wheel, looking with great interest at what by all appearances was a party.

Searchlights swept the cloudless sky, fading into the heavens as they reached for the stars, an imposing stone structure was lit from below and swarms of people dressed to kill sauntered in anxiously as valets and waiters sashayed through the crowd with trays and coats.

"This can't be right." Cullen yawned, looking at the corner to make sure this was the intersection he'd been told on the phone.

"It just might be." She said, looking somehow more concerned.

"There is no way that the subject of the most daring and high value heist in over a decade is being displayed here, where all these people could just call the police and report it." He stretched, bumping an arm into her impossibly warm side as he did.

She bit her lip nervously, a troubled hand rubbed her forehead as if trying to iron out the concern raising creases along its normally smooth surface. "Cullen, I want you to get in this seat, turn this car around and get as far away from here as you can."

"Why are you always pushing me away?" he exploded and in the closed space of the car it was a bellow that surprised even him, echoes of his father calling in his mind.

His ire fell on deaf ears, barely even registered to her and in that long moment between his question and her response. Watching the fearful way Enola regarded this benign looking party and all its charms, a cold knot of fear twisted in his stomach.

"Take out your phone please." She asked without even sparing him a glance.

He did, the battery was dangerously low from his night on the street and today's exploits.

"Look up where we are." Her voice had taken on a dreamy quality as she looked on, waiting patiently for him to obey.

Cullen did as he was bade, thrown off balance by her placid countenance. He'd have assumed any person dumb enough to raise their voice to Enola Sloan was likely to regret their lack of control for the rest of their days. But here she was, calm, cool and waiting for him to see something, something she could not or would not explain.

The mirror image of the picture in the windshield flickered on the screen of his phone, a black banner that read: Hell-Fire Caves in drippy red script flashed across the screen at the top and tabs for events, rates and tours beckoned on the side.

"The Hell-Fire Caves…" he read out loud and tapped the History button, he got as far as 1700 before his phone, having reached its limit, died in his hand, the screen going black.

Still, Enola said nothing.

"I thought the Hell-Fire Club was in Ireland." He replied, missing her point.

Enola shook her head, "…there were many outposts of that particular…club." She swallowed hard, and gripped the wheel the whites in her hands blooming as the metal underneath groaned in her clasp. She immediately released the wheel and turned to Cullen, her eyes wet with tears as her hands sought his own.

"Please….go." she begged.

"Not on your life." He stated sternly.

"How about on your own?" her eyes had taken on a wild quality, rolling about in a fearful dance.

"Enola," he held her hands firmly in his own, yanking on them to center her gaze on his, "tell me what's going on."

"I don't know!" she wailed as her breath hitched in her lungs, "I don't know what's going on, I don't know who's behind all of this and I don't know what's going to happen!" she drug a few deep breaths into her mouth raggedly, clinging to what little composure she had left, "What I do know is that terrible people committed unspeakable acts in this place centuries ago, Cullen. And it is no coincidence that the door is here tonight."

"You believe the Hell-Fire Club has…returned."

She swallowed again and wiped her eyes, "It would certainly appear that way."

"And they have the door in there...for some reason." He followed this this thread with her, feeding off her evident fear.

"Yes." Her eyes wide.

"And that is dangerous?" he continued.

Her eyes locked with his again, "Very."

"Then let's go get it back, Enola." Cullen's eyes took on a shadowed cast, "I don't know why I'm here either, but I am, we are...and I feel, no, I know that should be enough, I want to finish this dance."

A smile stole away some of her fear at his reference, and as they sat in that car, hands clasped Enola thought for a long time before saying, "If that's the case," she began looking him over critically, "then we're terribly underdressed."

Cullen's eyes roamed over the crowd that was flowing into the entrance of the structure, which had taken on an ominous presence in Enola's fear of it. Tuxedos and gowns, masks and jewels, hand in hand the couples were dressed to the teeth. He regarded his jeans and shit-kickers sadly and nodded in agreement.

"So what do we do?" he asked, clearly out of ideas.

"We borrow." Enola's eyes were fixed on a Mercedes that was coasting past the already full lot and ridiculously long line of limos to a dark street around the corner. She threw the car back into gear and pursued it as it rolled to a stop on a deserted cul-de-sac likely used for deliveries to the bustling venue during business hours.

As the man exited the vehicle and walked around to the passenger side to help his wife out, Enola walked toward them asking, "Would you happen to have a charger?" she laughed, "our phone died and we're quite lost." Her breath chuffing out from her mouth in the chilly fall air.

"Sorry," the man answered curtly in an American accent, "no charger."

Enola kept walking, "Thanks anyway."

He ignored her now, but kept a wary eye as his wife rose from her seat, once he'd shut the door and locked it Enola was on top of him. A quick open handed strike to his face had him slumping to the ground as blood trickled from his nostrils, the wife however, she took gracefully into a choke hold and with an amazing amount of care, strangled until she passed out.

She checked both their pulses and nodded at the timid thrumming she felt inside, then turned her attention to the woman's clothes. Cullen came up behind her, his mouth open at the expediency with which she'd dispatched them both.

"Why didn't you just hit her too?" he asked, standing over the three in shock.

Enola stopped for a moment, looked at the unconscious woman critically, "I didn't want to mess up her face."

Once again Cullen was completely lost in the mysteries of Enola Sloan, who would steal a woman's clothes, and knock out her husband, but drew the line at shattering her septum.

"He's not going to undress himself." She admonished, pulling the shoes off the woman's feet and moving for the stockings.

Cullen knelt next to him, put his hands to the jacket and pulled back. "I feel so creepy!"

Enola gave him a look of utter impatience, "You're telling me that I have to knock him out for you and undress him?" Without waiting for a reply she jerked his limp arm from the cutaway jacket and rolled him easily to the other side. It only seemed to take her moments to have him stripped and with the same effort she would have exerted to lift a blanket, she scooped the man in his underthings up and placed him considerately in the front seat, reclining the headrest so he would be comfortable.

Cullen was just buttoning his shirt when Enola had finished putting the wife, also in nothing but a bra and panties next to her husband. Considerately turning his back to afford her what little privacy he could on a public road, he managed the cuffs well enough but became hopelessly frustrated at the cummerbund. Without thinking twice he turned to ask her assistance with the flimsy thing and in that moment, Cullen got his first good look at her.

He'd just always assumed her modesty was camouflage for some tragic birthmark, burn or less than perfect body. The sight he drank in blew all those theories out of the water and knocked him senseless.

In an age where women could be almost foolishly thin, she was lushly built with opalescent skin from head to toe. A nipped waist with a cruel scar low on her left side flared to her rounded hips and sumptuous bosom. Cullen's mind flashed back to the pin ups of the 50's and 60's, their long legs and bright smiles window dressing on the sinful hourglass figures of those buxom beauties. His mouth watered as his throat went dry and though he knew he should turn away but every fiber of his being howled for him to touch her.

She had leaned against the trunk of the Mercedes to pull on the black silk stockings she'd borrowed from the now resting Mrs. As she smoothed the smoky film up her thighs, she stepped daintily into the arched velvet pumps and was moving over to take hold of the gown she'd tossed over the roof when Cullen seized her wrist.

His face held an expression she'd not seen on him or any other man in an age, and that was by design. She covered up and blended in as best she could in this world. Because as tightly as she held that leash, there were some ways, some acts when even she was helpless to control it.

Cullen was beyond reason now, and as he hauled her against his chest he pinned her back against the side of the car. His hand greedily pulling her thigh around his waist as he cradled her face and pressed his mouth hotly over hers. Enola allowed her arms to twine around his neck, savoring the feeling of his touch, of his body against her own. His lips fused with hers and as his tongue teased hers in a sensual dance, a low moan emanated from deep inside of her throat.

That primal sound being coaxed from her at his touch sent Cullen ablaze and he felt a surge straining against the trousers he'd donned. That unearthly thrumming he'd come to know as only hers was singing from her now, her skin ablaze in passion and traveling between them in agonizing waves that threatened to buckle his knees beneath him. Drunk on the scent of rose and the sweet taste of her soft mouth. Cullen yanked her hair free of the elastic she'd bound it in this morning and twined his fingers in the silken strands crushing her mouth on his own.

A ragged gasp was torn from her lips when he pressed his mouth to the soft hollow behind her ear, trailing hungry kisses to her collar bone as he went. He filled his hands with her full breasts and teased the scorching flesh. Placing his mouth over the tightened peak and drawing on it, his eyes rolled into his head as she put her hands on either side of his head and sighed.

The pounding in his ears rose to an almost deafening roar and her body was arching tightly with every desperate breath as she clung to him and fought the tightly leashed animal inside of her. One wrong move, a single misjudgment and she could kill him, in the throes of her ecstasy he could be paralyzed. Her thoughts were scrambled when his questing fingers parted her thighs and found the fabric between them drenched in her wanting heat. As his knuckles drug against the sensitive flesh through the damp fabric Enola's hands seized the roof of the car, gripping the metal in trembling fists, curling it in her fingers like paper.

Driven by her response to his touch, Cullen's fingers frantically worked at the fly of his trousers his mouth on hers again, drinking deep of her lips once more. Once he'd freed his aching flesh from the damnable fabric, his hands clawed at her panties, drawing them desperately down her thighs.

He heard glass shattering and saw it rain on the pavement a scant moment before her iron grip was over his hands. "No." she gasped.

Cullen tried once more in vain, but he was frozen in her clasp, his eyes met hers and saw the need blazing inside of her. The hot flush riding up her skin, bruised lips and blushing cheeks…she wanted him, her breasts heaved as she sought to slow her breathing.

Enola once again had hold of that delicate thread which held the stampeding strength inside of her at bay. It rattled and knocked within her, demanding she release it to run free as it chose. She knew better…

Chapter 15

The enthusiasm from the party below drifted up through the floorboards of their room, which was lousy with bushels of white flowers and flickering candles. As Adam gently set his wife on her feet, Gilda eye's wandered over to an arrangement near the window, picking up their sweet scent as the chilly night air coasted over their blooms. A fire had been lit in the hearth and the heat was creeping across the knotted floor toward the fur draped bed at its center. Fanny had considerately turned it down, a single white rose perched on the sheets near the downy pillows.

Gilda's eyes flew to Adam's where they fairly blazed with love as he ran a single finger down the side of her face to tuck the wildly curling strands that had come loose in the night behind her delicate ear. Stealing a kiss from her gently he continued to look her over with wonder, "In all my years I've never seen a lovelier bride."

Shaking her head at his fervent compliment and looking down at her table cloth skirt, she realized she did feel beautiful, and lovely. The bulging bridal purse caught her attention and she smacked it with an open palm, causing it to jingle loudly. "I'd say we made out like bandits."

"It's certainly more than we came in here with." He agreed, hefting the thing in his palm with a surprised expression at its weight. "Generous people on the sea."

His hand let go of the pouch and slid along the belt to her waist. Pulling her close to him, he took her free hand and placed it on his stubbled cheek. Closing his eyes at her touch and taking in a sharp breath, he asked softly, "Are you scared?"

Gilda knew to what he was referring, her mother, ever the sage of advice and knowledge had been quick to explain what she could expect from her husband on her wedding night. Of course as she'd detailed the act it had been

Nathaniel's lithe body she'd pictured in her mind. The reality, she thought as she regarded the towering frame of muscle she'd reduced to a gasping boy with a single touch of her hand, was far more appealing.

"I will never fear you, Adam Flynn." She vowed, pulling his mouth to her own, not for a tepid peck though. Gilda had tasted the tiniest hint of passion in this man, and she wanted it, whatever that meant, tonight.

It was all the encouragement Adam needed, and with a savage growl from deep within his chest he pulled her delicate frame against his own and crushed his mouth on her sweet lips. Drinking deep of her as his hands went to the belt, it quickly fell to the floor with a musical thud as the coins in the purse landed. A desperate need began to seize him and with a yank the makeshift skirt was billowing on the floor around her pale feet. Pulling the shirt up over her head he was met with resistance from the dirty scrap of fabric that bound their hands. Without hesitation he ripped it apart, freeing them both and finally leaving her bare before him.

Gilda was quick to wrap her arms around her breasts in a modest flush, but Adam would have none of it from her. He took those dainty wrists in his hands and gently pried them away from her body, "Never hide yourself from me Gilda."

He felt her arms relax at his words, and he released her to see that in all the world, no woman was more finely built than his own. Pulling the leather thong Fanny had tied her hair up in, Adam sent her cognac curls tumbling down and around her in sultry waves. The edges skimmed her sinuous hips and tickled around her ripe breasts.

Unable to stand it any longer, Adam moved to run his hands through her hair, over her skin across every inch of her as he stole kiss after searing kiss from his delicious bride. Her nimble fingers made quick work of his shirt and when confronted with the chiseled wall of muscle she greedily pressed her hands against the planes of his stomach, marveling at the strength of this man. As her hands drifted lower to the trews, Adam's hands came over hers to halt them roughly, with a crooked grin, "We'll have to leave those on for a while or it will be over before it begins."

Gilda didn't pretend to understand, nor did she care. All would be revealed tonight, hastily wed on a cliff near Dunedin with a last minute reception, she wouldn't have traded it, any of it for the world. Adam laid her gently in the center of the massive bed, the fur that covered it had been warmed by the fire and tickled softly at the backs of Gilda's legs as she stretched along the length of it. After kicking off his boots, Adam joined her resting on his arms above her, once again letting his eyes roam over her in unabashed wonder.

In that quiet moment, Gilda laid a gentle hand on his arm and asked, "Why did you?"

His eyebrows rose in interest and fell into a sexy grin that once again revealed that dimple in his right cheek. "A few reasons," he curled a strand of her hair around his fingers, "I've never met a woman like you, not even close. You're strong Gilda...truly strong at your core and that's rare in this world." His hand had dropped her hair and had begun a tentative exploration of her body, starting with her arm. "The second reason is because that day, that awful day in the storm when I saw you die...it felt like I had died right along with you, a part of me went too and...I knew I could never be apart from you again and be happy...and finally," he was twining his fingers through her own over and over, "if we wanted to live together and make any kind of a life here...we'd have to be wed to be respectable."

"You could have always said I was your sister." She offered, savoring the feeling of his body laid next to hers. They'd slept alongside one another every night since the storm, but it was so different to be in a bridal chamber instead of sharing a pallet of moth eaten blankets out of necessity. The doors were open between them, and what lay inside was beautiful and delicate, mysterious and exciting...the beginning of a new life together.

Adam guffawed at her suggestion, collapsing on the bed next to her and shaking it with his laughter, "No one would have believed it Gilda, the way I look at you could never pass for brotherly affection!"

Gilda started to laugh with him, realizing how funny it would have looked, how mismatched they were in that regard, him all dark and brawny, her golden and slender. She supposed he was right and as their mirth wound down, they were both watching the firelight dance along the beams of the soaring ceiling in their attic suite. His hand found hers and held it, gently and rubbed his thumb along the backs of her fingers slowly, "Why did you say yes?" he asked in a soft voice that almost seemed like he was afraid of her answer.

Gilda thought a moment and answered plain, "I trust you."

Adam was roused by her simple but strong words, "You do...don't you?" she smiled at him and was rewarded with another soft kiss from her groom. He cradled her in his iron embrace then, wrapping the strength he had around her sweetly.

There, tangled around each other as the autumn breeze carried the gentle song of the fiddler's craft around them, Mr. and Mrs. Flynn regarded each other as they were, as they had been found and as far as they'd come together. Each accepted the other for what they knew and trusted in what would be, what might come did not matter for they would have each other.

Gilda could feel the strong, steady beating of his heart against her own, his warm skin and muscle all around her.

Those piercing eyes demanding that her own relent and allow him to see inside of her with no concession.

He placed another kiss upon her lips, watching her as he did so, relishing the dreamy expression she wore. "Gilda," he began with a pleading tone in his voice, nuzzling at the golden flesh of her slender neck, "I cannot wait any longer, and I'm needing you like I need air to breathe...I'm begging you please, without a second's delay....will you have me?

Gilda placed her hands on his shoulders, pulling Adam's head away from her so she could level her eyes with his, "Yes Adam, I'll have you, this night and every night."

A victorious grin spread across his face and with more passion he kissed her again, melding their mouths, his tongue demanding entrance to her sweet depths as his fingers twined in her hair. She lost herself in the sensation of his lips claiming hers, the weight of him atop her and those strong arms cradling her to him, to his will.

He jerked his head from her swollen lips, ran his mouth over her shell like ear, raising gooseflesh all over her body as he teased the nerve endings in the column of her throat. Awash in the sensations he was pouring over her, Gilda clung to him, her breaths coming in short gasps. A heat she'd never known was rising inside of her, answering the call he made with his soft touches and burning mouth.

Running his stubbly jaw along the tender underside of her breast, where the rounded flesh met her finely built ribs. Adam allowed his heated breath to tease the pale skin, his fingers to coax the wine colored tips to straining peaks as his bride arched tightly at his touch. Barely there kisses brought sweet moans from her hot mouth and when he was sure she was going to scream, he allowed himself the pleasure of suckling one, and then the other, relishing the trembling hands she placed on his head as he did.

His playful tongue tormented her, clinging to him Gilda was awash in the pleasure he lavished. Her breasts ached as they burned under his ministrations, when he drug his teeth over the sensitive side of her breast a surge rippled through her, the hidden strength she carried awakening to her passion.

Remembering the sound of her owns bones crumbling in her clenched fist, Gilda let go of his head, which was now bestowing tender kisses on each of her heaving ribs as he ran questing hands over and over her hips. Grabbing fistfuls of the fur that tumbled across the bed in their passion, she arched again as his sinful tongue laved at her navel and heard the answering rip of the pelt she clutched.

Calloused hands coasted along her silken thighs and her eyes shot to his own where a wicked grin was spread across his handsome face. Gently, but firmly his hands coaxed Gilda to open the legs she had clenched shut. Terrified yet titillated, the muscles within trembled as she wanted more than anything and yet feared the unknown. He must have sensed the internal battle, levering himself back up to her face, he kissed her in soft teasing, open mouthed bites that left her chasing his lips up as he pulled away after a mere taste again, and again.

All the while, his hand moved steadily yet slowly from the knees she bent up from the bed, toward the source of that liquid heat he knew he would find, if he could just convince her to relax, to release. In spite of her passionate response and the flush that colored her entire body, those thighs were like bands of steel and short of prying them apart, Adam had no idea what would coerce Gilda to drop this final veil, to lay herself bare before him.

Halting everything, and waiting for her to rouse from the passion he had conjured for her, when those blissful eyes opened to his own they stared each other in gasping silence for a heartbeat. Adam placed his hand on her knees once more, "Trust me." He whispered.

He saw her take the deepest of breaths and without moving her eyes from his, he felt Gilda drop that final fig leaf and release the last battlement of defense she had. Open to his touch, Adam swore he'd never known a sweeter surrender. Gently, slowly to the point that it might drive him mad, his hand traveled up the porcelain flesh of her thighs to the dusky curls at her core. He inhaled sharply at the slick heat his fingers found and as his knuckles grazed the sensitive flesh Gilda moaned and clutched at his shoulders with such strength it surprised him.

Delving deeper, allowing his hand to become familiar with the most secret part of her, Adam clenched his jaw against the urge to rip his trews off and rut on her, though every piece of him howled for just that. He would not hurt his darling bride on this night, or any night. Watching her experience passion for the first time, seeing her writhe in the heat he alone could bring to her surged through his chest in proud waves.

Unable to stop himself and desperate for more of her, every piece, he lowered his head to those damp curls and tasted her nectar with long sweeps of his tongue. Gilda stifled a scream at the first touch of his wicked mouth and once again fought the raging beast inside of her that was ready to stampede through her embroiled body.

Adam's eyes rolled into his head at the taste of her, the fiery responses and her sultry gasps. As his hands splayed on her hips and raised her to him like a bowl of the sweetest cream, he drank deeply until he was nearly mindless with it, her sobbing moans a song that drove him on.

Gilda was aflame and in desperate need, of what she did not know, but wanting it to go on forever and end all at once was driving her nearly to tears. The raging bull within was a pacing mass of brawn, waiting for her to open the door, to let him loose upon this burning night. With all her might she resisted, against her every instinct and climbing passion she kept that door locked tight, terrified of what might happen should she relent for even a moment.

Unable to wait another heartbeat to claim her, to make her his, Adam relieved himself of his trews and lay above his panting prize, the blush in her cheeks almost red and her eyes wild. That finely spun hair of hers a tangled halo above her head, she gripped the torn fur beneath her as if she might fall and her limbs were splayed in a tumble across the silvery planes of the bed...she was gorgeous in her passion.

Rising above her and taking her tightly in his arms, Adam nuzzled again at her neck and as he found her sweet center and claimed his bride in a long, single stroke. The rippling heat of her clenched him like a silken fist and already his seed climbed inside him to release. Looking at her face, searching for pain or fear, he found only fire when his eyes fell upon her lovely face. She was burning as he was, on the edge like him and with a begging squeeze of her thighs and a rock of her body, she urged him on.

Needing no further encouragement Adam allowed himself to move within her, teasing her most secret flesh with his own, pulling soft moans and cries from her as he did. Her body rippled atop the bed, meeting his every thrust with the soft curves and planes of her own. And still she bucked beneath him, as if she still needed, was unsatisfied.

A heavy rain began to fall outside, the thunder rolling through the sky and over the sleepy town in grinding waves. The water pelted against the roof above them steadily and a brisk wind teased the flames of the candles that filled the room into a swaying dance.

Adam heeded her call and answered her primal need with stronger thrusts. Levering himself above her soft body onto his arms, his sweat falling upon her as the rain did outside. Gilda was unaffected, unaware of anything but the searing need inside of her, the plunging heat of her groom and the bull, always the bull, fighting her now to be free of the chains she bound him in. Her breath caught as another thrust sent a wave of pleasure through her, the next one, and the next one and the one after that left her wanting.

Closing her eyes and focusing on every sensation, every inch of Adam over and inside her, Gilda searched for the illusive prize she now knew she needed. That golden thread of pleasure that if pulled would send her unraveling into oblivion. The fire had been lit and she was helpless to stop it, she would be satisfied this night and behind her closed eyes she saw him. Not Adam, not her husband, not the man straining above her to sate her aching need but the bull, Esus.

Her cool eyes met the burning gaze of his own as a thunder clap shattered the sky and shook the walls, she looked at him, unafraid. The size of his hulking flesh covered in smoky fur, cruel horns curled from his head as his nostrils flared around her scent. Stamping his hooves, not in warning but in invitation, he beckoned her approach.

Running soft hands over the might of him marveling at the strength within she allowed herself to explore the being that resided within her. To feel every plane of him without fear or hesitation, he snorted as she leaned into his unrelenting body, allowed him to cradle her in his might. Curling the iron neck around her thin waist in an accepting embrace, she understood that she was his and he was hers...that they more than anything were together, were one.

Gilda's eyes had taken on a wild blindness beneath him and Adam's lungs were screaming as he powered into her, afraid he was hurting her yet spurred on at the same time by her arching body. He thirsted for her release, wanted it more than he wanted life and he set his jaw and dug deep, plunging into her with renewed vigor. Searching for a sign she was close, that she was enjoying this as much as he.

In the warm embrace of this wild creature she harbored, Gilda felt the heat of him seeping through her already scorching skin. He stirred around her, rousing her from the lassitude and completion of their companionable silence, the bull was hungry this night, as Gilda hungered. In his eyes she saw herself, saw that need and want, unashamed and proud he would take what he wanted and so should she.

Suddenly, Gilda erupted from the bed beneath him and in a flowing movement threw Adam to his back atop the bed. An unhinged quality had taken over her features. A savage wanting pulled at her normally sweet faces as she threw a slender leg across his hips and mounted him without a moment's hesitation.

He slid deep within and her head rolled back on her delicate neck, a guttural moan sliding from deep in her chest. Her hands went to his shoulders like iron hooks and as a streak of lightning cut the velvet of the night she began to ride.

The bull was running now, taking Gilda with him on his lumbering stampede, his big body rocking beneath her with every heavy stride. He bucked and tossed her above him, the panting breaths coming from them both as they raced together.

Adam was watching her in unabashed awe, running his hands up and down her sweat soaked body as she moved with reckless abandon. The storm outside was maddening in the sky, bolts of lightning chased each other to the earth and the wind was slamming the walls around them in a fury of howling gusts. Rain gave way to hail and as it beat the roof above them and tumbled in the open window a constant, unending growl of thunder consumed his ears in a threatening rumble that shook the floor beneath them.

And still she rode, her hair damp with sweat and eyes wild with passion. Sliding her sweet body atop his own as he gritted his teeth to hold fast until she found her pleasure.

They were close, as Gilda clung to her galloping mount she found that thread and grasped it greedily, urged on by the piercing roar of the bull beneath her.

Her motions took on a frantic desperation and Adam felt his bones creak under the force with which she loved him now. His shoulders screamed under her iron grip and he could swear she weighted ten stone more atop him as her hips ground into his own. He held...he endured, his own release clawing at him as this furious display played out atop him.

A shimmering heat blossomed inside of her, a terrible tightening that threatened to shatter her into pieces. Rising and rising to its feverish pitch, pulled every piece of her impossibly taught in a glorious agony. Gilda's entire body tensed around the sensation, pulling a groan from Adam in the distance, she cared not as Esus tore unrelenting toward release.

Adam felt that her sopping channel might crush his manhood inside of her then, the clenching of it was unendurable and he was about to pull her off him when a shuddering ripple tore through her, around him and he knew.

Sweet pleasure consumed her, racing through her entire body in delicious ribbons that teased her very soul. She moaned and screamed in her lust and lightning streaked across the window as thunder chased behind, deafening in its fury as the storm inside reached its pinnacle. Hail the size of his fists rolled heavily across the floor from the sky as the whipping wind drowned the candles and fire in the hearth and still she screamed in lusty pants as her body found its heaven.

Still the bull raged, pulling yet another climax from her as the first shattering one ended. She fell limply atop Adam, his chest slick with sweat and in the gentler throes of her second release he gripped her to him and found his own pleasure deep inside his splendid wife.

Sliding down the side of him, a lather of sweat shone on his fur and Gilda ran a sensual hand along his heaving ribs, over the curving horns in appreciation and with a guttural snort he sauntered away, pleased this night.

Chapter 16

After a tense moment between them, her breaths heaving in concert with his own, Cullen reluctantly let his hands drop. He turned his back once again, waiting this time until she came to him, the scalding image of her lush body burning inside his mind's eye. Some deep part of him bellowing for relief, for her and howling for release.

Tense moments melted into minutes and Cullen's heart slowed, his breaths calming in the cool of the night. Letting his eyes drift to the heavy moon as it rose over the gentle swell of the hill behind them, he felt that final clutch of need reluctantly give up and retreat.

An impossibly soft hand touched his arm and he turned, in those stormy depths he saw the roiling desire chained within, "Do you need help with that?" she asked softly as she reached for the now wrinkled and dirty cummerbund in his fist. Raising his aching hands into his hair to keep himself from reaching for her again, the scent of rose was teasing his nostrils and heating his blood anew. She was mercifully efficient and quick about it, stepping away again to inspect herself in the reflection of the unbroken window.

"It's too tight." Cullen remarked, eyeing the harshly outlined curve of her derriere in the navy velvet, ruches of the fabric highlighting the small waist that sent the seams all but tearing along her bosom and hips. Enola turned to look and shrugged after pulling at the fishtail hem in vain.

She shrugged, "There's nothing for it." her hands working to wind the still tousled strands he'd been clutching fist fulls of just moments before into a sedate bun at her nape. "This woman and I are totally different animals."

Cullen watched her fiddle and fuss, felt the lust subside and in its place a genuine affection ebbed through him. As she pulled a midnight colored cape with cream satin lining over her shoulders, she looked at him and asked, "Are you ready?"

"No," he replied in all honesty, "but let's do it anyway." Offering a courtly arm, they sashayed up to the entrance which was a busy as ever. Soft music teased out the great double doors at the front, red flood lights giving it an imposing appearance as they all flowed through them in a line. The anxious excitement bubbling up from the crowd as they approached, Cullen felt Enola's hand tighten in the crook of his arm as they walked through the doors.

Valet's swished the cloak off her creamy shoulders and Cullen winced at all that flesh literally pouring from the strapless gown. The swanlike lines of her neck, the drawn twin bows of her shoulder blades as she moved and swayed through the crowd. He took the claim ticket from the man without looking, he was too anxious to see what was to come.

His eyes scanned the dark room as they entered, only to see the banal and boring sight of every single gala he'd ever attended. A quartet played in the corner and amber lights crawled up the walls. Tuxedo clad waiters wandered with trays of champagne and canapes through the rafts of people that seemed to bundle up at every event. The air was overwhelmed with perfume, cologne and polite conversation as friends found one another and chatted excitedly over flutes of golden bubbles.

This couldn't be right, this couldn't be the place, filled to the brim with the types of people Cullen glad handed and bullshitted for a living. Their bright eyes and eager smiles almost a disappointment. Enola seemed just as confused by the pedestrian party, and Cullen watched her as she looked hard at the people around them, searching for something out of place, something wrong.

Placing his hand on her lower back and murmuring close to her ear, "I don't get it...what's going on here?"

Playing the loving wife, she brushed a gentle hand on his cheek, "Keep going, we'll know it when we see it."

Navigating their way through the soaring ball room to which they'd entered, past a bar and some beautifully decorated tables, the electric lighting began to give away to candles, flickering low in elaborate holders that hung from the ceilings and walls. Less and less people were about, as if this area was reserved and Cullen began to feel out of place in some subtle way.

A great archway of carved stone stood sentry over a worn staircase, the swaying candlelight dancing on the ancient ceiling as it descended into the unknown. Faces carved ages ago, frozen in agony, their open mouths and pleading eyes turned to the skies blindly. The patina of time gathered in the corners of their eyes and mouths, mossy blisters marred the flawless visages of these mute doormen. Feeling her hand tremble in his arm, Cullen smoothed his palm over her fingers to soothe her. Taking tentative steps toward it, the sound of angelic chanting floated up from below in disjointed phrases. The impossibly pure tenors and basses of a men's choir teased Cullen's ears and he could have sworn he caught a whiff of incense on the air from below.

Enola slid her shaking hand from its nest in his arm and clutched his hand in her own delicate grasp. Staring into the darkness fearfully before she looked at Cullen and swallowed hard, "I fear that once we go down there, we may not find our way back out." Her voice trembled around the words, a quivering lip shone fetchingly in fear, "Are you sure you want to follow me into the dark?"

Cullen brushed a soft kiss across her knuckles, "I would follow you into Hell, Enola." He felt his chest swell at the sigh that escaped her then. Pulling her along with him they began their descent down as the sound of heavenly chanting enveloped them. Candlelight gave way to darkness, and in the pitch of utter blackness, the voices were all Cullen heard, even over his own breathing and pounding heart. Down they went, on the worn and slippery stone steps that had seen thousands of years, untold people and the most unknowable of secrets.

They came upon a black curtain where a single robed man stood clutching a lantern of red glass out in front of him, the pulsing light inside like a beating heart in his hand. He looked on them passively with milky eyes and using a skeletal arm pulled back the curtain to reveal a chamber heavy with smoke. At the other side, a choir's loft was filled with robed singers their voices echoing sweetly off the stone of the room Enola and Cullen entered. As they approached through the rising wafts of incense that filled the space, the black blindfolds each man wore came into focus, along with the chains that bound their wrists to the gleaming oak rails that lined the loft in which they stood.

The shackled siren's harmony floated through the smoke allowing not so much as a rattle of a single link of the chains to mar the notes of the hymn. So completely awash in themselves and their song, it was likely that whatever soul passed through here went unnoticed. Their cheeks were damp with blind tears as together they wove a chord so painfully beautiful that no mortal should ever hear its perfection.

Cullen felt Enola's hand tighten on his own once more and he winced at the sharp pain, relaxing as she quickly released. Hastening her past this bound choir with a hand at the small of her back, the censors that oozed smoke were hanging near the next curtain and his eyes began to water either from the unhinging quality of the singing or the foreign scent of the Sulphur that threatened to consume every atom of air.

They were blissfully opened in a flourish and as a friendly man, also blindfolded greeted them warmly, another blind man politely asked, "Invitations?"

Enola gave Cullen a panicked look and his hands went to his jacket, frantically patting his chest and finding two sheaves of vellum in his breast pocket. He removed them and caught a glimpse of crimson script before the inquiring man swept them from his grasp, running the tips of his fingers over the expertly etched lettering.

"Mr. and Mrs. Ashby," he stated to a clerk in what looked like another cloak room off to the side. Only instead of hangers and rods, and shelves for hats, it was box upon box, wooden with small brass tags upon each one. Stacks and stacks of them inside the cramped space along the walls all the way to the ceiling of it. Among which the blindfolded clerk seemed to navigate solely by touch, running a gentle finger over each tag lightly moving along the grid formed until he arrived at the two he sought.

Deftly sliding the oblong boxes from the stack, the remaining ones clattering down in their absence. The clerk handed them both to his counterpart who laid them on a slender arm with a flourish and opened the hinged lids with the practiced skill that only comes from a lifetime of repetition.

"Brother and sister," he began as the lids revealed beds of sumptuous crimson satin, "welcome." Nestled inside each was a bracelet of sorts, one held a solid cuff of silver with a golden coil that wrapped around it thickly four times. Cullen stood obediently as the blindfolded counterpart placed it on his left arm below the cuff of his shirt.

The other held a black rhodium arm bracelet that resembled a jeweled tail, black diamonds running the length of it, glittering darkly in the sparse light of the room. Enola also waited while the sightless valet worked the six wraps of the darkly delicate thing onto her left arm. The pointed tail coming to rest in the hollow of her wrist, the rounded cuff cradling her elbow.

A crimson curtain was pulled back to reveal a great and soaring chamber with a hive like chandelier at its center. The lights appearing to swarm and swirl in the dark, the amber light they cast shifted and creeping along the stone floors and walls. As Cullen and Enola entered the curtain was dropped and the chanting that had become all but deafening was suddenly gone, drowned behind the heavy fabric.

In its place the tinkling of fine crystal flutes and the throaty laughs of secrets best kept in the dark. Fine shoes on cobble stone and the sultry whisper of satin and silk on skin. Cullen's eyes began to adjust to the constantly moving light and the disorientation it caused to see that this room was merely an antechamber. Like the face of a clock there were doors all around them draped with those asbestos curtains and guarded by a blindfolded sentry. While a mist of Sulphur crept along the floor to roll and wave along as it saw fit among the nimble feet of these mysterious guests.

Cullen's eyes fell on a couple as they hastened eagerly to an entrance arm in arm, the Sulphur fog stirring around their feet as they walked. The blindfolded sentry ran a gentle hand over each of their bracelets and politely pulled aside the curtain for them to enter. A hazy streak of purple light found its way around their silhouette as they swept inside, the curtain swinging heavily back into place and once again obscuring all to those who looked on.

"I think the bracelets are the key here." He murmured to Enola, who was watching an unusually tall man with shoulders broader than the door enter another room after such an inspection of the massive cuff that seemed a mere thread on his brawny wrist.

"I think you're right." She replied, trying to look at her own with the bemused admiration any woman has for a new piece of jewelry, "I count six on mine." She added taking

Cullen's hand gently in her own to press the palm of his hand to her face.

"Four." He answered, pretending to be completely caught up in their romantic interlude to any that may be watching.

"But which door is for what?" she asked, her eyes searching the chamber for a sign of what the rooms inside held.

"Only one way to find out," Cullen took her hand in his own and set his jaw with determination, approaching the door to the right of the one he'd seen the couple enter just scant moments before.

He held his breath as the sentry performed the same ritual with them, running claw like hands over their bracelets and silently pulling the curtain aside for them to enter.

The most delicious smell invaded his nostrils immediately, pulling a savage growl from his neglected stomach. Once they stepped through the darkened entry way Cullen was confronted with the most overwhelming spread of food he'd ever seen in his life.

Table after table was overflowing with a bounty of mouth-watering dishes. A table entirely comprised of roasts and ribs, steaks and loins all roasted to perfection with blindfolded butlers chained to the table with serving forks and knives at the ready. Enola looked at him with a bright smile, her own appetite making itself known when confronted with the lovely sight of potatoes in every preparation imaginable. A tower of cupcakes shone in the corner like a beacon over its constituents of pies and cakes, ice creams and candies all glittering beneath the flaming candelabras that soared above the feast.

In a darkened corner a bar the length of the great room was well peopled as blindfolded bar tenders slung drinks of every order to waiting guests with ease. A wall of illuminated bottles at least two stories high behind them.

The rolling ladder manned by yet another unseeing as he pulled the choicest vintages from their appointed places with ease.

"I'm starving." Enola stated, almost as if she were ashamed.

"Me too," Cullen replied, resisting the urge to lick his lips as a tray of hot corn bread caught his eye.

"Do we dare eat?" she asked fearfully.

"Oh, let's dare." Cullen said after a moment's consideration. People were milling about with plates in hand, taking what they liked and seating themselves near a roaring fireplace opposite the bar to enjoy their food. They hadn't had a bite since this morning in Enola's suite and his stomach was rumbling in a most undignified manner.

They shared a tense look and dove in, taking warmed plates in from the silver butler at the entrance to the endless buffet. Cullen was quick to venture to the table of a thousand meats, and took a New York Strip, some ribs, a few wings and even helped himself to ostrich, rare with raspberry reduction. Enola took a tender slice of extra rare prime rib, creamed horseradish and mashed potatoes with extra butter.

Moving to the seating area they were quickly shown to a quiet table in the corner where silverware and crisp linen napkins were waiting. A blind waiter asked what they would have to drink, Enola was quick to say water and Cullen followed suit. Icy tumblers with paper thin wedges of lemon floating in their clear depths were placed on the table and they were alone at last with their food.

Enola took a hesitant bite, and after a moment closed her eyes in ecstasy at the tender succulence that burst on her tongue. Needing no further encouragement Cullen dug in with both hands and was overcome with the most consuming feeling, like he was starving to death, like he would never see food again.

The juicy meat slid down his throat into his waiting stomach and such a feeling of blissful satiety washed over him he almost wept. Barely taking the time to chew before he shoved the next bite of meat in his mouth, he could only focus on swallowing it all, eating everything. Before he was even finished with the plate before him, he was thinking what he would get next. What he would eat to fill himself till he burst, anything to feed this feeling that was flowing through him.

Razor sharp memories of his childhood and the damnable lunch room at school clawed at his mind. Long tables of children munching happily on sandwiches carrots and cupcakes, while his siblings and him shared a some stale crackers that they used to scrape the remnants from a jar of mayo. The ache in his empty stomach had been a familiar companion then, with its voracious cohort shame and tonight they roared back to life. Wailed for food, as much as he could spare in exchange for silence.

And silence he would have, gulping bite after bite in a frantic grasp at peace, at the wonderful sensation of being full and happy of having everything he could hold and more.

A firm hand on his arm startled him out of his revere and when he looked down he was horrified to see that he had totally abandoned the silverware and was holding the steak in his hands as he tore at it with his teeth. Dropping the remains of the meat with a gasp, he quickly dipped his napkin in the untouched glass of water and began mopping up his hands only to have a valet blindly supply a hot towel before sailing away to the needs of the other diners.

"What happened?" he whispered hoarsely, his stomach already churning sickly at the volume of food he'd eaten so quickly.

Enola shook her head, her eyes wide, "Look around you Cullen, you're not the only one."

Her words rang true and Cullen took in the sight he must have been just moments before. People seated at heaping plates of food, shoving it into gaping mouths that dripped with cream and gravy, their bare hands glistening with the fat from the meat they clutched hungrily. A woman at the table behind Enola was digging into an entire cheesecake, her hands coated in clots of the yellow custard as she licked it off her fingers greedily.

"It was like I couldn't stop." He said vacantly, hypnotized by a man cramming one sausage after another into his mouth as the juice ran down his chin. A bib was quickly supplied by the discreet and sightless valets that flitted about the place without so much as a trip or a dropped glass.

"Finished already?" an astonished voice asked as he hefted Enola's plate and was surprised by the weight felt on it.

"Oh yes," she replied girlishly, "If I eat one more bite I'll pop!"

The valet chuckled, "You may have as much as you like without fear of that, Sister." And with a flourish he gestured to a discreet door off the dining area.

Enola and Cullen rose from the table, not wanting to draw more attention than they already had and walked through the marble entryway into what appeared to be a restroom. Carrera marble floors gleamed beneath the burning sconces of heavily scented oil. Rows of onyx doors with white veins splaying through them lined the walls and as they ventured further into the chamber Enola heard the unmistakable sound of someone retching echoing off the walls.

As she turned her head to look, the portly man that had been stuffing himself with sausage entered, and smiled as he walked past them to an unoccupied cubicle. He quickly shut the door and began heaving up the food he'd just gorged on without a moment's hesitation. The sound of the contents of his stomach splattering in the water of the bowl loudly.

Cullen felt his stomach turn, the sounds coming out from the behind the door and the image of the woman licking custard from her fingers had him bolting into a door. Clutching the toilet and coughing up the barely chewed meat he'd just eaten.

Enola was quick to come in behind him and shut the door, rubbing his arching back as he emptied his stomach in muscle seizing heaves. She found that every amenity was available for such a thing and was quick to offer him a bottle of chilled water and mouthwash when he was finished. Standing over the small sink mounted in the wall, Cullen was washing the cold sweat that had come over him from his face and pull himself back together.

"I don't get it…" he said swishing more of the mouthwash around and spitting it into the sink, "why eat all that food just to throw it up?"

Enola's expression had taken on a grim tightness, the exuberant flush of a toilet from an adjacent cube stirred her from her thoughts. "It's almost a crime to be so wasteful, so decadent."

Cullen snorted and combed his disheveled hair back into its proper place, "Those gluttons out there stuff themselves to the gills, empty the tank in here and start all over again…disgusting."

"What did you say?" Enola asked clutching at his jacket.

"It's disgusting." Cullen repeated adamantly, tugging at the bowtie at his neck to straighten it.

"No..." Enola shook her head, "Gluttons, Cullen....those people out there are gluttons."

"Yeah...so?" Cullen snorted.

"So, we're in a lot of trouble." She replied woefully.

Chapter 17

The scent of a wild rain drying in the morning sun, the gentle tease of a linen sheet on her ribs as she stole those first waking breaths after a long, dreamless sleep and the heavy hand of her newly minted husband slung heavily over her waist. Mrs. Gilda Flynn's eyes fluttered open to the morning sky fresh as paint after last night's torrent. She stretched experimentally and only felt the luscious hum of muscles well used and singing from head to toe after last night's sprint. Rolling slowly over she met eyes with the rumpled Mr. Flynn or what was left of him, she could only smile at the well- loved, lop sided grin he offered.

"Did you sleep well darling?" he asked, running a soft hand over own.

"Like the dead." She replied savoring the goosebumps his callouses raised along her waking flesh.

"Well, you damn near killed me." He shook his head as if he knew he'd die happy and laid a warm set of lips over her own.

It didn't take long for the intimate mating of mouths to set light to their passions anew and as he laughed softly and rolled atop her. Suddenly a wince flashed across his face and felled him to the mattress in a slump.

"What's wrong?" Gilda nearly cried, "What hurts?"

He gulped dryly at the lump that had risen in his throat and tried again to raise his arms. The tiny movement of the muscles that swung iron tirelessly all day every day pulled a gasp from his mouth as they dropped limply. Without waiting for a reply Gilda quickly yanked down the sheet and stifled the shocked sound that threatened to escape her mouth. Black bruises on each joint of his arms shone in the new light like fresh ink, a tinge of red and green blossoming from the dark centers. His hips were speckled with purple skids and those powerful thighs carried a yellow tinge deep inside the muscle.

"What happened to you man?" she nearly howled, running gentle hands over the painful spots seeking to soothe the hurt within.

He laughed again softly, "YOU happened to me Gilda, and I swear it was worth every agonizing second."

The night flashed through her mind, the storm, the shaking walls and falling hail...Esus. Oh lord the bull, she had ridden this man to death's door and for what? A shimmering moment of bliss? A little death that nearly killed her husband? She was horrified and appalled at the damage she had dealt in her lust.

"Oh Adam," she crooned, dropping the softest kiss on his pained grin, "forgive me."

He waved a consolatory hand limply, his brows knitting together at the twinge the simple movement raised through his whole arm. "Nothing to forgive you wicked vixen, I'd never trade it."

Gilda brought a troubled pair of hands to her wrinkled brow as the gravity of it all came crashing down upon her. Confronted with the wounds her passion dealt she understood, she conceited, this thing within her, the beast that sheltered could not be trusted and it was her burden and duty to restrain it, whatever the price.

Adam looked at her with that satisfied expression, "I don't suppose you feel bad enough to help me down to breakfast Lass?"

She felt bad enough to almost carry him down the crooked stairs, although his vanity demanded he at least stagger to the table on his own bowlegged and limping feet, but just barely.

Shamus took a suspicious draw off his pipe, let the smoke slip almost unnoticed from the bowed lips he hid under that tremendous beard and called, "Fanny! Get your arse in here and tend to this wounded man!"

Fanny swept in with all the grace of an elephant, a harried look on her face as she dried her chubby hands on the sail like apron that spread tightly across her hips. She took one look at Adam and dropped the damp cotton in shock at his appearance, "Sweet morning lad, what did she do tae ye?" With a mother's concern she fussed, pulling and touching all over, assessing the damage as he groaned beneath her examination.

Turning to Gilda with her hands on those imposing hips she asked, "I don't know what ye did…"

"But will ye teach her? Shamus barged in, a deep laugh shaking the belly that hung over his belt.

Fanny shook her head, a smile beaming from her ruddy cheeks as she laughed. "I've seen my share of wounded brides, limping from the love her groom treated her to…but never a groom felled by his bride."

Gilda stepped close to the towering woman to add, "I'm also afraid that I may have…torn the fur on the bed."

Fanny's eyes went wide at this confession, "The wolf pelt?"

Gilda nodded, true regret seeping in her eyes as she did.

But Fanny tossed her head back and brayed, clapping a mighty hand on Gilda's back when she came up for air. "A hell of a wedding night Mrs. Flynn, ye break the groom and a storm blows through that sinks three ships and burns two houses to the ground."

"Fire?" Gilda asked looking at Adam in shock as he slumped pathetically on the bench.

"Lighting dear," Fanny offered, guiding Gilda to the kitchen as she explained, "just minutes after the two of you went upstairs, a storm like we've never seen whipped up and all but blew this town into the sea."

Gilda followed under the heavy arm of her hostess, her mind adrift in the coincidence of it all. A storm had killed her at the stony lake, offered her to the bull, and here, last night a storm raged on as she and Esus rode to their pleasure.

"No matter, Mrs. Flynn." Shamus offered as he pulled a draught of whisky from the barrel behind the bar, "We'll have yer man on his feet in no time, the lovliest bride in all of Dunedin deals the heartiest…affection."

Fanny swatted at him with that huge hand and hustled Gilda back to the kitchen, "Pay him no mind, lamb." Already cracking eggs over a steaming skillet. "Yer a bonny lass, and it's no surprise that ye'd be a lusty thing in bed…those eyes of yers, they speak volumes."

Hiding a blush and reaching to help, Gilda lost herself in the simplicity of cooking breakfast. It seemed an age since she'd been tasked with something as small as a meal. The smell of sausage stirred her memory and in place of the imposing Fanny, her mother appeared. All ivory skin and downy hair, emerald eyes and that silvery voice singing as she cooked. Those perfect hands almost too delicate to work handling pot arms and wooden spoons, asking Gilda to bring more water from the well.

Tears pricked at her eyes then, and too tired and worn out to fight Gilda let them fall…for her parents, for the memories and all that was lost.

"Great Gods Fanny!" Shamus bellowed, pulling her from her thoughts, "Can this girl set foot in yer kitchen without ye making her cry?"

"That's enough from you today!" Fanny hollered back, nearly flinging a plate of sausage and eggs at him as he turned to leave. "Come back and I'll make ye cry yourself!"

"I'm sorry Fanny," Gilda offered, running hands over her damp cheeks in distraction, "I don't know what's come over me."

Fanny touched a finger to her nose and tossed a wink Gilda's way before she sauntered out of the kitchen with her arms loaded with toast and bacon and potatoes. "No matter Lamb, tears never rusted a single heart in this world."

Settling in next to Adam, Gilda took a lady's serving of everything, biting daintily at first and then hungrily shoveling it in and chasing it down her throat with mugs of Shamus' ale. She finally noticed that the table had fallen silent while she helped herself to a third serving of potatoes and when she raised her eyes only to find three baffled pairs fixed on her Gilda blushed fiercely.

"It all just tastes so very good, Fanny." She offered after a long pause.

Ever the jolly soul, Fanny threw her head back again in trademark fashion and brayed at Gilda, smiling and shaking her head, "You're a marvel Mrs. Flynn!"

"What will ye do with yerselves today?" Shamus asked, wiggling his eyebrows indecently as his bow lips hung over the edge of his mug in a smile.

Fanny swatted at him with that enormous hand, "Not until I get a look at what's left of that room ye ox! For all we know the bed's ready to break after the thumpin ride Gilda treated it to!"

"We need to take a turn around town anyhow," Adam interrupted mercifully, "I was hoping to find a place for us on our own. As lovely as your inn may be, my bride deserves a home. Do you know of any that would make a fair place for us to live and work my trade?"

"What is it you do exactly?" Shamus managed around a bite of crisp bacon.

"Blacksmith." Adam replied, smiling warmly at Gilda.

"Always work for a smith, dear." Fanny nodded emphatically, "can ye make chain for anchors?"

Adam nodded, "Of course, anything you like."

Fanny was rising from the table like some specter of clean plates and as she gathered all the remnants in her great arms she offered. "Out the door and to the right down a ways, there's a house for rent that was the ferrier's...the landlord is the butcher, you two should get on like a house fire."

Gilda and Adam shared a surprised look before she crowed over her shoulder, "Go on! Tell him Fanny sent ye! A walk would do you two good!"

Fortified with Shamus's private stock, Adam was once again standing tall and walking with the wide legged swagger of a man satisfied. The soft smile pulling at his lips all but setting his face ablaze with love and affection. Although Gilda was dressed once again in her trews and boots, they were recognized by every face they met and greeted with a hearty good morning as they sauntered hand in hand among the cobbled streets of what was to become their home.

"Nice place this." Adam observed as he stepped around a herd of children running wildly through the street, a scrappy dog on their heels barking shrilly. The simple houses rose above them and twisted sharply to the right, leading the happy couple into the bustling marketplace of town.

A fishmonger's stall was dripping with the scales of his early morning catch, their gaping maws hanging open for all to see. The tailor's window was dressed with a pretty white dress, the neck scandalously cut low to reveal a lady's bosom just below the squared neckline. The silken weave of the fabric hung from the dummy like a dream and Gilda brought a distracted hand to her throat at the sight of such a lovely thing. "You'd be in it for three seconds before I tore it off you with my teeth." Adam murmured coarsely in her ear, catching her gaze in his own.

Gilda shook a distracted hand at his breath tickling her ear like she would a fly, "I don't know what you're talking about." And with a haughty turn on her heel moved away from the pretty sight.

A florist, a baker an apothecary and even a furrier, his lush pelts hanging neatly behind him. Dunedin was a thriving metropolis if their marketplace was to be a pulse point on the economic system of the town.

Ambling ever further hand in hand, they finally happened upon the butcher's stall. Near the cliff wall that led to the sea, a trough in the stone street sloshing the blood of his trade to the churning waters of the bay below. A rail thin man in a simple white apron was making quick work of a side of beef as an anxious and sallow skinned woman looked on, directing him to leave the fat for the crows.

He only nodded, the grey wisps at his temples dancing as he did, the tortured look in his eye wishing for this customer to find another purveyor for her meat. Wrapping the ruby cut in a piece of coarse cloth that he tied with string. She stingily counted out his pay and without thanking him sped away with the parcel clutched to her chest as if someone would steal it from her.

Wiping his hands on the blood stained apron, he raised a tired but hopeful gaze to Adam, "What can I get you today sir?"

Adam smiled in spite of himself, "Fanny sent us to inquire about the house for rent."

His bushy eyebrows shot up at this news, "You two must be the bonny Mr. and Mrs. Flynn!" he threw his well-muscled arms wide as if in celebration. "I arrived at your reception after you two had….retired." His grin spoke volumes and with an arm thrown around Adam's shoulders he nodded to his son to take his place as he led the way to the house in question.

"Strangest thing," he began as they left the marketplace proper, "the prior tenant couldn't keep any animals in the place." He gestured with blood stained hands at the two story home with shuttered windows and a red front door. To the side was a one story shop with heavy shingles and wide swinging door.

"Didn't matter what he did, how he barred the shop, they'd always find a way out." He chuckled then patting his pockets absently for the key, which he fished out with a smile. "One morning he was just gone, into thin air like a draught of smoke…" a distracted look traveled across his face then, pondering the strangeness of it before shaking the expression away, "I don't know the way of it, but its brought you two here."

The cast iron key grated heavily in the lock and with a flourish he opened the door, ushering Gilda inside gallantly. "Nice space for a pair just starting out," he continued, following close on her heels, "two bedrooms upstairs for anyone else that might come along." He tossed a wink at

Adam, "the stove and fireplace are over here and since the tenant left all the furniture you may as well put it to good use."

Gilda left the men to discuss the money matters and found herself at the back door, a sea grass yard that backed to the cliffs of the ocean, its grey depths glowing in the morning light after last night's stirring. She opened the heavy door with a creak and was met with a merry gust of salty sea air. Vines of flowers clung to the eaves, thriving on the sun, and a well just like her own from home stood pertly on the corner of the lot. The damp stones gleaming wetly from the sweet water that seeped up from the untold depths inside. She turned to see Adam leaning in the doorway watching her, arms crossed over his mighty chest and pushing the muscles forward in a most distracting manner.

He swung the key from a single finger, "Welcome home Mrs. Flynn."

Gilda moved to run to him and he held out his hands quickly, "Wait."

She stopped, puzzled only to find herself swept up in those mighty arms, only the slightest wince crossing his face as he carried her over the threshold. He set her firmly on the flagstone floor in the kitchen and kissed her soundly, gathering her up in those brawny arms and laying kiss after sweet kiss on her lips, cheeks and eyes.

Gilda twined her own hands around him, clinging to his shoulders and loving the feel of his body pressed to hers. "Lucky this house was vacant," she mused in between the biting tastes of his mouth. "We may have been terminal tenants of Fanny and Shamus."

"I'm the lucky one you lovely devil." Adam murmured, his voice all gravel and silk against her ear, "In the whole of this town, you are the most exquisite woman." His hands began to flex against the small of her back, pressing her against him more urgently, "fiery, fearless and so wickedly lusty."

His lips were on the column of her throat placing kisses so soft she wanted to scream, twining her fingers in his hair and roughly pulling his mouth to her own. Gilda slaked her lips over his and shoved him harder than she meant to against the wall. Pulling a gasp from her husband and a startled coughing from their landlord who had returned with the keys for the shop in his hands.

"My my, Mr. Flynn" he cleared his throat nervously, giving Gilda a wide berth as he handed the winded Adam the key, "now I see what all the fuss was about." Taking her hand in an almost frightened grasp, he laid a gentle kiss on her knuckles, "Eli O'Mally, Mrs. Flynn, your servant."

Gilda curtsied in spite of her ridiculous dress, "Gilda," she said, "and thank you, Eli."

He smiled like a young boy and nodded again at Adam, "If there's anything else you need, you know where the shop is." And excused himself quickly, pulling the door discreetly behind him.

The bemused expression on Adam's face reduced her to giggles in mere seconds. "By sundown tonight this town will paint me positively indecent!" She covered her flaming cheeks with demure palms only to have her husband pull them away firmly.

"What did I tell you last night?" he asked in all seriousness.

Images of their wedding night flashed through her mind, the heated flesh and damp sweat. Gasping mouths and seeking hands, and that bull galloping her over the edge without remorse. Throwing her arms wide in abandon, "Never hide myself from you." She echoed to his delight.

Kissing both her palms with the tenderest regard, Adam jingled the key merrily and left her among the dusty confines of the house to see what shape the shop might be in after being left vacant for untold time.

Chapter 18

Enola hastened a waxy faced Cullen from the purging room back into the dining area proper, the gluttons happily stuffing themselves to the brim knowing sweet relief from their excess was a brief stroll away. She was careful to keep him well away from the savory scents that wafted over from the serving area.

As they skirted the glistening tower of sweets, a clear voice announced, "We have a challenge!" and suddenly she and Cullen found themselves in a swarming crowd pressing toward the tremendous bar. Cullen clung to her iron arm desperate to stay close to her as the throng swelled them ever closer to the brass rail and weathered wood.

Two men faced off as The Unseeing bar tender began to deliberately and in a well-practiced manner line up shot glasses. One after another of various liquors, some he recognized and others he could have sworn smoked when confronted with the open air as they trickled into the crystal. Bottle after bottle, shot after shot were drawn as the crowd pressed and settled anxious for the show that was to come.

Cullen lost count and could only marvel at the menagerie of spirits spread across the bar. The opponents, a slight man with a smoky eye and haggard scar on the side of his face removed his jacket with grace to lay it carefully across the stool near which he stood. The younger man, dark and exotic to look upon, almost reminded Cullen of a scimitar in his dangerous beauty.

The reverent hush fell over the crowd as they reached for the first of countless shots. Gently and respectfully touching the rims together before tossing them back without tearing their sneering eyes from one another.

Quickly, the next ones went down in much the same manner and as glass after glass was swallowed by each man.

Cullen saw the unmistakable gleam of boozy sweat break out on the Scimitar's forehead and he began to swallow harder with each gulp of foul burning liquor. Still they drank, the cloudy eye of the opponent unflinching at each one, taking it as if it were his first, as relaxed and casual as if he were on the deck of some fine yacht.

Cullen found himself hypnotized by them both, by their relentless self –abuse and the strangeness of it all. His earlier illness was replaced with a new kind of nausea, the sort one experiences for someone else. The type of sickness you bear out of pity and empathy because you're powerless to do anything else.

A fierce grasp at his arm pulled him from his thoughts, and with a breathy voice Enola drew his attention to something he had missed. "Cullen...look." She raised a brow and tilted her head meaningfully.

His eyes fell upon the wrists of both of the men as they sloshed shot after shot down their throats. The older man wore a cuff like Cullen's with only three coils of that scaly tail wrapped around it...the Scimitar wore nothing on his own.

Their earlier zeal for this display was waning quickly and even the steely constitution of the scarred man began to waver. Slower and slower they reached for what had been poured, taking longer pauses to dote on ceremony. Almost leaning against each other through the rims of the glimmering crystal glasses that they touched together each time. Freezing in an exaggerated arch with the empty glasses to their lips though they were hollow now, anything to delay the next drink.

The Scimitar began to sway on his feet as if the floor had come to life, Cullen watched the Adam's apple in his throat tremble and shake with hard swallows. Recognizing the signs of a man on the losing end of a fight with a bottle, he expertly escorted Enola from the line of fire. Stepping behind the crowd of fascinated onlookers that seemed to have doubled since the last time he'd looked. Then the unmistakable gag echoed through the room, followed by the deafening crack of crystal on marble floor and crowned by the sickly smack of liquid pelting the shards of glass.

An exuberant yell rose from the crowd at this, and both Enola and Cullen looked back just in time to see the young man being hauled away by the servants, a gooey string of drool hanging from his once handsome face.

The horde dispersed immediately likely since the show was over, and the two of them rode a wave of the well-dressed heathens back out to that maddening great room, too shocked and confused to deny the swell of them all. Cullen found his fingers twined in the slender softness of Enola's, her brows knit together once again in an expression of concern and fear that set his empty stomach twisting.

By twos and threes they entered other rooms, the Unseeing running hands over each bracelet before pulling back those heavy swaths. "Did you ever read Dante?" Enola asked, a sadness in her voice pulling the corners of her lovely mouth in a grim frown.

Cullen could only shake his head at this inquiry, "Why?"

"We've stumbled into something akin to his divine comedy," Enola began, drawing him near to her and angling his body towards the door next to the one they'd just exited. "At least I think we have...."she almost whispered holding her wrist out for inspection along with his own.

Their bracelets gained them entry into a dark room with throbbing music pouring from the speakers. It was shocking how loud it was in contrast the serene silence of the outer room. Strobe lights flung angles of light in every color across the walls and the writhing forms that were stretched on vinyl couches, their limbs entangled, skirts raised and trousers around their black socked ankles.

His jaw dropped and Cullen pushed himself against Enola as he realized the man he thought was leaning against the wall by the door was actually pinned there in ecstasy while the head of another man was thrusting in a tell-tale rhythm against his naked crotch.

"Lust..." Enola mouthed over the pulsing music as she grabbed his hand firmly and turned to pull him toward the door so they might leave. Cullen's eyes danced over the naked bodies that strained and stroked against one another. Their low moans and guttural giggles lost in the thumping bass that flowed from an unseen source he could feel in his bones. A row of curtained rooms set against the wall filled his vision and just as they began to leave the velvet drapes of one fluttered open. His eyes were filled with the horrific vision of a woman splayed naked on a table of greens as a pig rutted at her, pulling unfettered screams of delight from her gaping mouth before the fabric settled once again over the entrance and he was yanked outside in shock.

Cullen winced at what he just saw as Enola all but carried him back out into the blissful quiet of the antechamber. The image of that woman and the flopping ears of the hog between her taught thighs burned in his mind.

"Cullen!" Enola whispered harshly, looking around to make sure no one was watching, "Are you listening to me?"

"No..." he moaning, rubbing his eyes hoping to rid them of the ugliness, "I mean yes...what?"

Seizing his wrist in her hand and holding it up to his face, "The nine circles of Hell are alive and well at this party Cullen, only instead of suffering for them...people have gathered here to wallow in the pleasure of committing them."

He focused his eyes on hers, finding a serenity in those stormy depths once again. "So why the bracelets?"

Her eyes grew wide, "I have a theory...care to test it with me?"

"Do I have a choice?" he asked.

"Always," her eyes softened on his again, "choose to leave. Now."

Pulling her close to his face and fixing his eyes on hers, "Never."

Enola sighed at the answer, not in surprise but supreme frustration. "You may hate yourself for this later Cullen, in a way that you cannot see to forgive yourself for...are you sure?"

Ignoring her and once again straightening his bow tie, "What's the plan?"

She was silently counting the doors, her mouth moving in a breathy whisper as she did, "We're going in there." She began pointing to the fifth door, "and we're just going to see what happens."

Cullen took a deep breath and tucked her hand in the crook of his arm, "Alright," stepping confidently toward the entrance, "let's see what happens."

This attendant was a withered old thing, his face a road map of wrinkles and his hands had long yellowed nails curving from the gnarled fingers. They coasted over Enola's bracelet but paused over Cullen's, "Are you challenging, Brother?"

Cullen's eyes flew to Enola's and she shook her head in some miniscule manner, moving to pull him away, but before she could.

"Yes." Cullen affirmed, "Challenging."

"Excellent, Brother." The wrinkled man grinned, his sagging skin pulling into a horrific mask of glee, "the moon is right."

Cullen nodded, forgetting no one could see him but Enola, who was fuming as the curtain was drawn back and they were confronted with an acrid smell beyond recognition. Her hand squeezed his arm painfully as two Unseeing appeared out of no-where and took his arms to escort him inside.

The floor was tiled with midnight squares, decorated with stars of no perceptible pattern, a crescent- moon mezzanine gave way to a vast forum below that was absolutely packed with people. As Cullen was hastened down the curving staircase with Enola on their heels his eyes leveled with a wild array of people, from all corners of the Earth. A nude man with skin like oil, covered in dry flakes of white mud danced with a rooster around an open flame, the flailing arms of women dressed in white rising from the floor the crouched on at his feet in a circle.

A woman with matted hair lay in a silver box as all manner of snakes slithered over her naked flesh, at a low table a person so old their gender was a mystery handled the oversized cards of the tarot to a well -dressed patron who was listening with rapt fascination. People laid on beds of nails and hung from the ceiling by hooks in their flesh, they were eating fire and spitting blood to read the clots, it was a carnival of heretics.

Heresy

Cullen thought and relaxed for a moment, he could fake a vision, pretend to speak in tongues. After all, what evidence did these people have that what they said they saw was in fact real? He turned to look back at Enola, a triumphant grin on his face as he felt the surge of pride that for once he was taking the lead, helping their cause and not relying on her strength. But her expression of concern only deepened at this contact and something in her eyes warned him to be wary.

He was led to the center of the forum which cleared of the crowd as a mighty gong was rung from a corner.

"Brothers and Sisters!" one of the Unseeing called in a clear voice, "tonight we shall be graced with a challenge!"

An audible gasp swept through the room, and Cullen felt his stomach drop with dread.

"It has been 212 years since one of us has dared this feat beneath the Crone's Moon!"

Enola's eyes all but rolled out of her head and one by one, the great burning sconces of oil were extinguished on the soaring walls of the room, dropping the space into a consuming blackness one section at a time.

"Choose your partner, Brother." The Unseeing bade and without hesitation Cullen held his hand out imploring Enola to take it before any that looked on saw it trembling in the gathering gloom. She obliged, tugging nervously at the too tight fabric of her borrowed gown once more as she squeezed his hand reassuringly.

As the last fire was smothered and pitch consumed the room a flaming beacon slowly approached one daunting step at a time. His breath began to hitch, and his nostrils burned at the strange stench coming with it. Closer the man drew, holding a golden bowl of dancing flames in his hands, casting strange light over his blindfold like veins as the light shuttered over his visage.

He reached Enola and Cullen and knelt, holding the vessel up on straight arms in a supplicating gesture. The other

Unseeing lit a single candle in the fire before dousing it with wine which flared in a volcano of sparks before it guttered in the amassing liquid.

In the flickering light of the single flame, Cullen's eyes adjusted to peer inside the bowl. Two ashen and burnt orbs rolled sickly in the murky slush.

"One for each of you," the Unseeing said filled with pride, "no challenge goes unanswered Sister, even for you who has met a challenge of her own in this circle."

Enola took a deep breath and leveled her eyes with Cullen's almost watching to see what he might do, if he might run. Cullen knew she would fight her way through this place one person at a time if they had to. But they didn't, he didn't have to let her do that for him. And with a final glance at her, he reached into the bowl and took both of the crusted yet strangely loose balls from the bowl.

Handing one to Enola they threw them in their mouths and the gelatinous liquid that was barely contained in the charred exterior burst on his tongue. Oozing down his throat in a eerie consistency he was sure would never leave his mind, he saw the determined look on Enola's face as she swallowed again and again, a stiff cord in her neck rising in the shadows.

A round of applause erupted from nowhere and as the Unseeing handed Cullen the candle and retreated into the darkness he was left alone in a pool of golden light with the lovely Enola. It seemed natural to put his arm around her, huddling around the dancing flame, their only defense against the dark.

His eyes were scanning the room, the nothing that enveloped them for a clue of what was to come next, what they should do. But before he could manage a whisper the unmistakable sound of a quartet tuning up pierced the silence like a knife.

The staccato of a violin heralded the opening of a waltz and without hesitation, Cullen placed a firm hand at the answering arch of Enola's back. He swept her into a graceful frame and with the candle clutched in both their hands began to lead her into a box step as the other strings began to sing the unmistakable song of three four time.

"What are we doing?" Enola hissed, her feet stumbling over the hem of the skirt as she fought and pulled around in Cullen's arms awkwardly.

"We're supposed to be dancing," Cullen chided pressing a little harder on her back, "if you would let me lead that is."

He could feel the brawn in her body flexing at his touch, the surging heat she harbored searing through the velvet of her gown. The flame of the candle swinging wildly as he sought to give her the anchor she needed, the support to hold onto while he guided the way in the dark.

"Close your eyes." He said softly, "and stay in my arms...no matter what, stay with me."

She opened her mouth to protest for a half a heartbeat and surprised even him by closing her eyes tightly, clenching so hard on his hand he worried she might snap the candle and extinguish their only light.

But she relaxed, a sigh escaping his lips.

"Listen to the music Enola, listen to my voice" he murmured allowing for broader steps as she fell into the contagious one, two, three- one, two, three that rang off the walls, "just like that."

Keeping her eyes closed, she followed a little easier now, starting to glide over the floor in front of his feet like a dream. The candle was beginning to burn smoother now, and he could swear he felt the tension she chained inside ease by the smallest measure.

"That's right, we just have to dance." He soothed, turning her in a counter clockwise motion, guiding her back against the unbroken dark where hundreds of eyes watched eagerly for what he did not know.

Enola's eyes opened to meet his, and that familiar thrumming began to surge from her and into his limbs, through is body and back through her. On a circuit now as they spun and stepped around the floor, some kind of grit scratching under the soles of their shoes as they matched time with the unseen musicians.

A consuming heat began to ride up his body, setting his flesh afire and at the same time chilling his very bones. Sweat began to pour from his face and down his spine, soaking his shirt.

"What's wrong?" Enola asked, a look of abject worry on her face.

Cullen could barely speak, drowning for air all he could do was gasp and watch his vision blur as beads of sweat gathered on his eyelashes and sputtered into his eyes. A spectrum of swirls catching the briny liquid, throwing the curtain of black into a thousand moving shadows that drew toward them. Pressing in on their small pool of light, the air so hot he swore steam was rising from beneath his collar, damp now with sweat and his hair hanging limply in his face soaked through in strings. He dared not stop though, determined to meet the challenge or drop dead trying, Cullen continued to swirl along the floor with Enola.

Edges of black seeped ever closer into his vision, a contracting iris until all he saw was the blurred form of Enola in navy velvet, and suddenly he saw nothing at all.

Chapter 19

Gilda looked around what was to be her new home, dusty and dark she tore through the shadows and cobwebs furling open the shutters and letting the crisp air chase away the musty gloom as she went. A simple table sat near the stove with four chairs, there was a rocking chair in the parlor along with an upholstered chaise and several chests, tables and lamps. A china cupboard still boasted plates and cutlery fine enough for the likes of the blacksmith's wife.

Her cheeks flushed at that thought, and as she continued her exploration of the house that was newly hers. She stumbled upon some simple linens and tablecloths, crockery and of course all the walls still had the paintings upon the hooks.

There was an imposing stag over the river rock fireplace in the parlor, his chest broad and antlers jutting from his head with a ferocious pride. Amber eyes fixed on some unseen opponent among his wood as a shy doe and fawn hid behind a copse of birch behind him.

In the kitchen an impressive bowl of fruit complete with a bottle of wine and garland of flowers wound around it. A pomegranate bursting with crimson flesh and seeds staining the linen colored blooms with its bloodred juice.

Upstairs she found the two bedrooms Eli had mentioned, one stood empty and the other boasted a sturdy looking tester bed, the mattress and blankets however were in need of replacement. A flock of moths took to the air as Gilda smacked her palm on it and she was quick to throw open the window that overlooked the back yard for them to escape.

Without thinking she picked up the mattress, blankets, pillows and all and shoved it through the wide window to flop onto the grass below with a downy smack on the flagstones that lined the house. Adam was upstairs in a hurry, a wild look of concern on his face.

"What was that?" he asked, moving to Gilda by the window and taking her hands.

"Just that moth eaten mattress and blankets."

He looked below puzzled, "I would have done it for you."

"No matter," she waved a dismissive hand at the heap below, "I didn't want to hassle you with it."

"It must have weighed a more than you!" he insisted, looking again at the massive envelope of feathers.

"Stronger than I look I suppose." Gilda floated a breezy kiss over his lips and left the room without waiting.

Adam followed her down to the kitchen where she was hefting their bridal purse, "We have just about anything we could need...." She flared an inquisitive brow at him, almost teasingly.

He took the bait and once again went to her, unable to keep from touching her in some way, loving the hum of her body when his fingers coasted over her bare flesh, "Is there something my bride wants?"

"Well," she began in an excited and surprised tone, "a new mattress is in order, and I saw some lovely pelts at the furrier, some candles, bread, wine and meat."

"Done." Adam said, agreeing with her sensibility. "Anything else?'

Her eyes went to the ceiling mischievously and she took a step toward him where she boldly put her mouth over his own, "Nothing...for now."

He chuckled against her sweet lips, unable to help himself when it came to bundling her up once again in his embrace. "I love you darling girl." He whispered, kissing her softly, "Did you know that?"

"I do now," her eyes smiling in a way that curled his toes, "and I love you, strong man."

With that he poured a generous handful of coins into her hand, "If they need more than that, you're being robbed and you'll tell them to see me to settle the account."

"I'll be fine." She assured him with a gentle pat on his scruffy cheek. "This isn't my first market."

Sweeping out the door into the chilly October air, Gilda smiled back at her husband once more before sauntering back to the bustling marketplace. Anxious to meet all the new friends she would make, and of course, to make the house behind her a home.

Eli's stall was the first one she happened upon and after being received once again by the gracious Mr. O'Malley and being introduced to his eleven children ranging from 16 to 6 months, all of which, with the exception of the two youngest, were in some capacity working with their father at his trade. His wife Leda was a short little thing with chubby cheeks and flaxen hair wound on the sides of her head in massive golden buns. In spite of her size a voice that could stall a storm erupted from her as she commanded one of her brood to stop fooling around with a goat, the child froze in fear and quickly ran to his father's side for protection under the squinty glare of his mother.

"How may we be of service Mrs. Flynn?" she asked with a knowing grin.

Gilda couldn't stop the smile that spread across her face at the moniker and knew Leda understood the giddiness of being a bride perfectly well herself. "A roast I think for tonight Eli, and plenty of fat if you please, I'd like to make gravy."

Eli smiled and with three quick swipes produced a sumptuous cut of rump with a healthy ribbon of creamy fat running down the side.

Gilda nodded at the lovely thing and as she dropped the coins in Eli's hands, he smiled and handed the wrapped package to one of his older sons. "To the blacksmith's house Henry, tell him its bought and paid for and ready to wait in the cellar." The boy took off, tall and lanky like his father without hesitation.

Leda came from the confines of the house carrying a willow basket on one arm and a chubby babe on the other. "For the rest of your sundries and with best wishes." She handed it to Gilda with a smile.

"I couldn't accept it," Gilda protested in spite of the prettiness of the almost lace like handle, "it's too lovely and too much after all you and your husband have done."

Leda crossed her arms in mock consternation, "I'll be offended if you don't."

She relented and took it from her with a smile, "On two conditions, we share a meal soon and you call me Gilda."

Leda nodded with Eli's approval and as the entire O'Malley clan waved her away, Gilda set off to find the furrier, hoping he'd have the pelts and a mattress to fit the enormous bed in that house.

Hamish certainly did, and for a man that dealt in fur Gilda struggled to see even a single hair on his head or face. A deliberate and quiet man, he greeted her with the slightest of bows, listened intently to her request and led her to a room in the back of his tremendous shop.

There hanging upon great ladders of cedar were pelts of every description and color, bushy ones with coarse streaks of color blazing through them, the fine light hides of deer and cow, and even a shaggy bear up near the top, glowing darkly in the mid-day sun. Hamish was quick to suggest a wolf pelt similar to the one Gilda had ripped at Fanny's, she winced at the memory and looked around for something else…something lighter.

Her eyes felt upon a creamy swath of buttery sheepskin and knew she'd found what she was looking for, ever the accommodating purveyor, Hamish swiftly took her to the other side of the shop where his mattresses lay in beds of fragrant chips to keep the moths away. Familiar with the bed he had a mattress that would suit and after Gilda paid for the pelt, mattress, pillows and some simple linen sheets he set to loading her wares in his wagon to deliver.

Gilda made her way and introduction to the baker, the local farmer whose cart boasted the loveliest carrots and pumpkins Gilda had seen this side of Eden. She even stumbled upon a dairy farmer and had gotten a charge of sweet butter and cream. Waddling home with the great basket biting into her arm from the load, she looked happily down at her wares. Anxious to share her day with her husband, she all but ran home.

But as she walked into her house, instantly hit with that fresh scent of the ocean that now blew through every room, she felt that Adam was no longer home. Looking in the shop and seeing he's swept out the moldy hay that littered the floor and taken stock of the tools on the wall, she assumed he'd set out in search of what he needed to work and got busy herself.

Lighting the stove and marching into the cellar to retrieve her roast, she placed it in a deep lidded pot with peeled potatoes and onions, salted it and added a dash of pepper and set it in the oven to cook slowly as it heated up.

Hamish had already come and gone, leaving her sheets and pelt folded neatly atop the downy heap for her to make as she pleased. Flipping and folding them into place, she plumped the new pillows, covered the mass with that soft sheepskin and set a candle in the holder on the table by the bed.

The afternoon breeze had more of a chill to it now, and Gilda closed all the windows in the house. Satisfied that the dank of neglect had been blown out and went down to the parlor to light a fire. As she did something new caught her eye, something ghostly white in the dying light of day.

The dress she'd admired at the tailor's window, its creamy satin and long sleeves so feminine, so lovely. Gilda reached to touch it and pulled back, shocked at her dirty hands, if she was going to wear something so fine, she would be clean when she did.

Drawing another pail from the well and placing it in a great pot to heat, she looked closer to see that a pair of ribboned slippers accompanied her gift and a single rose, starkly white against the grain of the table.

Blessing the tinker who'd sold her the soap, Gilda washed in bits with an ewer and basin and even managed to wash the tremendous and embarrassingly dirty tresses that tumbled to her waist. She was sitting in front of the fire, dressed in her finery bare footed and humming a tune as she combed her drying hair with a tortoise shell comb when a familiar voice pulled her from her dreamy state.

"I knew you would be a vision in that gown." Adam said, standing in the doorway admiring her.

"How long have you been there?" she asked, rising quickly to greet him.

"Long enough to know you're all I ever want to come home to for the rest of my life."

Chapter 20

The searing heat was replaced with a bone chilling cold that settled deep inside Cullen's soul. Within this blackness there was nothing to see, no noise to hear, only the burning chill that seeped through his body and twisted the nerves into a chorus of agony.

His legs throbbed, and his arms screamed as every breath he drew threatened to shatter his icy lungs like glass. There was nothing outside of the pain within, and the lonely emptiness of a vast nothing he traveled through sightless and lost.

Panic set in when he felt that final sinking loss, when the awareness that wherever he had gone, Enola did not follow. Accustomed to her reassuring face, that burning heat she carried within and the boundless strength she harbored, the acute loss of her absence frightened and wounded him to the core.

Time had come loose and his mind flailed blindly to grasp at something to hold onto, a point of reference for him to maintain. A roaring began to build in his ears and his teeth chattered wildly at the cold that was blistering his skin with its consuming frost.

That's when he heard it, a shattering that pulled him from his own loathing and fear and gave him something to focus on, a direction in which to travel. He followed, worried that there would be no other clue to guide him, but he was rewarded with yet another burst of glass. Then a deep and rolling chuckle followed by a slow and almost musical grinding.

Frantically Cullen followed the sounds his eyes moving in the sockets yet seeing nothing for their strain and then, in the distance a small light grew larger. A fire danced in its slowly dying swoon, throwing light on a shadow near it.

More of that fear ran through him, and yet he was powerless to stop. It was the only way, and he was supposed to see this, whatever it may be. Cullen drew closer in spite of himself, teeth rattling, muscles screaming and skin ablaze. His gaze feasting on the growing light from the dying fire and fearfully creeping over the shadowy figure, who was lying in a most casual fashion his legs crossed and a wine bottle in his hand.

He was propped up on something lumpy and strange, a bauble dangling from his neck and sparkling in the dim before his eyes. The stranger took a long pull from the bottle, emptying it down his throat in a noisy gulp and with a disgusted exhale he pulled it from his lips and hurled it at Cullen where it traveled through him and shattered in some unseen area beyond.

"Bitch." The man murmured in a harsh voice, reaching beyond Cullen's tunnel of sight to retrieve another bottle. He pulled the cork with mossy teeth and spat it angrily into the fire where it hissed until the wet burned off and took another pull from the neck. Rivulets of wine running down the sides of his face to drip off his neck and stain his grimy shirt.

He smacked his lips and let the flames take his gaze, "11 years of service...loyal, discreet service....and what's my thanks?"

He drank deeply again and let out a wet belch that echoed off the walls heartily, "Services no longer required...I am to take my place in the lodge among my brothers and sisters!"

He reached above him then, his fist twisting above his head where he leaned and with a yank and some ripping he flung a dress onto his lap. A white satin gown with gold trim that covered his legs in a cloud of beauty. His eyes burned at the sight of the thing and as he set down the bottle he clenched the delicate gown in his hands and began to pull it, savoring the sound of the seams as they tore loose under his fury.

His rage seized him then, and with frantic grunts and wild gestures he began to tear at the thing in earnest, yanking tattered strips of it away from the rest. Grinning cruelly as he did, a sheen of sweat broke out across his forehead and he was panting before too long. Surrounded by a pile of stringy fabric, the gown unrecognizable now as his elbow struck the bottle of wine at his side and knocked it over, spilling the red contents across the stark white scraps.

"Bitch!" he screamed again, catching the neck in this hands once more and taking another gulp of what remained.

He leaned his head back again into the strange pile he sat against, his throat working in a knot that he struggled to swallow as his eyes searched the ceiling. "I never believed that she would come...."

His voice thickened then, and Cullen could swear he saw a tear escape his wildly rolling eye to roll down his cheek. "In my time, after so many...."

Without raising his head he began to kick the ruined satin into the dying fire by his feet, the flames stuttered against the fabric for an instant and began to melt the finely woven strands as they blackened and singed in their heat. He took a mouthful of wine and spat it in a cloud of mist at the flames where they bloomed in a roar of heat.

He leaned forward then, piling the fabric on the renewed fire with zeal, orange petals that happily feasted on this exquisite fuel rising higher and higher in the dark. He pulled another mouthful from the bottle and blew it once again into the flames, the heat surging from the ball that exploded from it seeping into Cullen's frozen limbs.

As the light flared to an incandescent corona around him, Cullen's eyes met the stranger's and he knew he'd been seen. The man's face twisted into a cruel snarl, his eyes burning into Cullen's with distain and disgust.

"Well, well," He bit out, rising from the ground with a stagger that he over corrected before finding his feet. "Look who came to visit."

He took a staggering step, threw the bottle to shatter against the wall beside him, red lines dripping sickly down the damp stone. Reaching out with those grimy hands, he seized Cullen around the throat in the fire and began to scream in his face.

"You are damned....damned by blood, by destiny and that muling bitch...DAMNED for eternity...you give her this for me, will you!!!"

Over and over he screamed into Cullen's face, his bloodshot eyes blazing with the fire within until he could endure no more and surrendered to the black that threatened to drown him. The fingers dug cruelly into his throat and he didn't care. The words he screamed pierced his ears and rattled in his mind and he didn't care. The scalding cold took over his limbs once again and still, he didn't care....Cullen wanted to drift, to be lost and to submit.

And as he felt that final light inside begin to sputter out, he was awash in a familiar heat, a haunting thrum that echoed from within. His skin came alive and in a gasp that bowed his body in a painful arch of desperation, his eyes opened once again upon the visage of Enola Sloan.

She had him cradled in her arms, the darkness around her a glorious backdrop to her worried beauty. He hummed with her essence and soaked in her warmth. Her voice seeped inside his roaring mind, faint at first and growing crisp as he woke slowly to this world. He heard her and was finally able to meet her gaze and gasp in horror at his own hands clasped around her ivory throat.

"What happened?" she asked, squeezing him with a fear that he relished because it was real. Loving her because he was clawing with all he was worth at her throat and she only cared for him.

"I'm damned..." he managed in a hoarse voice, his stomach dropping at the revelation that whatever had happened, wherever he'd gone, it had been real. His hands dropped limply to his sides and landed on the floor with a thud.

A cacophony of applause erupted from the darkness that surrounded them, and as the sconces were once again lit a crowd of adoring people pressed in on them as he laid on what he realized was a salted floor. A hundred happy and anxious voices echoed off the walls of the chamber and in his head, hands reached out to touch him, seeking to taste even a crumb of the oblivion he'd touched.

Enola leaned over him, keeping the majority of them at bay as he struggled to find himself. Having enough of it all, she rose in that too tight dress and took him with her as if he weighed nothing. Throwing his limp arm over her shoulder, she began to press her way through the crowd only to have it part in awed silence.

But not for them....from the other end of the pavilion three Unseeing came, two leading a third between them by the hands. As he drew closer Cullen could see fresh stains of blood dripping from beneath his black blindfold and when they were face to face he recognized him.

The Scimitar

The bloody blind man knelt reverently at Cullen's feet and kissed his shoes with adoration before leaning back on his heels to raise his face upward. In his trembling hands, a new cuff with an extra ring gleamed.

"My eyes gave you The Sight and for that, I am grateful, undeserving and your eternal servant in the circles to which you descend."

He opened his mouth to reply, and he fell silently into oblivion, the darkness a sweet reprieve from the place he had so eagerly entered..

"Cullen!" he heard her voice before the cold water hit his face, he inhaled some of it and awoke sputtering water and choking.

"What happened?" he asked, tasting a sour sludge on his tongue.

"You passed out." She replied, they were in another bathroom…not the purging room though. A vast solitary chamber of black with lights that twinkled in the ceiling like stars.

Bringing a limp hand to his face and rubbing it quickly, "I remember being strangled."

Enola dabbed his head with a damp cloth and looked deep in his eyes, "And then?"

Cullen closed his eyes and strained to recall, "He told me I was damned."

"Who told you?" she asked.

Cullen shook his head, "I've never seen him before…but he knew me."

Enola bit her lip at this revelation, "Can you stand?"

He took the hands she offered without a twinge of masculine guilt, grateful for her strength just then. As he looked her in the eye he remembered the final image before it all went dark, "Did we eat that man's eyes?"

Her expression took on a pensive concern, almost as if she didn't know what to say, settled on saying what needed to be said and wrapped her arms around him in case he fainted again. "Yes, we did Cullen. And for your trouble you've earned a new bracelet and a blind butler for life…he's waiting outside."

Bile rose in Cullen's throat and Enola interjected with, "Don't bother, you emptied the tank in the ballroom."

For some reason hearing the eye wasn't in his body any longer quelled his desire to vomit and when Enola was convinced he wasn't going to hit the floor like a safe, she let him go to look in the mirror.

A haggard masque of tortured years looked back at him, bags under his eyes and sweat soaked hair, a sallow tinge had affected his skin and he almost looked thinner, sickly compared to when he'd tied his bowtie in the rear view mirror outside.

It felt like a lifetime ago, being out the in the fresh air, not knowing about this place. His ears never having heard the torturous beauty of the Bound Choir. His nostrils free of Sulphur and sin, unaware of the horrific hunger that the gluttonous revered. Ignorant of the taste of eyes and untainted by the evil that had reached out of the abyss to caress him so cruelly.

Staring in the mirror he understood what Enola had meant and why she'd insisted at every turn he leave her. That he go home and he stay away. The wounds he sustained in this hole would never leave. He would bear the scars for the rest of his life and beyond, Enola had only wished to spare him this damnable place, shield his soul. Before he could stop it, Cullen hung his head over the obsidian sink and cried in great heaving sobs for the innocence he'd lost.

He almost hated the Cullen that had walked into this place with Enola on his arm, confident and excited, unaware and stupid...so fucking stupid about it all. What made him think he was any match for this place, for these people and whatever they worshipped in these pits of decadence? His whole life he'd lusted for an experience that was incomparable, to test his mettle and to push the limit...arrogant he would succeed because that's how it always ended in the books he read over and over again.

It was all wrong though, this was a foul place far from all that was right and good in the world and for the first time since he'd met her, Cullen understood the fear that tore at Enola's eyes.

His body was wracked with sobs and snot dripped off his face to the sink, he couldn't stop, couldn't breath and just when he felt he might crumble to the floor with the weight of it all her arms came around him again. Her heat like summer sun seeping through his jacket and shirt to the skin of his back, breaking the clouds, calming the storm that raged inside. She slid her hands down his arms and over his own as they clung to the lip of the sink and he could feel her heartbeat through his whole body, a mighty drum that commanded his own fluttering organ to march it its beat, to slow, to obey.

Sweet relief flooded his limbs and Enola was the tidal wave washing over him again and again. His mind fell quiet and his serrated nerves went smooth. His breathing slowed until all he knew, all he felt was the beating of her tremendous heart and the power of her soul. She rinsed him clean and made him new, a power surging from his back through his chest so enormous he thought he might burst from it all.

She pulled away suddenly and he heard the staggering of her heeled shoes on the tile as she sunk to the lip of a soaking tub weakly. He looked again in the mirror and saw Cullen from ten years ago, bright eyes and taught skin. A healthy glow that came from within and the vigor that raced through him…he felt ten feet tall.

Enola's feet skittered out from under her and she sunk to the floor in an awkward slump. She had gone pale and he went to her on the floor, taking her hands and pulling away at the clamminess he felt in those normally burning palms.

"What did you do to me?" he asked, smoothing her messy hair from her sallow face.

"What you needed me to….we can't go back now Cullen, the only way out is in." she gasped in a breathy voice.

"Now what?" he asked, afraid for her, running hands over her yet unaware of what to do.

She looked at him in all seriousness, "Do you still feel sick?"

He shook his head, confused.

"I need to eat." She said and held up a weak hand, asking with her eyes for help.

Cullen rose and pulled her up, astonished at the lightness to her, the gentle clasp of her fingers and the trembling of her legs below her.

Placing a supportive yet discreet arm under her as they went to the door, he was surprised to see the still bloody face of The Scimitar waiting for them as he opened it.

"Your servant, Mr. Ashby." He offered with a courtly bow.

"Mrs. Ashby is hungry," Cullen said in a gruff voice, "Please make sure a table is waiting for us."

With another bow he was gone and through the curtain as Cullen made casual progress to the door with Enola who had a determined set to her jaw in spite of the fact that she was moments from losing consciousness.

"I'm sorry." He offered in a quiet voice, realizing the cost of his recovery.

"I'm not." She breathed.

"Is it always like that?" he asked, "Does it always make you weak?"

"One way or another," she wheezed, "I pay what is owed."

Chapter 21

Gilda moved across the parlor to her husband and wrapped her arms around those broad shoulders, he winced at the contact and she felt the pang of guilt rattle through her once more. She had hurt him terribly last night, but in spite of all of it, his amber eyes ran over her face in the firelight with a wonder that she wished would go on forever.

He placed those large palms on either side of her face and broke into a grin, their noses all but touching as he did. Soft kisses rained on her cheeks and nose and a throaty chuckle erupted from deep within him. Gilda could feel it shaking through her own flesh, and she opened the eyes that had slid closed under his romantic overture to see what the fuss was all about.

Adams eyes were fixed squarely on her, his handsome grin wide as the sea behind them as he laughed.

"What?" she asked, feeling silly in spite of herself.

Adam shook his head and quieted, "I just never thought I'd see the day I all but ran home to greet my pretty wife."

"Were you quite wild?" Gilda asked with wide eyes, it wouldn't have shocked her in the least to discover a trail of ruined women in his wake.   He was a fine man in every way, and it was a certainty that doe eyed girls followed him wherever he went.

"Quite." He offered sparingly, his eyebrows raising in memory. His hand slid down her neck slowly, admiring the silken flesh of it for a moment before he cradled her slender hand in his own palm. "Practice for you my darling…although I'm afraid I didn't practice well enough." His crooked grin highlighted the ham handed attempt at levity, and Gilda turned smartly in his arms and all but floated to the stove.

With a towel on her hand she carefully opened the heavy door and the sumptuous smell of meat seeped through the air. Adam rubbed his hands over his stomach and followed, looking to pick a potato from the pot before she could replace the lid, Gilda was quick with a smart slap to the top of his hand.

"You'll burn your fingers, man!" she snapped, and shoved the pot back inside the piping hot oven and saw to stoking the fire.

Adam just stood there watching her for a while, those gold tipped curls swinging down her back and the dreamy expression on her face as she pulled two wood hewn mugs from a cupboard to pour wine. The curve of her waist and answering flare of her hips, those delicate toes peeking out from beneath the airy hem of her gown.

He looked at his dirty hands and moved outside to wash, but she stopped him with a pail of steaming water and a cake of soap, a linen towel on her arm. Adam moved to take it from her, but the slightest retreat stopped him. She pressed forward with an unspoken plea in her eyes, he backed up until he found his legs bumping against one of the chairs at the table.

He sat with a twinge of pain in his hips and thighs, trying to hide it for the sake of his pride. She was disinterested in his pride at the moment, and with the gentlest of hands. Her fingers curled around the hem of his shirt and pulled it over his head. His arms screamed at the motion, but he managed. She pulled his boots off and tossed them by the door and took to him with her water and soap, towel and touch.

He'd never had a single soul tend to him with such reverence and gentility, the heated water was just the right temperature for his chilled skin after his jaunt through town. Adam allowed his head to fall back on the chair and his mind to wander as his wife washed him for dinner, humming softly as she did, a song he didn't recognize but adored as it tumbled from her sweet lips.

She dropped his feet in the bucket when she was done with him and he all but groaned in pleasure. She was inspecting his shirt a frown on her face, "I hate to put it back on you, its filthy."

"I was so caught up in buying yours, I neglected to see to my own" he managed in a gravelly voice.

The wilting look she tossed him as she took the shirt with her to some unseen area of the house was comical to Adam. "You've already made yourself at home I see."

She came back with a mug of wine in her hand, "This is our home, after all."

Adam drank deeply, "Only because you're in it."

Gilda moved to take his feet from the cooling pail of water and lifted his legs easily and she did. With a soft kiss on his lips Gilda fluttered around the kitchen, laying a plate loaded with meat and vegetables in front of him with a noisy smack on her lips on the crown of his head.

"Eat man," she ordered, coming right back with a loaf of bread and the dash of butter.

Adam all put wept at the meal she'd laid before him, such a simple thing to have done and yet it pulled at his heartstrings, the kindness in this woman, his woman. As she ate daintily, keeping an eye on his plate and his mug, quick to reload either should she think he might need more, Adam all but stuffed himself to the gills and when he finally leaned back from the table a belch rolled out of his mouth before he could stop it.

Gilda shook her head and smirked, "Ate everything but the plate." She observed as her hands began to gather up the plates and forks.

Adams hands over her own stopped her, "Don't." he said softly, "I'll do the washing up, you stoke the fire and I'll be there in a minute."

The look that crossed her face was one of sweet surprise, and without a word she left him to clean up their meal. Seating herself on the sofa near the fire, watching the flames dance in the hearth as the wood crackled and hissed. Her eyes fell upon a blister of sap, and as she watched it heat, tremble and finally burst in a shimmering explosion of molten amber, she realized it was the same color as her husband's eyes.

His hand on her shoulder yanked her from her reverie and with a jerk she looked up at him, placing a pale hand on her thundering heart. "You scared me!" she breathed, shaking the cobwebs from her mind.

He sunk into the sofa next to her, eyeing her with a shy look on his face and with just a moment's hesitation, burrowed his head into her lap and looked up at her. Gilda smiled at the boyish sweetness in him and this gesture. Who would ever guess that this mountain of a man, this brawny mass of muscle and strength could be so sweet, so shy?

She let her fingers twine in his hair, combing through the strands over and over in a slow rhythm as she found herself humming once more, her eyes drifting over his drowsy face and back to the fire.

"Can it always be this way Gilda?" he asked softly, his calloused palm once again coasting over the column of her throat.

She looked down at him and smiled, "Always."

"I'll hold you to that." He warned wryly.

"I would expect nothing less." her eyes rolled to the ceiling.

They fell into that companionable silence once more and Gilda felt him drift away into the lifeless repose of a person who has not rested, truly rested in a very long time. His jaw went slack and his limbs soft, beneath his eyelids they tiny twitches of a mind at work in a dream someplace. Content to sit and watch the fire a while, Gilda let her own mind drift as she held her sleeping husband.

An unnatural sound carried on the wind jerked Gilda awake, Adam's head was still in her lap, his body curled around hers. Bringing a distracted hand to her head and marveling at drifting off so suddenly like that, she looked around for the source of the cry that had jarred her.

The fire had all but gone out, the coals beneath glowing weakly in a desperate search for more fuel. Carefully she crawled out from under Adam, lest she wake the worn out man from his much needed rest. Throwing another two logs on the fire she watched, expecting them to light, yet the coals remained engrossed in their desperate hunger, the logs unmarred. She bent to the hearth, blowing a careful stream of air deep into the slumbering heat, but no flames rose to her call.

This fire was cold somehow

Another call rang off the walls around her and she looked wildly for the source, swearing it must be in the house with her, it was so loud and clear. Her eyes flew to Adam once more, he snored softly, unaware. The walls began to shake with the thumping of some great unseen force, she looked to the windows that lined the street and saw only the dense swirls of ocean fog churning behind the glass. It was a moonless night and frost piqued the corners of the sill in lacey frills.

Moving to the kitchen, the bread Adam had left on the counter was molded and sunken in the middle, as if it had spoiled overnight. The smell of vinegar crept from the bottle of wine because it had turned. She seized the knob of the back door, heard the hinges sing out with rust and thrust herself out into the fog, blind to everything but its smoky veil.

Even the sea had gone silent, and its normally abundant roar was still in the cottony quiet of this strange night. She moved slowly in her bare feet, the chill of the flagstone beneath her feet biting her skin. Taking one halting step after another, carefully patting the ground in front of her before she moved, Gilda made precious little progress. Echoes of the endless night in that hole shuddering through her mind. To be blind, to be lost…to be once again alone.

A snorting behind her raised the hair on the back of her neck and she spun blindly, terrified of what she might see. Her breaths came in nervous pants and she felt the bull inside of her strain once more, felt the chains pull and rattle under his power. He was awake this night, but not for passion…he was wary.

The fog swirled and gathered, and from its pale cloud a black hoof stepped stately, bringing with it the proud chest and head of a mighty stag. His great antlers twisting to the sky, droplets of mist glistening in his chestnut fur and with every footfall, the very ground beneath him shook. Streams of steam blazed from his flared nostrils as he regarded Gilda in front of him, his eyes the fiery color of the amber from the sap.

Something about this animal was wrong, and being near it and at the same time nowhere frightened Gilda. She fisted nervous hands in the satin of her gown, and gasped as the fabric fell away in mottled clumps, moth eaten and old.

Soon she wore nothing at all, the finery she'd been given nothing more than grey dust around her feet.

Naked before this unnatural creature, she sought to cover herself and get away. She took a halting step back and felt her stomach drop as the searching sole of her foot swung wildly in air. She had reached the end of the yard and was perched precariously on the edge of a cliff. There was no place to go, nothing in front of her but the stag and his imperious gaze.

He sniffed at her, bringing that tremendous head and rack of points and whirls dangerously close to her. He quaffed her flesh with great guttural snorts, licking at his nostrils with a slick brown tongue. Up and down her body he pulled great puffs of fog and air from Gilda's body, as if searching for something. The sides of his body expanding in a disturbing bow of ribs and icy fur as he gulped greedily at her.

Suddenly his head jerked away, a primitive expression of terror in his eyes. Rearing back he let loose an ear piercing bugle, those burning eyes rolling in their sockets in fear. He reared back on his great haunches, the front legs spinning madly, the black hooves like knives that sliced the air.

Gilda slapped her hands over her ears at the nauseating sound, wanting away from the startled thing. He called over and over again, as if to some unseen brethren for help for assistance. To alert them to this intruder to the danger he'd scented on her this night, before she could do them harm.

He landed on those hooves once more, shaking the ground with his might and behind his great and glistening body, in the fog Gilda could see the tell-tale swirls of movement. Obscured in the fog, in the deafening silence, they gathered. Crowded and pushed closer and closer to her, to the stag who bugled once more in a victorious fashion, tossing his head arrogantly before he leveled those flaming eyes upon her once again.

With determined steps that rattled through the soles of her feet, he advanced the unseen foes behind him following.

The bull roared in a rage, furious at this intrusion and their brash advance. Gilda was too scared to hold the chains any longer....they were coming for her.

Chapter 22

After Enola had been seated at a table among the shameless eaters that gathered to binge, Cullen all but sprinted to the buffets. Loading a plate with rare meat, watching the blood ooze across the plate in the candle light somehow knowing she needed it this way, nearly living, hardly dead. Hastening back to her as she drained a tall glass of dark beer, her throat greedily pulling it into her stomach as the Scimitar waited patiently for her to finish. The foam from the head clung to her lip and she handed the glass to the blind man without a moment's hesitation, "Another and one for him this time too." Their delicate butler blindly floated away with a gentle nod and before Cullen could hand her the weighty plate she seized it from his hands, dropped it in front of her and dug in with a ravenous joy that he adored and feared at the same time.

It wasn't Enola eating the scraps of meat she all but ripped with the knife she clenched in a fist that threatened to bend the silver it held. Her eyes were brighter than he remembered, almost searing from within with a light, an energy that was hypnotic and strange. She all but destroyed three slabs of prime rib and two more pints of ale as Cullen watched, sipping his own absently. The ethereal glow that was uniquely hers had returned with a rosy vigor, and that desperate hunger in her face faded. She pushed the plate away with no small amount of satisfaction and finally focused on Cullen's eyes once more.

He could almost hear her heart now, that enormous beating coming from her body. It soothed him to recall the surging power of it all, the thrumming that raced through her veins was a wellspring of serenity and strength in all this madness and wrong.

"Tell me what you're thinking." He asked as she eyed the half full pint near his hand.

"We have to keep going." She said, reaching for it without asking, "But we need to find a better way, or I'm afraid you won't last to see the end."

Cullen winced at her blunt words and at the same time felt the tug at his soul as she never once thought about the danger to herself, the risk she was taking, it was always him she sought to shelter.

"I agree." He straightened the cuffs of his shirt and looked around, "But how?'

"Perhaps I can be of some assistance, Brother?" The Scimitar emerged from the shadow in which he'd been discreetly waiting for their next command. "It would be my pleasure to indulge your darkest wish."

Enola and Cullen shared a look, he had sworn himself to them, but in a den of sinners what good was an oath?

"We wish to descend," Cullen offered sparingly, "as quickly and easily as possible."

The Scimitar nodded graciously, "I understand completely," he pulled Enola's chair out for her smoothly, "follow me and we shall find the way."

They silently followed him through the steaming tables of food, constantly replenished and served by his Unseeing brethren. Out of the curtain, through the antechamber and toward an untried room.

With The Scimitar as their escort, the sentry tested their bracelets and opened the curtain upon what looked like a casino. Well-lit and lush the burgundy carpet glowed under gilded candelabras as they lit the tables below. Great, round things with Unseeing dealers offering every game imaginable. A craps table was crowded with jolly onlookers as the shooter rolled the bones for seven the hard way and cheered as he won, doubling their money and his in the process. A pit boss with a gnarled cane strolled through the fairway, casually scanning the players for anything untoward, his hands clasped tightly around the titanium staff.

The Scimitar didn't stop however, and led on toward a roped off area to the side. Enola and Cullen passed through into the smaller room with a fire roaring in the corner, a balcony over some obscured sight below to the other side. They were deep underground now, the stony walls were dripping wet with ground water and coated with beards of moss and nitre. Even the air had an unturned odor to it, as Cullen exhaled he could swear he tasted dirt.

"The main area offers gambling for money only, but in here the exotic and rare are put on the table, winner takes all." He murmured as they stopped to watch.

There were only two tables in this place and at the one nearest to them every chair was held by a person of extreme, almost painful beauty. Men and women who were exquisite to look upon, all chiseled jaws and flawless skin looking closely at the cards and one another. What struck Cullen odd was that there were no chips on the table, no bets laid, just the discards in the center as they moved through the game. It came down between two ladies, a blonde with a heart shaped faced and the mouth of a cherub, the other a raven haired siren who's eyes could cut glass.

The moment of truth arrived and the blonde lost, breaking into tears as she realized her error, the victor was quick with a box cutter to mar her face with a cruel cut that ran from her ear to her lip. Snagging the perfect bow as a ribbon of crimson blood dripped from her highly arched cheek.

 Cullen was quick to look at the next table, where two men were at the end of what looked to be an all-in game. Baccarat, Cullen surmised from the dealer's gestures with the long flat pallet. On one side of the table a toffee skinned man with a beard that dripped to his belly was eyeballing his opponent, sleek and bald in a fine suit.

He stroked the wild chocolate colored hair at his chin and gestured for another card, wincing as it revealed his loss. Jerking to his feet he knocked the upholstered chair on its back behind him and he furiously strode away, then back and away again.

"Another game perhaps?" the sleek man offered, folding his hands diplomatically on the felted table before him.

The bearded man was beyond conversing and with a frantic gesture of his hands he motioned in dismissal, "You have taken them all, everything!" He shouted in clipped tones. "What else have I to give?"

"I'm sure I can think of something." The bald man grinned with oddly white teeth.

After a moment's consideration, he refused and gestured to the Unseeing with a wave, "Come, come….don't make him wait."

The grating sound of a vault door opening echoed through the air drew their attention, although the other players hardly raised an eye as a line of three children came from the unseen room. Nude and oiled with their hands behind their necks in silent obedience, they ranged from pre-pubescent to around five years of age. The two boys and single girl walked with cast down eyes as they went to their new master with the unseen stink of fear coming off their exposed bodies.

Cullen moved to stop him and felt the iron grip of Enola's hand on his elbow which he ignored, "Sir!" he said in a pleasant voice, "I couldn't help but notice your good fortune."

The man stopped and smiled eagerly, "Yes, quite the windfall, I was about to take them someplace where we could get acquainted." He turned on his heel once again to leave but Cullen followed.

"I don't suppose you would be willing to humor me with a game of cards for them?" he asked casually.

The bald man turned and regarded him critically, "What have you to offer? I am a man of singular taste."

"Nothing as fine as what you have already won, but I'm sure you can think of something?" Cullen was in his element in this room, the greasy dealings of shifty souls who were always looking out for their own interests at any expense. It was better to let them tell you what they wanted rather than offer too much and leave money on the table.

His pale eyes shifted from Cullen to Enola and widened momentarily in interest, "Your wife?" he asked.

Cullen nodded without hesitation, which stunned him slightly and the man approached, looking very closely with appreciation as he walked slowly around her. "Lovely...beautiful skin." He ran a cursory hand down her arm and wrapped long fingers around those delicate wrists, holding them up to admire in the light. "Exquisite bone structure." He murmured, almost to himself.

He finished his inspection and with a sudden turn faced Cullen once more, "If you would deny me these delicious partridges and all their charms for yourself, then you will offer your wife to me, to whip until that fine skin cracks and she begs me to stop in the Circle of Wrath where I'll hang her by her Achilles tendons and break her thumbs with a hammer."

The breath escaped Cullen's lungs in a paralyzing wave of shock, he couldn't decide which was worse, the fact that he thought of it at all, or that he thought of it so quickly. Was there some other woman with a whiplashed back and broken thumbs who had served as currency at this table? Could he stand even the idea of such a thing happening to Enola? Was it worse than those poor children, what they may experience and what had already been done...Cullen found himself lost in a swamp of morality while the wolves waited for him to drown.

He was unaware of just what to do when Enola gave him the slightest of nods, and Cullen smiled obligingly, "Your terms are acceptable."

The gentlemen sat at the table as the Unseeing dealer set the table for a new game, Cullen felt surprisingly at ease as he settled into his seat. He snapped his fingers and The Scimitar was at his side like a dream. "Gin and tonic please." He asked, eyeing the bald man casually, watching the way he leaned far back in the chair, the way he stroked his hand over the crimson tie at his neck and allowing it to glide to the breast of his jacket which he gave the slightest of tugs.

His mind drifted back to the floating card palaces of the Mississippi where he cut his teeth, and learned his con. Sitting in the gently stirring air of a riverboat casino with men that called themselves The Colonial or Bo and underestimated him for the simple fact that he was poor white trash. Cullen had tried not to take it personally, and used their judgement to his advantage. Letting them think him simple and safe, Hell, Cullen's favorite was to let the men take all of his chips, get up to leave and sit back down with a some weepy story about his Granddaddy's pocket watch that he brought back from the war and he'd slap a pawn shop piece of shit on the table and clean house as they swarmed to take the last thing they could get from him like a pack rabid wolves.

His whole life he'd been on the bottom, the loser and the last one anyone saw coming. Just this once, with those kids and Enola riding on it, he'd like to win. To show that dirty little boy with the bruised back who had to put cardboard in the bottoms of his shoes to keep the mud from seeping in the holes that it could happen, when it mattered.

His drink was set sedately by his side, the ice tinkling in the glass as a wedge of lime glowed in the light, Cullen could barely bring himself to drink it he was so nervous. But then he saw Enola once more, she hadn't moved from the spot she'd been in when he'd struck this deal. Her eyes met his and all that anxiety washed away, and he felt it again, that heat running through him, stirring his blood and awakening his soul.

This was a bad place, with evil people but he could do this, none of them knew where he came from and they didn't care. Looking at that strange woman as she gazed back at him with that inexplicable expression of serenity. Even in all this madness, he realized she would never ask, because it didn't matter in the least where a person started out, only how they ended up.

Several interested onlookers trickled past the rope to watch and that suited Cullen fine, let them watch as he trounced this asshole in the grand tradition of The South...politely. The Unseeing dealer set up the cards with his pallet, two in front of each of them.

Cullen raised a polite hand, "Please, you first."

The firelight was gleaming off the bald man's head and that insipid smile as he flipped over a King and the seven of hearts.

"Seven" the unseeing announced to the onlookers that had gathered, to Cullen's intense wonder. If they had no eyes and were blindfolded, how was it they saw? Knew? It was a question for another time, the bank showed his hand.

"Also seven." The he called flipping over a three of spades and four of clubs.

Cullen chewed his lip and flipped the six of diamonds and six of hearts.

"Two." The Unseeing stated almost apologizing.

The bank and his opponent would likely stand pat, seven was pretty damn good and considering there were already two sixes on the table his odds were slim. But what else was there to be done? Cullen had started this dance and was determined to finish. He made a small gesture with his fingers before he realized his dealer was blind but a card was pulled from the shoe and slid to him anyway.

Cullen reached out and flipped over the six of spades.

"Congratulations, sir." The Unseeing nodded with a smile as the bald man's face fell. The grin evaporating into abject shock and anger.

"Impossible!" he screamed, the echo of his outburst bouncing off the damp stone walls. He threw the chair and stormed out of the room, the modest crowd that had scrambling like roaches to get out of his way.

Before Enola could reach him at the table a small hand tugged at the sleeve of his jacket followed by a small voice, "What would you ask of us master?"

Cullen's eyes fell upon his prize, the trembling three, naked and scared with their hands behind their backs. Those wide eyes watering in fear of what he might ask, too small to fight and too alone in this world.

He snapped his fingers and spoke knowing The Scimitar was listening, "They eat whatever they want until they're full....then bring them back to me."

If the request was odd no one showed it, and as their blind guide hustled them away to a feast unlike any they had tasted a hand fell on Cullen's shoulder like a hammer.

"You play well." A Russian accent growled.

His eyes followed the heavily scarred hand to an arm the size of a tree trunk and up and up and up to the imposing shoulders of a mountain of a man. His grin was wide and the yellowed teeth were crooked and crowded in his mouth. His shorn hair was speckled with bald spots where the hair strangled in the scar tissue. The neck that held the hard and weathered face was thick enough that Cullen doubted he could get his hands around it if he tried.

"I would like to play." he stated simply, his guttural voice thickened like motor oil in the accent.

"For what, exactly?" Cullen asked, sipping his drink as he rose and realized he could only gaze upon the buttons of this enormous man's vest as he did.

"For the only thing that matters here." He replied, holding up his wrist and the massive cuff that wrapped around nine times. It was dented and chipped, tarnished and old. This man had earned this cuff and was unlikely to lose it easily.

"We have a challenge!" The Unseeing dealer announced and Cullen felt his stomach clench. He recalled the withered crone's voice telling Enola that no challenge went unanswered in this place. He was without choice, his victory had taken him to this point, it was just another step in the dance he was learning as he went.

Cullen stretched out a hand that was enveloped in the tremendous grip of his opponent and shaken vigorously. "Surely you have no objections to my lady luck watching?"

His eyes fell on Enola and with a snort he dismissed the idea that her presence would disturb him even a little, "Your lucky lady, your unlucky man...what do I care?"

Enola swept in between them as if he were the gentlest of men, "Might I know the name of the man my husband is about the best at baccarat?" she asked, her voice a low and even purr.

This caught his attention, obviously taken aback by her boldness, "Anatoli Zubov."

"We're the Ashby's." Cullen injected, extra heavy on the drawl.

"American." He snarled, "Spoilt and weak, puny and small...all of you let machines fight for you."

He sat at the table, the chair creaking beneath his tremendous weight, "At Black Dolphin, I fight...fight to eat, to sleep, to live to breathe."

Cullen had no response to this comment, didn't even know what Black Dolphin was, but Enola did.

"No one just goes to Black Dolphin Mr. Zubov, how did you get your invitation?"

They were staring each other down and Cullen thought he saw a moment of confusion cross his face before he replied, "I like to hurt people."

Her head cocked at this comment, but she remained as cool as she ever had as she took a sip of Cullen's drink. "And how did you get out?"

"There is only one way out of Black Dolphin...I died." He said folding his massive arms across the wall of muscle that was his chest.

"And yet here you are." Enola marveled, "that must be a fascinating story."

"Hell Fire Club brought me here to fight in the pits," he continued, "that's where I earned this." He said thrusting his cuff into the light proudly, "by fighting to the death."

She took just a second too long to answer, "Congratulations."

"Enough of your mouth, let's play." He muttered, frustrated when he couldn't scare Enola.

Cullen did his best to hide the smile that was playing on his lips, this guy was all about the head game, the big scare. You'd be crazy to beat him because he'd kill you and yet, Enola had reduced him to a frustrated boy with a single word. He'd have to remember that one for next time.

He took his place across from Anatoli and waiting for his cards, Cullen gestured once more to his opponent politely, "After you, sir."

Anatoli flipped the tiny cards with his giant fingers, queen of diamonds and nine of clubs.

"Natural!" the dealer called as the crowd gasped.

Cullen told himself to calm down, he could still get to nine, there were a lot of ways to get to nine and he would if he had to dig his way there with a teaspoon.

He flipped his cards, seven of hearts and seven of spades.

"Four." The dealer all but sighed.

The dealer showed his eight of hearts and Jack of diamonds.

"Eight...dealer stands."

Cullen was surprised the blind bastard waiting for him to do it, surmising that he could hear his fingers itching for the card in the stagnant air of this place and as the card slid along the felt on the pallet to him he spared one last look at Enola.

One last look at the only perfect thing he'd ever seen in this world, one last glimpse before this card changed everything and made it happen or ended it all.

When his eyes fell on that damned two of clubs his heart fell to the floor.

"Six, the dealer called, congratulations Sir." He offered to The Russian.

He'd lost...it was over and Cullen heard the silent footsteps of the Unseeing coming to take him in the back and tear out his eyes. The last thing he thought was what it would be like to see without seeing, and where they all lived when the party wasn't on.

Chapter 23

A soul searing scream shook her awake and as Gilda's eyes took in the golden light of dawn she also saw Adam's face in her lap looking up at her with an expression of terror on his handsome features. The shattering wail went on and on until she feared her ears may bleed from the sound, tears running down the sides of her face in hot rivers as it went on and on. The panes of glass shuttered in the windows and the doors rattled under the strain of it.

As she realized she may faint if it didn't end she felt Adam's hands on her shoulders, his mouth moved in the familiar shape of her name, and yet she heard nothing, the shrill keening took all her hearing.

He shook her softly at first, then more violently, hauling her soft body from the couch and around the room like a rag doll. The pane of glass in the rear window shattered and with a panicked look Adam pulled back a hand and laid a searing slap across her face, then another and another but still it went on.

Finally Gilda realized the sound was coming from her, clapping her hands over her own mouth so hard she felt her jaw creak under the grip and mercifully the awful, mournful noise was finally smothered. She allowed herself to take a breath, deep and shuttering her whole body in Adam's wild clasp, their eyes locked as she kept her hands clawed over her mouth, lest she start screaming again.

"WOMAN!" he bellowed, dropping her angrily to slump on the ground, "What vexes you?" He took several frightened steps back and eyed her with a suspicious glare that paralyzed her heart.

Afraid to move her hand, tears welling in her eyes from hurt tumbled down her cheeks as she shook her head in confusion.

Raking an angry hand through his sleep addled hair, he began to pace around the stilly silent room, keeping his eyes on her as he went. He would stop for a moment, open his mouth as if to say something, think better of it and begin storming around the room again. "I've never heard man nor beast make any manner of the sound that came from you..."

Gilda had no answer for it, knew she couldn't explain what she'd seen in her vision. It would sound like madness. She feared the loss of their tender union, it was so new and delicate, it seemed that anything could shatter their fragile bond. Her cheeks stung from his slaps and she could feel her jaw swelling at the joints from her own force. Although she'd slept all night she felt weary and drawn, knowing that she'd taken no rest in dark of that specter's world.

She had two choices, she could tell Adam everything and hope he understood or explain it away and make sure it never happened again. Looking at his fretful face as he watched her like an animal uncaged, Gilda knew her choice was clear.

Taking her hand away from her mouth tentatively, she drew another breath with a shutter and in a hoarse voice whispered, "I'm so sorry darling....I dreamt of that awful night at the lake."

It was a lie, an ugly one at that and Gilda hated herself for it instantly. She was betting on his guilt over that moment when he chased her feverish and dying out to die on that strange water as he watched.

The next thing she knew she was in his arms, those tight bands of muscle clenching her to him desperately. She felt his breath hitch under her arms and knew her arrow had landed, she released a deep sigh and let her head fall to his shoulder. After a moments embrace he pulled away from her, cradled her already bruising face in his hands and she saw tears running down his face, but he was smiling in spite of them.

"I forget all you've been through lass, I forget what you've seen." He kissed her salty lips, their tears mingling as their cheeks brushed damply and before he could rise from the floor to help her up the front door busted open with Eli and Shamus in various states of dress, hair mussed and bleary eyed from bed. Eli clutched a butcher's knife in his hand, Shamus toted a large and gnarled club, weapons at the ready they looked around for some unseen foe and when their gazes fell upon the couple Shamus let the club drop by his foot where Gilda saw he was wearing only one boot.

"Blast it Eli!" he bellowed, shoving the thin man's shoulder in agitation, "Ye drag me from bed saying death itself has called on the Flynn's and here they are cuddled up on the floor kissin!"

"I heard it Shamus!" Eli defended, "I heard the most horrible scream come from this place...like the wind was watching the sun die..." he ventured further into the house, looking for the foe.

Adam rose from the floor, pulling Gilda with him with a grunt, swearing it was the shock of waking in a dither that had made his muscles strain under her weight. "My apologies men," he began, curling an arm around her waist and cuddling her to him, "Mrs. Flynn was having a nightmare."

The two men offered a befuddled look in unison, their eyes shifting to Gilda, and back to Adam in confusion.

"A nightmare?" Shamus echoed.

"She woke up me, my wife and every child in the house because of a nightmare?" Eli asked, running a distracted hand through his gray hair.

Adam only squeezed her to him closer as he nodded, the two men looked once again at Gilda and each other. After a moment's silence, heavy and tense Shamus let out a guttural sigh of resignation. "Well, come on then." He shook his head and gestured with the club out the door, "If Eli will bring the bacon, Fanny'll fry it and we can hear just what you're talking about."

Gilda's hand clenched on Adam's arm in protest, but he patted it gently, seeking her eyes as her own bounced between Shamus and Eli. Seeing her hesitation and outright fear, he dropped the club with a floor rattling thud and went to them. "No one is going to hurt you …not while I'm drawing breath, not while you're here…not in your home."

"That's right," Eli joined him, the knife glinting in the burning morning sun, "we take care of our own here."

Adam sought her eyes once more, imploring her to trust him, to trust them. It was hard to say no to those warm eyes that crinkled when he smiled at her. His touch a whisper under her aching chin, "Come on girl," he whispered gruffly, "they came here ready to kill."

Gilda's eyes took in the ridiculous sight of it all, of them all rumpled and half- dressed and a tiny laugh escaped her raw throat. He had a point, a good one. They'd come to her aid unaware of what waited inside and that meant something. With a small nod and a sigh she consented and as Adam quickly dressed in that filthy shirt and boots, she slid her feet into the delicate slippers and followed Shamus to the Inn once more where a frantic Fanny waited the news.

"Gilda girl! What's happened to yer face!" she crowed as the quartet slunk through the door, descending on them and shoving to Gilda she took her screaming jaw in her hands and turned her face into the light, "You've bruised her face ye brute!"

With a loud smack she slapped Adam's back angrily, "What could she ha done to earn those?" All but chasing him through the Inn, landing blow after blow as Adam ducked and dodged her great swinging hands, trying to explain but being drowned out by her own endless tirade. Shamus finally grabbed hold of her in a great bear hug effectively neutralizing her for the moment.

"It's a long story you fearsome nag...I bet if we feed them, they'll tell us."

A stilly hush fell over the remnants of the breakfast table as Adam finished his tale about what he and more to the point, Gilda had endured to reach their charming town. Three pairs of eyes regarded her with a bewildered awe as she nibbled on what was left of the bacon Eli had supplied.

A flurry of questions erupted from the trio suddenly, they were specifically interested in what had happened in the lodge, something she hadn't even told Adam about in any great detail. Partly out of wanting to keep it from her mind, and most because of the strangeness of it all.

"How did you get there, lamb?" Fanny asked in that concerned tone.

Gilda could only shake her head, "I don't remember, I went to bed like I had every night of my life and I awoke underground with a man who stripped me down and locked me in."

"If he locked you in, how did you get out?" Eli was quick to interject, pointing one of his agile fingers at her as he did.

"There was only one way out," her mind went back to that stinking hole, and all the horror she'd crawled through to survive it. "I crawled through a tunnel...I don't know for how long but there was a door at the end."

"A door?" Shamus repeated in disbelief.

Gilda nodded as she took the mug of ale Fanny had refilled for her, "It wasn't like any door I've ever seen."

"Why not?" Adam even asked now, looking at her puzzled.

"It was so large and perfectly round, I thought I imagined it." She sipped at the sweet ale and felt the ache in her jaw lessen.

"Then what lamb?" Fanny coaxed, "Go on…"

"There was only a knocker…so I knocked and it was opened by these people…"

"What did they do to you?" Adam asked, almost growling at the question.

"They were so kind to me…dressed my wounds and put me to bed, but it – it was strange there." Gilda recalled their gloves and the blindfolded serving girls who put her to bed.

"Strange how?" Eli asked.

She searched their faces in hesitation, did she dare tell them all she'd seen? Was it wise to drag these people into her mess, her problems? What if they should come looking for her here and hurt them. Flashes of the swamp and Nathaniel…and that man she drowned took her miles away, made her unsure.

"It's alright Gilda…" Adam stroked her hand almost reverently. "You're safe here."

"They wouldn't touch me with their bare hands, even the doctor wore fine gloves as he tended to me, soaking them with water…and the servants…." She drifted off remembering their swift hands, as if they could see in the dark.

"Yes?" Fanny all but shouted, her clenched fists on the table in anticipation.

"They wore blindfolds when they dressed me." Gilda finally admitted, lowering her head in a silent request that the subject be dropped.

Her request was honored and with an ominous glance between her dining companions, they all cleared the table to retire to the kitchen where they could talk about what they'd just heard without Gilda in attendance.

It suited her fine, watching the three men follow the hearty swing of Fanny's hips into the confines of the kitchen and away from her ears. Although the damage had been done, the images of that night as fresh as paint burned in her mind. The congenial smile of that well- dressed man and his humble apology, the opulence of the room in contrast to the abysmal hole she'd crawled from...and that room, that painfully beautiful room.

Shaking her head to clear it of the past, Gilda rose with her mug in hand and wandered around the main floor of the Inn. Looking at the rough -hewn tables, long and worn from endless nights of drinking and mirth, the grain of the planks almost shining from the nightly wash of ale they'd endured over the years. A small shelf on the wall had a carved figuring of a dancing goat with a candle nearby, and so many paintings on the walls.

A ship steered through a storm over the bar, its sails straining under the gale of the wind as waves clawed at her hull. There was a portrait of a young woman, Fanny perhaps or a distant relative, they shared the same features and a merriment of temperament that could even be captured in oils. Gilda ran her hand over the rounded stones of the fireplace and raised her eyes to the great framed picture over the hearth....

She felt her stomach clench as her gaze fell upon a boar, its tusks muddy and bedraggled with limp reeds and twine. It stood on sturdy legs, its broad body ready to charge out of the frame and into the room, its amber eyes almost glowing in the dim of the room.

Gilda's mind flew back to the chamber in the lodge, and that strange hare that had regarded her as she drifted off to sleep, then the stag in their rented home and now this...it couldn't be coincidence. These strange paintings, those insidious eyes and why the meaner creatures of this Earth?

She felt the bull stir for a moment and in a head swimming gasp she realized that last night, wherever she'd been, it was these animals, these familiars that had sought her out, crowded her to the edge of the town with the intention of pushing her into the salty depths.

Chapter 24

The too light touch of the Unseeing was already around his shoulders, removing the glass from his hand and pulling him to the horror of life as a blind prostrate bound to this other world he'd dumbly stumbled into on the heels of a woman he hardly knew. Panic was starting to seize his mind and freeze the gears in smoking terror, Cullen wished for shock to set in mercifully and hoped the unearthly serenity of The Scimitar was not just an act.

He was knocked out of his self- loathing by a splintering thud, Enola had removed her bracelet from her left wrist and smacked it hard atop the cards. As the wooden legs of the gambling table all but bowed under the force she exerted on its felted surface, she leveled her cool gaze with The Russian and in a low voice that raised gooseflesh on Cullen's skin in spite of the feverish panic, "Double or nothing I take you down in the pit."

Anatoli couldn't have stopped the mighty laugh that escaped his body if he'd tried, placing those anvil hands on his hips he let the amusement of a mere woman challenging him shake his muscled form till tears rolled down his cheeks. But once he'd wound down the Unseeing announced in a clear voice, "We have a challenge!" and as if by some silent announcement, people flooded the room to witness what was to be a rare treat.

"It is to the death," The Russian shook an almost sad finger at her, "and I always liked killing women best."

Enola only allowed that sphinx like expression to lay on her features, "Our lives for your cuff, acceptable?"

He raised an impressed set of eyebrows at her brash reply to his obvious threat and nodded. "I'll see you in the mud."

He stalked off, removing his jacket as he went and in a flurry the Unseeing were around her, "This way, Sister."

One gestured grandly, sweeping her through the swelling crowd that had gathered.

Cullen grabbed at her arm, his eyes wide with astonishment, "Enola…please."

She halted in the flock of blind men that were scuttling her along and ran a soft hand down the side of his face, "…don't watch." Then she was gone, out the roped off area to face some unhuman animal in combat on his behalf and Cullen was sure that he would die from the shame before Anatoli could kill her.

The Scimitar was at his side, with a fresh drink and a cool towel, "If I may be so bold Master…she honors us with her blood as the pit has not seen a fight in quite some time."

Cullen mopped his head with the towel and slung it over the shoulder of his companion, knocking the drink back hard and wincing at the juniper bite of the gin. "And why is that?" he asked, knowing he'd hate the answer.

"Because he killed all bold enough to challenge years ago." The simple reply all but rendered Cullen unconscious, the thought of her near that mad dog was making him nauseous.

"You should be proud." The Scimitar cajoled softly, "she will be remembered always as the bravest among her Sisters."

His words were of little consolation and before he realized where he was going, he felt the sumptuous cushion of a chair beneath his shaking body as his eyes fell over a dirt ring below. Voices rang out behind him, taking bets on The Russian, seeking to gain at Enola's certain demise and while the rest of the Brothers and Sisters clamored for a good seat, the opponents entered the ring and were welcomed with a resounding cheer.

The Russian had removed his jacket and shirt along with his shoes, standing like a wall in trousers, the suspenders tight along the expanse of scarred muscle that comprised his stomach and chest. Enola entered like a dream, in her lovely gown all curves and velvet in high heels, almost gliding over the mud.

There was no announcement, no pomp and circumstance of the boxing rings in Vegas. They were just locked in there together, the carved wall to the back brown with a crust of dried blood. The torchlight trickled down on them as an eerie silence took hold of the room, and the final deafening thud of the doors being shut and barred.

Enola regarded The Russian sedately as he took a wide stance and held those hammer like fists out to his sides. He was drawing great deep breaths that caused the planes of his body to expand and contract like some fleshy bellows. Cullen could see the prominent bulge in the crotch of his tuxedo trousers and realized he didn't like hurting women, he fucking loved it and the sheen of sweat that broke out over his snarling face announced that it had been too long since he'd enjoyed this singular pleasure with a specimen as lovely as Enola. She remained unmoved at his display, allowing him to flex and strut as he pleased, her arms resting easily beside her curving form in the tight confines of the borrowed finery.

The suspense was suffocating Cullen, and even as he watched Enola calm and centered in the ring, he felt himself spinning out of control. His breaths came in jagged gasps and a lump rose in his throat that was as immobile as a boulder. He pulled at the bowtie in a frantic tug, tossing it to The Scimitar as he took the next drink offered in a single gulp.

He wanted it to begin, to already be over…to have this be some awful dream from which he'd awake in that doorway in London beneath the early morning drizzle. Anything but this horror about to unfold in front of him being a reality.

About the time the air could have been cut with a knife The Russian began to move, slowly at first. To one side and then another as Enola was quick to counter in a delicate swirl of navy skirts along the mud. Drawing close as he teased from one flank to another in the ring, leaving deep indents in the soil, he was close enough to steal a kiss but still he waited with wild eyes running over Enola's body in the torchlight that surrounded them.

Suddenly he erupted with a lighting fast right hook, in spite of his tremendous size the man was quick and the crowd gasped as his fist glanced off Enola's jaw when she took a step back a second too late. The smack of his knuckles on her flesh echoed through the place as her head was snapped to the side so sharply it shook her hair loose in a tumble around her shocked face.

Cullen's heart stuttered at the sight of her taking that punch, her arms flailed out wildly as she sought to keep her balance and he let his fingers claw into the arms of the chair he sat in, gritting his teeth. That sound send his mind reeling, and for a brief second, he wasn't in the Hell Fire Caves any longer. The stench of rendered flesh once again choked him and booming thunder of his father's rage was followed by the lightening of his fists. That ugly green carpet rose up to his ten year old face and the world upended around him as his sisters screamed in terror. Rolling in time to see the blackened shadow of the old man coming close to give him the business Cullen felt his iron grip on his shoulder and jerked only to be met with the dulcet tones of The Scimitar, "Master, you mustn't stray too far."

In the ring Enola stumbled on her feet but recovered quickly, regaining her center and tossing her locks behind her as he followed like a freight train with a left jab. This one she deflected neatly, turning into his body to spin behind his massive frame and knock him face first in the mud rather elegantly which raised a surprised chuckle from the onlookers that watched.

Shock was painted all over his face as he pushed himself quickly to his feet, she'd surprised him with that one and he was a little angry now. A flush of red on his already taut features painted him downright devilish. He took a low stance as the clods of dirt fell from his damp chest, Enola matched his posture which sent the velvet of her gown straining under her widely spread legs.

The Russian didn't bother with a punch, he simply hurtled himself at her, likely to knock her pretty face in the mud as payback but when he reached her low set stance their arms tangled up like the racks of two battling stags. Instead of her flying back into the loam as Cullen was certain he expected, her feet held underneath the charge, pressing a raft of mud up behind them in a great heap of sludge as they grappled.

A crying rip heralded the skirt of her gown giving under the strain of her legs as she pressed against the onslaught that was The Russian at full speed. The jagged tear in the fabric went all the way up to her hip and a roar erupted from the lookers on at the sight of all that delicious flesh.

The Russian had given up on knocking her over and twined his arms around Enola tightly and set those mossy teeth into her shoulder yanking a howl of pain from his opponent. He ripped a chunk of flesh from her with a jerk of his head. Ribbons of blood ran from the gash, over her breast and down the front of the gown between them. The animal swallowed the bite as he stared her in the eye and Cullen looked away as his gut twisted in horror.

He quickly looked back in time to see Enola swing her own head into his heavy brow and the bone crunching sound that rang through the place rendered all who watched silent. She had split her eye right above the brow line and more blood ran but The Russian stumbled backward with a hand at his head. She'd hurt him and he was confounded and angered by it.

Enola wiped the blood from her eyes with her arm, smearing it up across her forehead and into her hair. An expression Cullen had never seen on those lovely features had started to spread, he told himself it was the blood, it was her jaw swelling from that punch but he knew he was lying to himself. It was her eyes, they weren't like her challenger's. It was something savage in her, something that was enjoying this fight and wanted more.

She was on the move, headed straight for her target, but he was quick with one of those right hooks that had landed so well before. This time Enola caught it stopping the blow like a wall in her ivory hand and with practiced ease she extended the arm out. Dealing a sound strike to the elbow joint she bent it the wrong way and pulled a roar from the large man's mouth as the bones broke and the arm hung at a sickening angle to his body.

He jerked away from her, spun and clotheslined Enola's swanlike neck with the bulging muscle of his uninjured arm, flinging her across the ring and into the wall where the stone behind her fractured under the impact thickly.

That sound echoed around in Cullen's head until it became glassy and sharp, he once again was years from the here and now, watching as a thousand shards of mirrored glass exploded around him. The back of his mother retreating to another room to hum to herself and knit until this lesson was ended, either by Cullen losing consciousness or his father losing interest. The mirror dug cruelly into his back and before he could move away his father reached for him to shove his flesh against the biting edges.

It was The Scimitar once more, holding Cullen in his chair with gentle but firm hands. "Don't leave her for dead just yet, Master."

Enola fell to the ground in a slump as Anatoli advanced and just when he was about to pounce she landed a kick to his ribs so hard the heel of the shoe pierced his body and hung in the flesh. He staggered back a few precious steps before Enola was up and back in his face. An open handed strike that sounded like boards clapping broke his nose sending a spray of blood across her face and chest in a crimson mist.

Without hesitating she swung both arms out and around to clap his ears with open palms, rupturing his ear drums and ruining his equilibrium. As the watery fluid trickled down both sides of his neck Cullen watched in optimistic horror, realizing she was going to take him apart, piece by piece if she had to.

The Russian staggered drunkly at her, seizing her throat in his only usable hand, the sickly gag that was pulled from her had Cullen reaching for another drink, thankful for the soothing touch of The Scimitar.

He lifted her from the ground by her neck and as her feet flailed wildly under her she finally hit pay dirt with that damn shoe, raising a scream from him and causing him to drop her to the ground as he yanked the thing from his body and a spurt of blood erupted from the wound.

Enola charged, the muddy and tattered skirt flying behind her as the all but destroyed stockings clung to her legs in holes and runs. Cullen could swear he felt the ground shake beneath every step and watched as her feet sank deep into the blood soaked mud, leaving the other shoe standing in a low trough as she came for her prize.

He grabbed her by the hair and hauled her to the ground where he straddled her body and swung once, twice, three times on her lovely face with his left arm. He was pulling back for the coup de grace as the stunned Enola found her wits and with a buck of her lithe body that sent him flying above her like a rag doll, rolled a very surprised Russian beneath her. Her weight somehow pressing him deep into the mud below.

A wild look of panic crossed his face as he locked eyes with her and her small blood caked hands found that hole in his side. An ugly snarl took over her face as she forced her fingers into the wound, and The Russian went oddly still in horror for a moment as her hand went even deeper into the torn flesh, probing for something inside then in a flurry his massive hands began to claw and shove at her to no avail.

Panic sent the great body thrashing beneath her in the soft dirt, kicking clots of it up in the air to rain down on them in their fatal embrace. Cullen could see the muscles bunching in her arms as she dug even deeper , her wrist and arm vanishing inside the man as he pushed at her to no affect, she may as well have been carved from stone.

Agonizing seconds ticked by until finally, in a horrid flourish Enola all but ripped her arm from the broken body of Anatoli Zubov with the pale and slick length of his intestine clenched in her wet little hand. It strung from him in kinks and curls as she pulled what was inside outside to wind around his neck and with a pull that pressed the chubby pink rope thin around his neck, Enola began to strangle Anatoli with his own innards.

He clawed at his flesh weakly, his features pale and waxy from what must have been a most unnatural sensation. Still he battled for air, lashed at Enola who was unmoved in her focus, he even managed one more blow to her face which landed with all the impact of a drop of rain.

She held fast to her rope and Cullen felt his stomach clench at the hungry almost amused expression her features wore as she wrung the last drops of life from this man. He was an odious creature to be certain and it was nothing less than he deserved, but the brazen way she enjoyed his final thrashings sent ice water through Cullen's veins.

The hulk beneath her went still and when she was satisfied he was dead and she had won, Enola allowed her head to drop to her chest, those iron muscles to unclench in her arms and back, still sitting atop the remains of Ataoli Zubov as every person in the mezzanine waited, holding their breath.

With a great sigh of her body and so slow it hurt Cullen to watch, Enola rose from the ground, the divots her knees left in that battle churned mud low enough to hide her calves. Staggering to her feet in the tatters of a gown, she turned and the crowd roared in excitement.

Her right eye had a doughnut of blood around it already, nearly shutting it with the swelling. Blood trickled from the crack in her forehead and gushed from the bite in her shoulder. The lip he'd been kissing scant hours before was ballooned out in an odd shape and she was limping as she circled the body to yank the impressive cuff from the corpse with her blood soaked hands. A foreign expression took her features, one that was breathing deep of the carnage and pain, a savoring of this battle and even respect for her fallen opponent while she relished his hideous death.

Holding Anatoli's cuff high over her head as everyone applauded, the Unseeing opened the great door to the ring and shuttled in to greet the victor. Cullen watched in a daze at what he'd just seen her do, the cruel way she'd murdered a man and left him in the dirt for the crows of this place. Enola, the woman who refused to ruin a woman's face if she didn't have to, and paid for the car she stole....had that unfettered violence always been there, just under the surface of her once lovely visage?

The Scimitar helped him from his seat and led him out of Greed and into Violence, down a long tunnel into a room where Enola was seated on a table as a doctor tended to her wounds. Their eyes met and she managed an odd smile with those swollen lips, Cullen rushed in happy to see she was upright and conscious, but he felt doubt panging in his mind, was this woman really any better than these animals she so reviled?

His thoughts were interrupted by the reverent whisper of The Scimitar, "Congratulations Sister, your demonstration in the ring has earned you both an audience with the Abbot."

Chapter 25

Adam emerged from the kitchen with a gentle smile on his lips, and Gilda regarded him with a frantic expression, seizing his arm in a grasp that pulled a wince from him she whispered in his ear quickly, "We have to leave, we're not safe here!"

His eyes took on look of confusion, "We're not safe here?" he repeated, his eyebrows raised in skepticism. "These good people have taken us in, welcomed us, given us a place to live and even listened to our problems...Gilda, if not here, where?"

She shook her head quickly, watching the door to the kitchen anxiously, "I don't know, but we must leave, please." Her eyes begged his and as Shamus and her beloved Fanny walked in through the door she felt that straining beast inside her, tense at their arrival.

Adam sighed heavily, looked her over as he shook his head, "You're tired, and you've been through too much these past few days, you need to rest."

"Of course she does!" Fanny burst between them, throwing one of those iron arms over each of their shoulders, "After what I've 'eard its no wonder she's all wrung out, take her home and its straight to bed."

"You two can dine with us tonight," Eli inserted quickly, "no worry there."

Before Gilda could politely decline, Adam thanked them and promised they'd be there at sunset. Leading her by her shoulders as they all but ran down the street he spoke in a tone of bewildered sadness, "You have got to stop all of this silliness right now, do you hear me?"

When he opened the door of their house and led her inside he stared at her, "Look at you, crazed and weeping, suspect to every soul that shows you kindness....do you suspect me as well darling?"

She replied softly, "If you loved me at all, you would believe me."

"If I LOVED you?" He roared, his face twisted in a mask of agony as he charged her, seizing her by her shoulders and ramming her back into the wall with a crash that shook the eaves of the place.

Keeping her pinned he ripped open his shirt, and pressed her hand against the frantic beating inside, "Feel that Gilda? It beats only for you...I think of only you, want just you and will accept nothing but what my heart cries out for....you."

Gilda's eyes flew to his and in that moment, seeing the desperation in his face and the pain in his eyes, she knew...he was just a man, like any other and she was unlike any woman on this Earth. Expecting him to believe her was like asking him to pluck the stars from the sky.

Adam said nothing, only spared her another glance before leaving for his shop. Gilda heard the forge roar to life and the singing of hammers on steel ringing through the still morning air. With that music to muffle her cries, she brought her hands to her sore and tender face and wept in earnest.

Great heaving sobs left her as she realized what she was going to have to do.

Gilda allowed herself the luxury of feeling sorry for herself for scant moments before once again, the bull inside her reared, reminding her that they were in terrible danger among these people. This town of strange magic and familiars that roamed the misty night.

Their eyes were everywhere, they listened for the slightest noise to escape this house and barged in at the tiniest hint of trouble. How could she escape such a well-crafted prison, not of walls and bars, but eyes and ears?

Her train of thought was broken when Shamus and a man she didn't recognize walked in with a plate of glass cradled between then with a strip of leather.

"Came to fix your window, love." Shamus announced, leading the man to the kitchen with no introduction.

Their boots crunched and popped atop the shards on the floor and as she listened to them set the window to rights she felt those great hands on her shoulders, turning to see the friendly face of Shamus smiling down at her, he said in a tone that made her blood run cold, "Don't fret Gilda, we have you now, and we're not ever letting you go."

Bringing a weak hand to her forehead, she feigned weakness and asked in a breathy voice, "Shamus, you'll forgive me if I retire to bed?"

He nodded eagerly and hoisted her to her feet by her arms, leading her up the small staircase gently. In a false swoon she leaned heavily into his great chest and stole a glimpse of a bronze ram, old and worn, hiding in curls of his chest on a simple chain...and she knew.

Gilda laid in bed on her side, watching the waves pump out to sea from her window. Refusing herself even a moment's sleep for fear that the Stag would come for her again, she waited for night to fall.

As the rosy fingers of sunset stretched across the sky she heard the footfalls of her husband coming up the stairs and her stomach dropped. He stopped at the door and Gilda could see him in the reflection of the window watching her, a sad expression on his face.

He surprised her by dropping to his knees beside the bed with a thud, "You look better now that you've rested." He offered hopefully.

"I do." She lied.

"I have a gift for you." He smiled mischievously, holding up one of his hands where a ruby ring glittered on the first knuckle of his pinky.

Gilda smiled at him then, and took it from him gently to slide on her own hand. As she admired the fiery stone in the fading light of day she vowed, "I'll never take it off."

He whispered softly, "You won't?"

Gilda shook her head, her gaze soft and kind, "Not as long as I live."

A smile spread across his handsome face once again and her sorrow evaporated along with the last rays of sunlight. "Eli's family is waiting for us for dinner." He reminded her with a small smile.

She rolled her eyes, and grinned, "Dinner with a family of 13, I can't wait." As she rose from the bed Gilda recognized the expression of lust rolling across his eyes, "Help me get dressed or we'll never make it."

His calloused hands roamed all over her body, coasting over her curves and edges stopping once again at the column of her throat as she arched into his touch. "Of all your pieces, this is my favorite." He murmured, placing a gentle kiss on the tender spot below her ear, "so elegant and graceful, like an ivory swan."

Gilda took his face in both her hands and kissed him sweetly, slowly savoring the taste of his mouth and the tender dance of his tongue with hers. "Now, help me to dress," she stated to his dazed and lusty gaze, "A girl cannot live on love alone."

Adam hesitated a moment longer, helping himself to once last glimpse of her lush and curving body before helping fastening her into her gown, the tiny hooks a challenge for his large hands.
As she tossed her hair behind her shoulders and offered her hand to his he winced at her bruised cheeks.

"I shouldn't have hit you so hard…" he offered, holding her face in the dying light.

Gilda shook her head as if it didn't matter and the fact was it didn't, not anymore.

They strolled hand in hand to Eli's and the cozy house that was rotten with children and familial love. Leda had set a lovely table of pork loin with roasted vegetables, and as the each and every O'Malley took their place at the table, hair combed, faces and hands scrubbed it struck Gilda odd that they didn't bow their heads to pray.

Eli poured the wine and served the meat, saving the tenderest piece for Gilda, and not his own wife. As she ate she realized that the children were watching her with rapt attention and awe, she stopped eating and offered a confused look to Eli who cleared his throat in a fatherly warning.

"I apologize," he offered around a bite, "they're just curious about you."

"Why?" Gilda asked as she watched Adam help himself to more of the salty meat and potent wine.

"They heard you can read and write." Leda was quick to supply.

Gilda's gaze had found the portrait of a wolf over the fireplace, its amber eyes a menacing challenge over their meal. It snarled at her from a frigid wasteland, the glowing eyes of its pack members behind his tensed frame.

"Gilda…" Adam nudged her as she had become distracted.

Finding herself once more, Gilda smiled, "That I can and maybe after dinner, if you approve I'll teach them how to sign their names."

They children burst out in a buzz of excited whispers and laughs, Leda and Eli smiled indulgently with a nod, "If they're very good." Eli admonished, taking another bite of his meal. She ate slowly, and sparingly only allowing herself a full helping of the bread pudding Leda had slaved over, it was her mother's favorite and she couldn't help herself.

As the men smoked pipes around the fire opening another bottle of wine under the watchful gaze of that abominable wolf, Gilda sat with the O'Malley children who were old enough and one at a time, taught them the letters of their name and the way of writing them.

As each one sat watching her as if she were a magician while her delicate hands etched out the letters carefully with a charred piece of coal on the very parchment Eli wrapped his wares in and then encouraging them to copy, to imitate. Leda had finished washing up and stood behind her, the O'Malley baby on her hip, a mystified expression on her own face as she looked on.

After all the children had their pieces of parchment with the letters Gilda had written and their own wiggly attempts beneath it she patted the bench next to her and said, "Your turn, Leda."

This pulled a furious blush from the woman, "Oh! No...I couldn't!" she fluttered quickly as if Gilda had asked her to raise her skirts and jig on the table.

"Go on!" Eli jeered from his chair drunkly.

"Let my wife show you how clever her hands really are!" Adam joined in a blurry voice, his comment drawing a drunken laugh from his cohort before they both set their attention on yet another bottle of wine.

"I promise it won't hurt, Leda." Gilda offered, once again gesturing to the bench.

Setting the baby in his cradle she joined Gilda, careful not to touch her as she sat.

"You have a very pretty name, and L's are one of my favorites." Gilda began as she swooped out an elegant letter under her student's rapt gaze.

Leda shook her head, "My word, like a ribbon in the wind...so beautiful."

"Your turn." Gilda said, handing her the smudgy lump.

She took it awkwardly, and Gilda corrected her grip, watching the anxious way her eyes flew to Adam when they touched.

"Now, its not about your hand," Gilda began reaching behind her to cup her elbow, "it all comes from here...move your arm and let your hand take the ride."

Leda make a wiggly and shallow L, her face lighting up as she did. "My word!" she exclaimed.

Gilda smiled, "Good! Let's get the rest of it, shall we?"

"Where did you learn to write?" Leda asked as Gilda etched out the e, d, and a that completed her name.

"My father made tombstones, and I wrote the names and inscriptions for him to carve."

An odd expression of amazement passed across Leda's face, only for a moment before she turned her attention back to the parchment, anxious to learn.

They went on that way, Leda the most attentive of her students, watching Gilda's motions closely and even asking if she would make an alphabet for her to practice with.

As she took the staggering Adam home late that night, he howled at the moon and sang a disjointed aire to the murky sky. Gilda drug him up the stairs and tossed him across the bed to undress him, starting with his boots.

He reached for her blindly, his eyes heavy from the wine and exhaustion, and she let his hands roam over her as he wished, falling into bed with him and gathering him up in her arms.

"I'm glad we're staying here." Adam huffed against her neck, struggling to stay awake.

"I know you are." Gilda murmured against his head.

"Are you mad at me?" he asked in an almost boyish tone.

"Not even a little." Gilda whispered.

He sighed then and she felt his body slip into the oblivion of sleep, his snores tickling her ear as his hands twitched.

She allowed herself to hold him as the moon rose over the sea, its silvery light gliding over the waves in the silent night. Gilda tried to memorize the way his arms felt around her, the sweet sound of his breathing and the taste of his lips and skin. She glutted herself on Adam Flynn and when she was about to burst, she slowly crept from the bed, dressed in the ragged trews, shirt and boots she'd arrived in and slipped into the night.

The streets were asleep, and silent save one...a woman with a broom and a bag was scrounging for food in the gutters of the marketplace. As Gilda came upon her they both froze and regarded each other fearfully.

"Don't tell no one I was here!" she whispered, "Don't tell them you saw me!" she begged, grabbing Gilda's shirt as she did.

Gilda took her hands and looked at the woman sadly, her face was dirty and her hands cut, scabbed and raw with dirt under the nails. She'd been stealing food at night, from gardens and garbage alike, but starving for her effort. About to shove her aside and move along Gilda was stopped dead in her tracks when the moonlight hit a necklace about the woman's throat.

Her necklace, the one her mother had given her, the one Maddox had ripped from her that night, that awful night. A simple stick of rosy gold that hung from chain glinted in the moonlight and stopped her heart cold.

"Where did you get that necklace?" Gilda asked harshly, grabbing her arms in a fierce grip.

"My husband gave it to me." The woman replied, a sour look on her face, "The only thing he ever gave me other than babies and a beating before he left."

"He left you?" Gilda asked, images of the man she'd drowned in the swamp flashing through her mind.

"Just never came home one night, and left me and my five boys to ourselves...no money to speak of, so I take what I can at night while everyone sleeps. Can't say I miss him, he was a cruel man, Maddox was....cruel and sick, but I don't know what's worse, the beatings or watching my babies starve."

Gilda reached for the bridal bag she'd hung off her trews and took out a handful of coins.

"I don't need your charity!" the woman scoffed proudly.

Guilt washed over Gilda in waves as she realized she'd been the one to widow this woman, the one to leave her children destitute... "Then sell me the necklace."

She regarded Gilda suspiciously then, "And you won't tell no one you saw me?"

Smiling Gilda replied, "Only if you don't tell them you saw me either."

She took the necklace off and handed it to Gilda as she took the coins, "Thank you, my son's thank you."

As Gilda put the necklace back on she shared one last smile with the widow and crept off into the night, away from this place and from her husband as he slept in the bed she'd bought and never shared.

Chapter 26

Cullen felt his hand sweating in Enola's as they followed The Scimitar down, further down still and far, far away from the noises of the Brother and Sisters as they frolicked among the damning levels of the Hell Fire Caves and finally to a pair of great oak doors. His servant demurely bowed and once again retired to the shadows until he was needed.

Enola's bruised gaze met his own, and he was terrified by what he'd seen in her, by what she'd done and at the same time in awe of her, of the might she carried within that he couldn't make sense of it if he'd wanted to. He feared and craved her in equal measure and as he tumbled further from grace he cleaved to this woman that he didn't trust but could not survive without.

She took his hands in her own battered fingers, the knuckles crusted over with dried blood and her bruised throat swallowed at that lump once more, in a trembling voice she asked him a final time, "Are you sure, Cullen?"

Without saying a word he raised his hand to knock, but before his knuckles could strike the wood the vast door was swept open silently by an unseen hand. A cavernous chamber was revealed, a fire roaring in a tremendous hearth with two chairs in front of it, one of them occupied. Mounted where a portrait might be, was a flat screen television showing the going's on in Lust at the moment. The unseen occupant clicked a remote and it was changed to the familiar Greed area, people gambling and cheering at the tables as they won and lost fortunes.

Enola pulled Cullen inside, her bare and still muddy feet marring the exquisite rug beneath them. The door swung shut and Cullen felt his arm tugged as Enola pulled his gaze toward the thing that had started this whole, tangled mess, in all its glory, standing in a corner was that damnable door. The ram glaring at them from his perch, challenging them to approach, the bloodred wood planks gleaming in the dancing light.

Before he could say or do anything, a velvety voice he instantly recognized purred, "Hello Gilda."

Mr. Baruch rose from the chair, a glass of scotch in his hand. Resplendent in a black turtleneck and matching slacks, he smiled and somehow became more even handsome than Cullen could recall, "And Cullen? What a nice surprise." He said in a tone that revealed it was no surprise at all.

Mr. Baruch barely spared a glance for Cullen though, before his mind could seize upon the fact that he was here, that he seemed to know Enola by a different name she confirmed his fears.

"Adam..." She whispered, her voice a gentle coo that trembled with emotion and disbelief, "It can't be you."

He set his scotch on a nearby marble topped table and moved toward her smoothly, "Let me look at you darling," he implored, taking both of her hands gently in his own, "I'd always feared that time would harden you and I see it's quite the contrary isn't it? Like a piece of sea glass, you have become even more lovely than I recall."

Enola allowed him to touch her, to hold her and even return his smile. "Adam, I can't believe...after all this time?"

He brought one of her hands to his face, seeming to relish her touch on his cheek before pressing a fervent kiss to her palm. "It's been far too long."

Before she could reply he pulled her into his arms, burying his face in her neck and inhaling deeply, his eyes rolling up into his head. Enola didn't fight, to Cullen's surprise she wrapped her arms around him, leaned into the embrace, when he saw her hand cradle the back of Mr. Baruch's head he snapped and jealousy reared up inside of him.

"What the fuck is going on here Enola?" he bellowed, pulling her from Mr. Baruch's embrace roughly, "How do you know him?"

"Enola?" Adam repeated ignoring Culling entirely, "Is that what you're calling yourself these days?" Contemplating it for a moment before asking, "And the surname?"

"Sloan." She replied without hesitation.

"Enola Sloan," he said slowly, savoring the name as if it tasted good, "I like it...befitting the stature of such a winning creature like yourself."

"And Baruch?" Enola thought a moment, "Like the philosopher?"

"Exactly, darling." Mr. Baruch replied, retrieving his scotch for a taste. "But where are my manners?" he asked himself with arms thrown wide, "Please, drinks for my guests and something to wear that's more befitting my bride."

The Scimitar and another of the Unseeing flew into action as Cullen choked on this last word, *bride*.

"Enola," Cullen said seizing her hands in his own, "I don't understand....are you? Did you?"

She only shook her head with disbelief, "Cullen, I swear I didn't know."

"That is true," Mr. Baruch confirmed, "she did not. Point of fact, I wasn't even sure until this very night that I had finally, after centuries of searching, found her."

As The Scimitar offered a gin and tonic to Cullen, which he took because he was too flabbergasted to refuse it, the other Unseeing put on a pair of gloves and began to remove Enola's tattered gown from her body.

She brought her arms over herself in a modest huddle only to have Mr. Baruch bark, "No!" he set down his glass with a slam and rushed to her, seizing her arms and in an intimate voice, "What did I always tell you?"

Enola hesitated for a moment before allowing him to pull her arms wide, revealing her battered body to him plainly, "To never hide myself from you."

He rewarded her with a kiss, gentle and sweet on her mouth, "That's right, not even ever."

Cullen's rage flared again in concert with the lust of seeing her so exposed, her long legs and sinuous hips. It was quickly cloaked in a black velvet robe, the Unseeing cinching the waist with a black satin belt before handing her a glass of beer.

"If memory serves," Mr. Baruch offered a toast, "ale was your favorite."

Enola offered a toast in return and as they both drank sharing that oddly intimate gaze Cullen snapped. Throwing his glass to shatter in the fire he screamed, "What the FUCK is going on?"

Mr. Baruch regarded him with surprise, "You remain a sublime disappointment."

He approached Cullen then, a consolatory arm around his shoulders, "I thought for certain, you would be able to bring her to heel, one way or another...what with your bloodline and all."

"My bloodline?" Cullen repeated as another drink was supplied discreetly.

"What did you say, Adam?" Enola asked, taking a step toward them, the fog starting to lift from her eyes.

"You didn't recognize him?" Mr. Baruch asked, almost giddily, "I would think that of ALL the people on the Earth, you might see a little trace, some familiar feature in the ancestor of the very first man you killed."

Cullen's stomach dropped and his eyes flew to Enola's as he saw her own surprise at this revelation.

"You can't mean..." she said, her hand beginning to shake, tossing beer on the rug beneath her in foamy dregs.

"I do....the O'Keefe clan has a rich history in the Hellfire Club and Cullen here is a Legacy Supreme on account of his ancestor Maddox being the one to bring you to us in the first place."

Cullen looked with horror at Enola and as Mr. Baruch seized his face between his fingers, "That's right Cullen, Maddox was so delightfully cruel, he savored fear like most men would wine, and was a master of pain in his own right. You cannot imagine how happy I was to find you, hustling in that abysmal hole in Georgia....and then how completely disgusted I was to discover that all of that instinct and fury had been bred out of you like some fucking poodle."

Dots of black began to creep into Cullen's vision but a smart slap to his face brought it back in painful clarity. "Stay with me boy!" Mr. Baruch hollered into his face in a reeking gust of scotch, "I did enjoy our....time together...you were most accommodating." He sneered.

"Leave him alone," Enola warned, "I'm the one you're angry with."

"Oh?" Mr. Baruch let go of Cullen's face and moved back to her, "And have you also sampled our Cullen's charms...?"

"That's not even good conversation, Adam." Enola observed flatly.

Mr. Baruch only shook his head, "You're missing out darling, he's such a soulful and deliberate lover."

Enola remained unmoved by his taunting, but he continued "Am I to believe that in all this time, over all these years...there's been only me?" he asked a look of astonishment on his face.

She crossed her arms and poured the beer on the floor before dropping the glass to shatter crisply, "I want my door."

"Of course!" Mr. Baruch teased, carefully stepping around the puddle Enola had created on the floor. "And you shall have it and anything else you desire my darling, we're together now."

Enola was unmoved by his statement, "Why did you steal it?" she asked, "It's obvious you could afford it, why the ruse Adam?" He was caught up entirely in her, not truly listening to what she said, but watching the way she said it, the light dancing on her skin and the husky tenor of her voice.

As Cullen watched him leering at her he felt his blood boil at the same time the extreme shame of being so easily and expertly used threatened to drown him. The revelation of his ancestors having anything to do with this place, these people and knowing he descended from such debauched souls was sickening to him.

Enola's husband was standing before them, a man he had liked, had even loved in some strange and unanticipated way…he was awash in this pit and lost to himself. The gravity of Enola's story and her life came crashing in on him, if Mr. Baruch was to be believed she was over two hundred years old. A killer and some cog in the machinery upon which this garish world spun, she had hidden everything from him all along.

"Maybe I did it because I missed you?" he asked, a ring of sincerity in his tone.

"Did you?" She asked softly, moving past him to stand near the fire, ignoring the broken shards of the glass Cullen had thrown digging into her feet.

He followed, putting his hands on her shoulders and nuzzling the back of her neck, "I have waded through centuries only to find that nothing compares to you, Gilda."

She was fighting something inside of her, at every touch and caress she was resisting a powerful urge, Cullen could see it, that same wild look she had outside of this place by the car. Whatever it was that sheltered inside of her was on a tether that grew thinner with every breath. The mere presence of this man had her dangerously on edge, the air was thick with it.

"And the door?" she pressed, taking a small step away from him.

"An altar that served its purpose all those years ago, it brought you to me as was prophesized and will stand for all time as a testament to the power of our union and a doorway to The Bleak. We were meant for each other, and as much as you may loathe the fact of it, deep down inside at your core you know, you feel that we fit together as no others have or ever will."

Enola's swollen lip trembled at his words, but she held strong as she gazed into the fire, "A prophecy?"

Mr. Baruch pulled her to him then, a warm embrace and Cullen saw the way her head angled to his touch, the way her eyes slid closed as his warmth seeped into her. Like a soul long lost finally coming home, a deprived and lonely heart finally at rest...and he hated her for it.

"The Stonecutter's Daughter would crawl from Hell's Throat, stand stripped before the Ram who would be at last moved by her strength. For she alone could bear the son that would yank the stars from the sky and drag Hell from its depths." He murmured these words in her ear like a prayer, passionately and on the edge of losing control, his lips on the delicate skin of her neck, his breaths coming in pants.

"I don't understand." She whispered, her lips close to his as she clung at this shoulders with trembling hands.

"Did you believe it all a turn of luck, darling?" Adam asked as he steadied her tenderly, "Did you think for a moment that it was a random happening of chance that brought you to that pit, that place and me finally to you?"

Her eyes had gone glassy in confusion and disbelief, "I thought...I...you, the Lodge...." She drifted off as what she had regarded as the great tragedy of her life finally came into focus, crystalline and sharp.

"What did I tell you the night we met?" he coaxed, bending to meet her twitchy gaze as it fluttered around the room in shock at the revelation he was teasing her with.

She paused mere heartbeats before replying, "That you were drawn there."

"To you." He corrected, "Like the moon pulls the tide Gilda, I walked for hours in the night until I found myself outside of that place and saw you for the first time."

"Drawn." she echoed as if it was the only word she understood.

He gathered her up in his arms then, a tender bundle he'd treasured, lost and finally reclaimed, "Yes my love, drawn."

Pressed up against him her eyes cleared of their confused fog, "Who foretold of The Stonecutter's Daughter?" she asked in a voice gone small.

"300 years ago the founders of this sect, the most devout of the Hell Fire Club waited for the Beggar's Moon and each of them tore out their left eyes, ate them and saw what was to come."

"But why?" she asked as tears pricked at her eyes, "Why you?"

"Because I am midnight to the sun, the one good people fear and the wicked worship." He almost crooned to her.

"I don't understand." Enola wailed as her eyes scanned the room wildly, avoiding looking at this man from her past as he stripped himself bare and revealed his truth in all its horror to her.

"I have always been misunderstood, Gilda." He began, "I have played in this garden since before the age of man...I watched crude beasts straighten and grow through the millennia into something sophisticated, something worthy of my attention." His voice took on a strange quality as he spoke, a dark cast taking over his eyes as if someone had spilled ink in their depths.

"It was only by chance and happenstance that I came to be so revered and feared...the notorious evil to the son of light. A twisted and foul creature dwelling in some fetid hole to make those ivory towers they build all the more worthy of their precious savior."

"You don't mean?" she asked in a voice that had gone suddenly hoarse.

He sighed then, his head atop her own, "Every good story needs a villain Gilda."

Cullen swayed on his feet, only to be caught by The Scimitar who graciously saw him to another seat. His head was spinning with the idea of what this man believed himself to be.

"You know me Gilda," he said fervently turning her in his arms to face him, "you've seen inside of me, I'm no monster…simply a living being who feels and lives like you, who knows what it is to whittle away an eternity among the sheep of this Earth as they prattle and panic through the years of their small lives." He pressed his forehead to hers, "You alone are worthy to stand by me, to be with me."

"Why these people?" Enola almost wailed.

"I hated them for what they put you and all those women through, my treasure. Loathed the blunt tools with which they extinguished those new and shining lives. Disregarded their prophecy and rituals as stark ravings and nothing more…until you emerged from that place, until your splendid soul called to me from the depths." He was pleading with her now, begging for acceptance of him as he was and always would be. "And in that moment I knew, none of the sects that walk this Earth were right, but none of them were wrong either – and my violent devotees were right about you, about us."

"Why do you wallow among the lowest form of existence?" she pressed.

"I battled my nature for so very long, denied who and what I am for ages but came to realize that I cannot be anything but what I am…I play my part as you play yours…and destiny will make fools of us all in the end."

She brought a scabby hand to her forehead in what Cullen had come to know as an expression of extreme distress, "The door was a trap…"

"An invitation" he corrected, "….which you accepted." Mr. Baruch was pressing kisses all over her beaten face and bloody hands, cradling her to him gently, reverently. "I love you Gilda, so very much."

Her face was twisted in an agonizing mask of confusion before she finally threw her arms around him and pressed her mouth to his in a passionate kiss. They clawed and tore at each other in a feverish cloud that sent Cullen's heart to his shoes, he felt dirty for watching and angry for having to witness it at all.

Thunder rolled from the sky stories above them and shook the floor menacingly, Mr. Baruch tore open the neck of her robe and gently kissed the bandaged wound on her shoulder, "My fearsome bride." He crooned, "my wild love…we shook the pillars of heaven once, we'll do it again, forever, for always until the sky crumbles."

Cullen's eyes searched for another place to focus, anything but the intimate exchange before him. They fell upon the television above the fireplace and what he saw on the screen stopped him in his tracks.

In Greed, where Mr. Baruch had left the channel set, people were tangled in passionate embraces, their kisses and roaming hands searing each other's skin. A man laid atop a woman on the craps table, another pair of women were tangled beneath it in their own oblivion….it didn't make sense.

She remained silent in his embrace, desperate for more of him, all of him. Enola's eyes had gone wild in their sockets and she was beyond reason.

"Just tell me a single thing my darling and I'll lay the world at your feet," he bit her neck gently, "where is my son?"

Enola felt the bull inside her straining to run, to be set free as Adam's kisses rained down on her starving flesh. His sweet words and torrid gazes had set her on fire and like a woman starved she almost lost her mind at the sight of him after all the long years. Forgetting for a moment who he was, even the fresh realization of what he was seemed fuzzy and she knew with those three small words, that simple request, that it was all a lie, it always was and from the beginning this had always been about her son.

A sobering feeling of anger ran through her, chilly and cold it cleared her mind and sharpened her eyes to what she was truly bound. "Your son?' she asked sharply, seeing Cullen sit up a little straighter at her tone.

"I know you were with child when you left," Adam murmured, all but lost in his lust as he clung to her and kissed her still, his breath washing over her in pants. "Where have you hidden him away my clever girl?"

Flashes of that stormy night far from Ireland rattled her brain and fogged her vision. The driving rain, the relentless thunder and the blood...there had been so much blood that night. Her eyes burned with sorrow and shame, as her soul was torn anew with the savage pain. Enola had tamped it down so far, so well that she'd nearly convinced herself that it hadn't happened at all.

In a voice that trembled like leaves in the wind, she managed, "Dead." As she said it aloud, it was finally real and for the first time she wept for her son.

"What?" Adam asked, pulling his face to hers, an expression of disbelief rendering his handsome face haggard.

Tears began to roll down her cheeks, seeing her loss mirrored in his own, "He died in childbirth."

Her words resonated and with a soul shattering howl, Adam wailed as he sunk to his knees dragging her down with him. Crying violently at the loss of a son he'd never known and wanted so desperately was all more than he could bear.

He crumbled into her arms allowing the sorrow to wash over him, through them both. And for a moment they weren't Satan and the Stonecutter's Daughter but man and his wife mourning their child together.

"I'm so sorry..." he murmured over and over again, "I'm so sorry you were alone, that I drove you away." He clung to the hem of her robe and reverently kissed it, "I hate that you've borne the loss in solitude all this time...I was wrong...and at times I find I am unable to control myself in spite of my best intentions, even after all this time."

An eerie keening rained down from the crowded halls above, carrying with it all the sadness of a thousand lost souls who know not why they're crying. Enola's eyes flew to the television and she saw there among the gaming tables, people in despondent states, weeping and wailing as if the world itself had ended.

People rocked in each other's arms as they cried and attempted to comfort one another from the paralyzing wave that had taken them. Others clawed at their own flesh in searing grief, as if the tearing pain would eclipse the searing loss within if they dug deep enough and Cullen realized, they were just an extension of Adam...Mr. Baruch. They felt what he felt, loved what he loved, did as he bade...and now in his darkest hour of loss, they grieved.

She felt him settle in her arms as her own tears slowed and Adam raised a wet face to her own, "What was his name?"

She smiled at the question and replied with no small amount of pride, "Andre."

Adam's expression was one of pure love in that moment as he repeated, "Andre." Fresh tears teased the corners of his eyes and with a fervent tone in his voice, "Where is he buried?"

Enola took a long and jagged breath as she steeled herself, "His sweet bones rest in a corner of this Earth that you shall never see."

And just like that, the devastated father was replaced with a seething man on the verge of a rampage, "What?" he bit out.

"You heard me, Adam." She said sounding supremely exhausted in that moment.

He was on his feet, dragging her with him like a shot and he started to shake her violently, finally gave in to the fury inside him with a hard slap to her already battered face before he roared in her face furiously, "I WANT MY SON!!!"

Enola felt the sting of his palm on her tender face, saw the rage inside of him and felt that final irresistible tug from deep inside of her. A place she'd kept locked for all this time, an animal she'd shut away in fear was still ready, still hungry and after all these years…the time had finally come.

Chapter 27

Cullen leapt to his feet as Adam slapped Enola's face, "You son of a bitch!" he landed a single punch before the Unseeing emerged from the shadow to restrain him in a fearfully strong hold around his neck.

Adam cast a heavy look toward his wife, "You're going to come with me, without any trouble or your boy wonder here dies." A cruel looking dagger glinted in the firelight as the Unseeing pulled it from his robes and held it to Cullen's throat.

Adam was holding the glass of scotch with the all but melted ice cubes in its warm depths to his mouth with a smug expression of victory on his face. In a moment of fury Enola smacked the glass, breaking it across his chin as the shards made ribbon candy of his face and stung as the scotch seeped in.

He cradled his face and looked back at her with an expression of wonderment and awe, "Temper, temper darling." Without waiting for a reply from her he offered a single command to the Unseeing, "Make him bleed."

His sleeve was ripped off and the blade was drawn over Cullen's inner arm in surprisingly precise lines, the blood raising and finally running over the sides to drip on the floor. Over and over again they cut, as he bit his lip to keep from crying out, to be strong. As it reached the tender bend in his arm the nerves screamed in desperation and so did he.

She exploded toward them and hurled the Unseeing up and across the room to hit the wall where he died, she spun to see not anger on Adam's face but one of surprise and delight. He leaned forward cautiously, looking over his wife as if he'd never seen her before, like they'd only just met, "Oh my, but you are just full of surprises, aren't you Mrs. Sloan?"

She felt the bull flex inside her, remembered that night at the tree and those mysterious words. Esus had been one of them, they had been calling him, imploring him and begging him to shelter inside her, to remain until now, this moment, she was certain of it.

Adam whooped with laughter at her savagery, at the violence she'd carried, she'd been forced to kill The Russian however it was clear to him now, she had some secrets still. He was halted in his revelry however when she took a single threatening step on him and he caught the barest glimpse of what resided within his wife.

"Easy now," he held up his hands, dropping all pretense and the glass with it, "you don't want to do this."

"I think…." She began taking another step, the floor shuttering under her footfall, "that I want to do this more than I've wanted anything in my life."

"You cannot kill me Gilda." He stated plainly, and she knew he was telling the truth.

"I won't hold it against you." She said and advanced again, her eyes shot to the television screen where she saw the mindless masses organized and advancing with a single purpose….they were coming for her, to stop her.

Somehow, in spite of his greatest feat of convincing the world he didn't exist, The Devil controlled these people. As connected and as well dressed as they may be, at the end of it all, these polite people were just animals. She had precious few moments before they broke down that door to tear her apart, she turned to Cullen, "No matter what happens, stay behind me."

There was no time for argument, no concern for his pride, Cullen heard the groaning hoard coming for them and felt a chilling fear the likes of which no mortal soul should know. His trembling hands went to her flexing ribs and the instant he felt that wild thrumming inside of her he had to believe it was going to be alright, somehow.

The door broke open as Adam laughed wildly, clapping his hands in delight at the tuxedos and evening dresses that advanced into the chamber, screaming for blood in a fury only death would soothe.

She never hesitated, just threw herself into the mass and allowed the beast inside of her to take over. All finesse and skill went out the window as she grabbed the jaw of a screaming man and yanked it cleanly off his skull. The woman behind him was just as easily dispatched with a tremendous slap that sent her head spinning around the wrong way, her arms still flailing as she fell to the floor dead. The next man's throat was torn out cleanly sending a jet of blood across her and the room. An uppercut to the next one took his head off the spine, killing him instantly. She never stopped moving, just kept taking them as they came throwing them back into the doorway, making a dam of dead bodies that the rest struggled crest.

Cullen stood behind her, watching the horror of it all, a writhing crowd was bunched up in the corridor behind the door and they were getting impatient. She was keeping them bottle necked in the door, the bodies stacking up one at a time and they began clawing and punching at one another. Dissolving into a self-destructing mob they no longer cared who they killed, as long as the killed someone.

Adam's face fell in total shock realizing his army was really just a pack of rabid and starving dogs that had finally turned on each other, and left him once again alone with his wife. Who was covered in blood but ready for the real fight as she lowered her stance and leveled a dangerous glare at her husband.

"Come on you bitch…" he goaded, "Time to see what you're made of."

That was all the incentive she needed and with a charge that rattled the chandelier above them threateningly she collided with Adam in a crash that sounded once again like thunder from the skies above. She landed three hard blows to his face but he was right back at her with two of his own that had her seeing stars.

Shoving with all her might she pinned him up against the fireplace only to have him grab the poker from the mantle and clap her right in the ribs, knocking the wind out of her with a wheeze. She staggered back and seized one of the chairs, hurling it at him where it shattered around his body like glass.

Adam started laughing then, deep and loud with the poker out straight in front of him. "I'm really going to enjoy killing you Gilda....you've haunted me for far too long." He advanced swinging the poker so fast it whistled in the air and hit her shoulder with a sickening crunch as the joint inside shattered.

She howled with the pain of it and fell to the floor as Adam set his sights on Cullen, brandishing it like a bat he regarded his target with a business like grin, "We never did discuss your severance."

Cullen was smart enough to move back, and avoid the whistling swings Adam hurled at him. Meanwhile on the floor Gilda felt herself slipping away, in her mind's eye she saw him, Esus. Mighty and strong, his nostrils flared and eyes flaming with fury and lust to join the fight. All fear and regrets were gone, he was hers and she was his and with a crashing that seared her soul that final wall between them fell and Enola felt a strength unlike any she'd ever known seep into her. With a great drawing of air she was replenished and with the smallest flexing of her arms and legs she was on her feet again. All these years she'd been sipping from a cup, now she drank from the river and with a roar from deep inside, from both of them, Adam's attention was once again on her.

Cullen saw the rage inside of her, her eyes blazed with it and every step shattered the floor beneath her as she stalked across the room to her quarry. Knocking tables and chairs out of her way like blades of grass she took him on in a final charge with blood leaking out of her mouth and staining her hands. She looked like a monster.

Adam swung wildly with the poker but to no avail, the blows glanced off her body and when she reached him the power with which she struck sent him flying across the room like a rag doll. Adam sank down the wall weakly and clung to his poker in desperation. Seizing his shoulders with a deafening crunch of the breaking bones heralding her grip she charged full bore at the wall across the room, slamming Adam into it full force. His body buckling under the force she possessed. Turning and running at the opposite wall, shoving his crumbled form into the stone where fractures climbed up the walls as he hit and then again, and again as the whole structure trembled under the fury of her in a rage.

At the door the survivors of the mob were climbing over the dead bodies of their Brothers and Sisters, dropping from the heights of the Devoted Damned that littered the doorway to hit the ground running for the only thing they truly wanted. A murder of them scrambled toward Enola and Cullen, she managed to get him behind her and drop her battered husband to the floor. In a fury now she tore into the delicate flesh of these mortals like a hot knife through butter.

All pretense of the woman in which Esus sheltered was gone, what stood between Cullen and certain death was an animal unhinged. Roaring with the love of carnage as those delicate hands tore limbs from the crazed masses Cullen could only cower behind her and watch in horror. Blood streaked across the walls and his face as another head was torn cleanly from it's screaming neck, rolling sickly across the floor to the place in where he crouched, those blank and pleading eyes met his and the world went sideways.

As Cullen felt the world sliding away from him Enola hauled him from the floor and into her arms, their eyes met and he saw hidden behind all of that fury and might, his Enola, and he smiled.

Behind her, Adam rose on battered legs, the poker clutched in his crumpled arms and with a limping thrust his rammed the poker through Enola's ribs and into Cullen's gut…she turned and charged one final time at her husband, skewered to Cullen as she took Adam's battered body with them to the Hell Fire Door. Striking the ancient wood with his bleeding form, Enola locked eyes with Cullen and bit out, "Forgive me." Before she reached behind herself to shove the poker through her ribs, and Cullen's stomach to impale Adam on the wrought iron with them.
The Stonecutter's Daughter raised a weak and blood covered hand, reaching for the Ram to knock once more and throw open the doors of oblivion to The Bleak.

Chapter 28

A grey and strange place was all around them and yet the battle raged on, Adam's true essence revealed The Baphomet. An unnatural blending of man and goat, his once handsome face gave way to a bearded muzzle and curling horns. Skittering about on two legs and clattering hooves, he was unable to obscure his true form.

Enola was enveloped in the blazing power of Esus, her mighty soul burning beneath the brawn of the bull, his horns shielding her face, his chest guarding her heart and those proud hooves protecting her legs with every step.

Cullen felt his heart swell at the sight of her, something so savage at its purest and most clear as she pummeled The Baphomet in this slippery place of lost time and trapped loves. He felt the eyes of strangers upon him, saw the tentative faces of curious souls lost in this wasteland watching with great interest as the quarrel played out before them.

If she was strong before Enola was a force to be reckoned with here, every blow rattled and wounded the skittish goat as he ran and dodged. Blood leaked from his mouth and a horn hung broken from his head, those wild eyes pleading for help from some unseen ally, yet none came. She began to charge then, and the power of the bull aligned with the tremendous grace of the woman in which he sheltered to create a blindingly powerful melding of souls so exquisite in its perfection that it was painful to gaze upon.

Picking up speed to the point that she was starting to blur she lowered her head and picked up what was left of Adam, goring her opponent in a howling that seared the planes of this empty place. Tossing and shaking him on those cruel spears as the blood poured out of him in spurts and jets, she hurled him to the ground and knelt.

Taking his hand and raising her own, she opened her palm on her own horn allowing the blood to flow, did the same to his and clasped them together. Casting a cold glance at her husband she said, "The blood in my veins, the air in my lungs and my final moments on Earth, bind you to this place."

A greyish cast took over what was left of Adam, of the Baphomet and with those words he was bound to this realm, stuck and powerless as long as Enola lived. From the shifting fog that enveloped this place, the first tentative forms of strangers began to emerge. While Adams bonds began to take hold and chain him to this endless nothing, a crowd of women, nude and scabbed came into focus.

First only a few, then dozen and at last at least two hundred came forward from their place of refuge. Barefooted and naked, their greasy hair hanging over haggard eyes that burned with hatred and loathing for the man who's destiny they'd died for. Sparing Enola the smallest nod of appreciation, they focused on their prey and drug the now heavy and wounded Adam away into the fog to exact their revenge as endless and toiling as this place itself.

Enola stood and watched, the burning form of Esus wrapped around her calming, slowing in a way. Adam was long gone in the fog of The Bleak but still she watched the swirls of mist as if he might reappear, as if the fight weren't over. He did not return, and as she turned a golden light fell upon her face bringing with it all the memories and comforts of home.

As if out of respect the blazing animal retreated to that secret place that he regarded now as home instead of a prison. There was no need for the doors she'd barred inside of herself to keep him separate and away. The chains lay rusted on the floor and what remained was the bond they shared along with an understanding that only two souls occupying the same shell can know.

The porch she'd walked up countless times stood untouched by time before her as that deliciously warm and welcoming light beckoned her come, stay, rest. The door swung open and from it emerged the people who carried her heart, the bittersweet pain of hearing her mother's voice ask, "Where have you been?" rendering her all but mute.

Her grandfather hobbled onto the creaking planks, cane at the ready and a pipe in his weathered palm. Swirls of cherry and tobacco taunting Enola's nose and pricking her eyes with tears of memories she'd long avoided. Wanting to look away but unable to manage, even as her own heart threatened to burst with longing at the sight of her home, her people. She could not look away as the familiar silhouette of her father occupied this empty place as he emerged from the light.

Tall and elegant, his silvery hair curling over eyes that matched her own, Enola gave up all pretense and strength and let herself cry in earnest. Falling to her knees he regarded her with the kindest expression of love, "Don't cry brave girl, you've won this day." His voice was music to her ears, all the long years it was his voice that echoed in her ears, his wisdom and advice leading her through even the direst of times.

Enola let her head rest on the nothing that was the ground of this place as sobs wracked her body, "I'm just tired….so very tired."

"As is every woman, Gilda." He mused, "Now come along, enough sadness…someone wants to say hello."

Pulling her soaked and swollen face from its hiding place to meet the amber gaze of her little boy, Enola felt everything inside of her come unbound. "Andre!" She cried, reaching for him and her father grabbed the little boy out of the air as he all but leapt for his mother's arms. Hoisting him to into his gentle embrace he chided the little boy, "You know she cannot stay."

The emptiness inside of her screamed for the feel of her little boy, the child her own strength snuffed out before he'd ever drawn a breath in her world. "Hello darling." She managed in voice gone wavery with emotion.

"Hello Mummy," he replied, "I've missed you." He regarded her sweetly as he clung to his grandfather.

"I love you so much!" Enola said earnestly, "Never forget how much I love you!" She held the velvet robe in white knuckle fists as she knelt at her Father's feet, it was all she could do to keep from bundling her baby boy in her arms and forgetting the rest of this world, of time.

"I love you too, Mummy!" he smiled in a lopsided way that melted her heart. "Is it true you can't stay?"

Enola met her father's steel colored gaze, and knew as much as she missed Andre, he missed her more. "That's right darling, I'll never be able to stay."

"Won't you at least visit?" He pleaded, eyes large and liquid. Unaware of the cost his request would carry for her, to die in the world she wearily endured for the briefest of moments in her family's presence. Only to return to that hell anew over and over again for as long as the stars hung in the sky.

"As often as I can manage." She said softly through misty eyes.

Chapter 29

Cullen had been the sole survivor of the Hell Fire Caves Collapse, the shocking details of the real purpose behind that nights activities had been buried by the high and mighty Brothers and Sisters that had not been in attendance that night. He'd been sternly warned by a solicitor, signed the gag order and had taken his generous compensation without argument.

Medically he was fine, in spite of being impaled on a fire poker and to the astonishment of the doctors that treated him. He had walked away from a fatal disaster with nothing more than a scar to show for it. Mentally, and spiritually he was heartsick and broken, sleep was out of the question as nightmares of that night relentlessly chased him from any restful slumber. Images of Enola's dead body atop his own as he was sandwiched between their corpses turned food to ash in his mouth.

As soon as he'd been released in his tattered and bloody tuxedo, he'd wandered from the sterile confines of the hospital into the veiled midday sun of foggy London. Pushing his hands into his pockets because they felt so painfully empty without Enola's slender fingers inside them he encountered a crumpled piece of paper. Pulling it out into the muted light his stomach clenched at the claim ticket for the cloak Enola had worn, a brown stain on one corner, likely her blood rendered the thing brittle and crisp. Realizing it was all he had left of her and the scant hours they shared, he felt burning tears of loss brimming in his tired eyes.

Suddenly he felt so very small and alone, as if someone could snatch him up and place him in their pocket to be forgotten as well. People burrowed and bustled past him in a rush to see loved ones or get home and Cullen realized he had nowhere to go and no one to see. If he disappeared from the spot he stood upon who would miss him?

The endless throng of strangers stretched out before his weary eyes, infinite and unmoved by his pain. The suffering of a single soul made little difference to the tangled mass in which he no longer felt at home. But he had to believe it had mattered to Enola, that she understood his melancholy in this moment, for she had endured countless years of solitude of her own.

Because he could think of nothing better to do Cullen returned to New York, but his loft felt like a prison. The bed was hard and cold and no matter the time of day the light was wrong in that city, too bright at night and subdued by day. His friends drug him out night after night for drinks and dinner hoping to jumpstart the friend they knew back to life. But the overripe restaurants and twinkling lights that had once held such an alluring charm were now as cheap and tawdry as a back alley whore.

They prattled on about a television show they'd auditioned for, a job waiting tables, their parents back in Michigan, bills, boys, girls... Allowing his gaze to drift from the emphatic gestures of one of his companions as he passionately expounded on how important it was to live in the moment, Cullen snorted cynically and accidentally met the shy gaze of a pretty girl sitting at the bar.

She smiled coyly at him and looked away, then looked back and his mind ran the shuttering frames of that moment in the hotel tea room Enola had stared him down in when he'd tried to work her that first time. God she had been so terrifying in that split second, if he'd only known what she was capable of, what she would show him, he would have relished the scalding glare for what it was instead of cowering at what he feared out of ignorance.

The girl had mistaken his prolonged stare for interest and rose from her seat, sashayed across the room with an exaggerated sway of her hips where she sat next to him smiling confidently.

"Buy me a drink?" she asked saucily.

Cullen looked at her again, taking in her heavy eye makeup and caked on foundation, the cheaply made clothes she'd likely paid dearly for and the final insult was the acrid perfume wafting off her like a failed experiment in a lab. "Sure." He played along flatly, "How about some Silver Needles?" he asked.

"What's that?" she asked, tittering in nervous confusion, "A shot?"

Regarding her for a moment too long before dropping his napkin on the table and rising from his chair he replied, "No, just a wrong answer."

Her mouth opened in that expression of juvenile shock only young people can muster as he walked away from the table and towards the door. His friend caught him as he reached for the handle, "What the hell is your problem, man?" he demanded, stabbing Cullen's chest with a finger for emphasis.

Cullen reached for his wallet, took out a hundred and pressed it against his friend's chest, "Buy her a drink," he said jerking his head at the girl he'd just rejected, "stare at her mouth and ask about her Mom, what her dream home looks like and the words to her favorite song...then take her home and pretend like any of this matters." And with that he walked out the door and into the night.

He was always searching the sea of faces for hers, for Enola...or Gilda...whoever she was. He kept roses all around his place, hoping the scent would soothe his soul, but it only made him lonely for her.

He lost weight and the expensive clothes he'd literally sold his soul to buy began to hang off him. Finally an elderly neighbor, who he often helped with groceries said in a soft and wizened voice, "You can't make a living out of dying Cullen."

Realizing she was right he had started looking for work again, of course his lack of reference from Mr. Baruch as a direct result of his mysterious disappearance didn't help matters. He interviewed at a smaller acquisition house but just didn't feel right there, the people had name plaques on their desks and sat under fluorescent lights....how could he possibly go back to thinking a corner office was the best life had to offer after all he'd seen, all he knew?

The headhunter he'd connected with came through, asking a simple question, "Colorado or Arizona?"

Cullen had resigned himself to leaving this city that had raised him, he couldn't remain in a chapter of his life that was over any longer, it was killing him. Flipping a coin as he sat on the phone, he saw heads, "Colorado."

The guy gave him the details and told him good luck, Cullen booked a flight and found himself neck deep in the Mile High City the next day. Their downtown skyline was laughable compared to Manhattan, but the people had a laid back kind of way that he liked. Everyone seemed to own a dog and a Jeep and had the time to tell you where the turnoff for the highway was.
It was a drizzly November day and as he drove his rental car into the high country he couldn't help but remember that day in London when Enola had found him asleep in a doorway, the day she'd given him a tiny peek at what she really was.

Flashes of her in that other world, powerful and strong, melded so perfectly with that bull, bringing The Devil to his knees. Tears pricked at his eyes anew and he rolled down the window, letting the cold force them into retreat. He found the sedate and rustic looking office, shake shingles powdered with a dusting of the newly falling snow.

He opened the door which jangled the silver bell that hung from the frame as his nostrils took in the familiar and lovely scent of old books. In spite of the rustic exterior the floor was top of the line with books and manuscripts carefully displayed in climate controlled air tight vaults under special lighting so as not to fade the script.

Cullen was eyeing an original Don Quixote when a woman cleared her throat, "Can I help you?" She was petite with glacial eyes and ebony hair that was short and curling around her neck.

Cullen put on his best professional face and offered the head hunter's card, "Dan sent me to interview."

She scrutinized the card, and once again examined his face before a small smile broke on her face, "Up the stairs to the loft."

A curling set of stairs rose up to the top floor of the building with vaulted ceilings and a window that comprised the entire wall. An imposing desk sat against it, the high back of a chair to the entrance as he approached, he cleared his throat to announce himself when the familiar scent of roses hit him like a ton of bricks.

The chair spun and his knees turned to jelly, Cullen sank to the floor and she rose to help him, pulling him up with that unearthly strength.

"Enola?" he asked, placing a hand on her face in disbelief.

She regarded him with a critical look, took his hand in her own as her eyes ran over his thin frame and face, "I had a lovely funeral Cullen, it's a shame you had to miss it."

Epilogue

"Cullen!" he heard the voice and felt the light touch on his face, opening his eyes he saw her again, then the image of her impaled flooded his mind, causing him the clench his eyes shut, open them again and reach out to touch her once more.

"Enola...is that you?" he asked groggily.

She flared a brow and gifted him with a small smile and he felt his heart speed up at the realization that this wasn't a dream and he was once again with her.

"I saw your body....how?" he tried sitting up, and the room tilted crazily around him. She was quick to lay him back down on the leather couch in her office.

"A lot of people saw my body Cullen, but I have a tendency of finding my way back to this world, no matter what happens to it."

He started to cry then, really cry after months of longing and sorrow. The scent of her perfume and the way the winter light was filtering through her hair was a balm to his soul. He'd been starving to death in the world without her husky voice to chide and tease him. He'd been stripped bare in those caves, taken down to the bone only to be renewed and restrung better than before. The pain of being so exposed and alone without her was all the more acute now that it was at an end and he was helpless in the face of the tidal wave of tears that consumed him.

She pulled him into her arms and let him weep, enveloping him in her scent, her strength and all the things that had been haunting him, hurting him began to fade away. That thrumming he'd revered began to sing in his veins and the heat that seeped from every inch of her leached into his world weary bones and once again began the arduous task of coaxing them to their former state of strength and vitality.

"Were you badly hurt?" she asked, resting a cheek on the top of his head as she cradled his sobbing body with her own.

He shook his head and pulled away from her, horrified at the wet spot he'd left on her blouse from his tears. She rose and he was just taking her hand to join her when the tiny footsteps of a child running started up the stairs. He sat there on the floor as a small girl, maybe four or five reached the top of the stairs, her cheeks pink from the chilly November day, cognac curls pulled back in a pony-tail and eyes the color of the sea after a storm.

"Mummy!" she cried in joy and ran full bore for her mother, who scooped her up and rained little kisses all over her giggling face.

"I missed you darling! Have you had a fun day?" she asked, walking to her desk with the little bundle in her arms.

The little girl nodded fiddling with the carved buttons on her mother's blouse, "We went to the zoo, but had to come home because Candy said it was too cold for the animals."

A smiling woman with kind eyes behind a simple pair of glasses stood in the doorway, "Freezing cold." She accused with wide eyes.

"Nuff said." Enola replied.

"Mummy...who's that?" she asked pointed at the gobsmacked Cullen.

Enola put her hand over the child's chubby finger, "It's impolite to point darling....that's Cullen, he wants to work here. Cullen, this my daughter Sarite."

His brain stuttered for half a heart- beat before he clamored to his feet to approach the lovely child. Kissing her hand grandly Cullen bowed and said, "Hello Sarite, it's a pleasure to meet you."

She blushed and giggled but managed to reply, "It's nice to meet you Lully."

"Alright," Enola set the girl down with another kiss on her head, "Wash up with Candy, and I'll be there for lunch directly."

The twosome headed out the door and down the stairs before Cullen managed to cast a confused look to her, "You said your son was dead."

"He is." She replied, the cast of regret and sorrow flashing through her eyes for the briefest of moments before she continued. "And even though I was married to the prince of lies, and I'm certain he knows whenever one is told to him. I believe he has a problem with omissions." She offered folding her arms across her chest in a rare display of self-comfort, "He never asked for his daughter."

"Because he never knew about her." Cullen supplied.

"And he never will." She assured.

"I thought he couldn't die."

Enola cast a heavy look to the windows then, the icy rain running shadowy fingers down her face and Cullen gazed upon her greedily, taking in every inch of her. As his focus wavered around the achingly familiar sight of her profile something caught his attention across the room. Glowing in the bleached winter light, on a shelf pointed toward the window, stared the fearsome face of the knocker, its expression as menacing and brazen as that day in Sotheby's when his destiny had shifted.

Breathless for a moment at the sight of the two of them, the Ram and The Stonecutter's Daughter together at last, Cullen thought to say something but before he find the words to describe the perfection of this moment and its synchronicity Enola said in a voice that was almost a whisper ,"Everything dies Cullen, everything."

Printed in Great Britain
by Amazon